Dexter Petley lives in Burgundy where .... ime between writing, fishing and growing organic vegetables. His first novel, *Little Nineveh*, was published in 1995.

by the same author

Little Nineveh

JOYRIDE

Dexter Petley

FOURTH ESTATE • London

This paperback edition first published in 2000
First published in Great Britain in 1999 by
Fourth Estate Limited
6 Salem Road
London w2 4BU
www.4thestate.co.uk

1 3 5 7 9 10 8 6 4 2

A catalogue record for this book is available from the British
Library.

ISBN 1-85702-999-2

Typeset in Linotype Bembo by Rowland Phototypesetting
Bury St Edmunds, Suffolk
Printed in Great Britain by Cox & Wyman Ltd, Reading

for Lisa Darnell

PART ONE

The Dream-Car

I

*W*e made Ohio on the first day, newly-weds, me driving sixteen hours dark to dusk, three stops in 550 miles. Friday night in Streetsboro. We paid the toll and came off the James W. Shocknessy Ohio Turnpike, picking up a list of motels and campgrounds from the booth, choosing Streetsboro five miles up the highway. The day going wrong now. Instead of just fixing on somewhere to sleep we drove back and forth up Main Street searching for a diner. All the parking lots were like used car pounds. The only free space was at Tim N Donna's Motette N Steak House. The red neon tripped T BONE & LIVE COUNTRY. Parked up we didn't have the guts to pull back out so we took a window seat and ordered eggs with potato skins.

Tim N Donna's was packed out with bohunks having a time on T bones sticking six inches off the plate. An old man played piano in a Bob Hope suit with the fly down, plunking Golden Oldies like he was the singing dish-washer.

They had a six-some at the next table. Big men with beards and straining shirtfronts of distorted plaid, jean belts you could run a sawmill with. Their babes were straight blondes, chests busting out of glossy halters. One after the other they rose and took their purses to the bathroom. F said they went to puke it all up again. Watta Pair Brew Burgers, Spinach Leaf Vitamins, Bac-o-bits and Texas

3

Combos. F said 90 per cent of American women under thirty-five were bulimic or anorexic. Then Bob Hopeless thumped up a Kenny Rogers medley. The truckers choked along with mouthfuls of blood froth off the T bone.

– Still mooin's how they wannit, F said.

If ah c'd move ah'd git ma gurn an pudda innn the grou-ou-ouuuuund . . .

When they moved to gun talk and deep dish pies and hot fudge sundaes, F said, let's quit. We sat in the car staring through the windshield. Dust kicked up by all the cruising, the queue at the drive-up window. F called the Starlite Motel from the gas station. $28 a nite. Only triple twin doubles left. So we drove out to the campground a mile away, three forks in the lane, pot-holes, no passing. Farmland in gathering dusk. The tracks were all posted, the woods padlocked, dead and alive racoons along the roadside. The smell of dead skunk came on damp air from the fields. All the way across Pennsylvania that morning we'd seen skidmarked skunks. Some in pairs, but unless they'd been dragged there or crawled there to die together it was difficult to see how or why. F said if we were skunks she wouldn't leave me at the roadside, but she didn't know about hanging onto my tail and waiting for another truck to come finish her off. At the campground we hesitated. Might as well sleep rough.

– Whole slew o'places on the way up'd do, she said. But we went in the lodge and saw the manageress. Behind her log-effect desk she was going over the books with a bunch of keys round her size twenty neck. A Magna palled in an ashtray carved from a bison's hoof. She thumbed our attention to the price list on the wall. $8 to pitch a tent. We didn't own a tent. F said we'd sleep in the field.

– Please yaself, the woman said, sucking back a whole quarter inch off the Magna. Free country outside the fence. $8 apiece inside the fence.

4

The night sky clouded over and we drove up and down the lanes in pitch dark, scrutinizing the pull-offs, the tracks which led nowhere, till the flashlight battery ran down. Every place we stopped I said I couldn't sleep there. Too noisy, always a road running by and I couldn't sleep knowing there were cars. By then F was crying with fatigue and I was bloodshot and overheating but kept saying no. One more fork. Just one more. We'll sleep the next place. I was driving in circles and started cursing. Whichever way we went we'd end up on the same gravel lot outside the Baptist Church, parked beside its bus, THE BAPTIST MISSION FOR CHRIST'S SAKE.

F said, please try the barn once more. I didn't see anything wrong with it.

The barn was a mile back. Grass six feet high, wheel tracks under water. Inside was a bed of nettles pushed up through broken stone. Ten minutes later we were back outside the Baptist Church, chain-smoking with the lights off.

– Oh let's go back to the campsite, I said.

F shook her head, too exhausted. She couldn't think, she couldn't see. I could hardly keep my head from lolling. We'd been awake thirty-six hours, but we'd got away.

– I want to go to a motel, I said. It's better than sitting outside the church. We need a bath. We'll get nine hours' sleep in a motel, four at the most in a ditch. We've a long drive ahead.

The day we'd met was cold and dry. London. My afternoon walk had long turned to daily drudge. Highgate Ponds, cat ice in the margins, frosted dogshit. She was in the tea shop queue reading a tatty hardback. I'd never seen her there before. I'd been going to this tea shop a whole year and never spoken to any of the other dozen regulars. Even one of the waitresses refused to serve me for not smiling. Then my split second came. I'd only get one chance per lifetime to meet my own species.

My day began at 6 am in the industrial revolution, listening to 'Farming Today'. I was an outworker for a fishing rod manufacturer, whipping the rings onto carp rods under an anglepoise. I was paid two quid per rod and should've averaged ten rods a day, same as the women in the factory. But I was half as quick and twice as poor because I whipped each leg the traditional way. Tuck knots, taut thread, everything straight. Factory workers were told just to make it look like whipping. They glued the eyes then lined them up after they were all whipped on. Seven coats of yacht varnish held it all together. But they never met the anglers using them like I did. Two hundred quid each in the shops, those rods.

By afternoon I'd be exhausted and bitter and look like a thistle. As such I arrived at the tea shop. F had to share a table with some booklegger with black fingernails. He tried the old let me guess where you're from line as usual and guessed right. How did you guess? F said. He'd got friends in Connecticut and was good at accents. He said he was a writer. I choked on my toast about a table and a half away. F said: what do you write, exactly? He wrote articles on military books. Soon he was giving her tips on how to get a poem published. But he had to go, and gave her his card. She said no point, she was going back to Connecticut in a few days. And it was time for me to speak after a year's silence, all the regulars pausing over their *TLS* or half-million-word novels they'd spent fourteen years writing. And what had I kept under a bushel all that time? What was that silent poseur going to say at last?

– You didn't believe all that shit did you?

F was quite right to say: Excuse me?

I may or may not've repeated it. She said:

– Would you care to join me?

She told me later this was straight from Esme to Sergeant X in *Nine Stories,* J. D. Salinger. She even had Esme's crack across her watch glass. Before we left the tea rooms I knew the old world had disintegrated and gone.

Outside in the street we'd nowhere to go. F was staying with her mother who lived in a bedsit in Kentish Town with a fleabag dog and several pairs of bloody knickers always drying on the chairbacks. My landlady in Cricklewood was the puritan daughter of a Finnish pastor. I was the lodger in her daughter's old bedroom. It was unspoken, but no visitors. Till then it suited me fine.

F waited outside as I packed my camping stuff into a rucksack. We bought bread and cheese and coffee and already a new world exported its delights to me because I'd never had hummus before or even knew about olives and Greek yoghurt. We walked up to Ken Wood and settled among the trees, brewing coffee and talking, shivering over the petrol stove, ground frost on the dead leaves, then walking till a weak sun rose at dawn and we collected the corgi for its dump and jog over the Heath. F was used to being out too. Listen to me! Old campfire and covered wagon me. A traveller in a concrete jungle. Face grey as the sky, veins blue as the pavement. Eyes like joggers' phlegm. Look at that view – a city rising out the carbon monoxide as Jumbo Jets from the world's polluted cities roared down, one every fifteen seconds. Connecticut, she was saying. Night jogging in Connecticut with a dollar bill in her pocket, a pack of Camels and a compact disc of the Ramero Brothers playing Scarlatti Sonatas in E flat on their classical guitars. She took the rucksack off me saying she had the back to carry an ox over the Alps. Since aged five she'd hiked with her father in the Appalachians. His job to keep the trails open once. At midnight on a full moon she'd ridden her horse bareback over the school golf course through unspoilt snow.

I must've done things too. Just forgotten them till then. You don't have that many thoughts, and those you have are already known to you. In the end you're turning over your last minute . . . She got that, that in the end you've nothing left to remember. It's why she wanted to be a writer. She'd found these old newspapers in her parents' loft after their divorce. There was a picture of Caryl Chessman in the death cell at San Quentin lighting up a cigarette. He'd had nine reprieves by then. The caption said: CARYL CHESSMAN LIGHTS UP. NOW SMOKING 120 A DAY, HE IS JUST 60 CIGARETTES AWAY FROM DEATH. Chessman said he didn't intend dying till he was in the gas chamber. What about reprieve number ten? Well, he'd spend his time writing because prison was the ideal place for it and in ten years he might be good at it.

The next headline was CHESSMAN IS EXECUTED. He'd only been thirteen steps from the gas chamber when the final NO came by telephone. After the execution the Federal Judge said he'd've granted a thirty-minute stay to listen to the evidence if someone had asked him. Chessman was just a depraved thug anyway. He was a kidnapper, rapist, robber. He'd been on death row twelve years writing his best seller and studying defensive law. Became one of the foremost legal minds in the US. To save his life he dug up loopholes in the law no one thought existed. He could've gone on doing that so in the end they just took a vote and gassed him. F said writing was her loophole. I said she was mine.

II

*M*y old man rode a horse to school in New Zealand. Bareback, barefoot. He stole marbles with his toes and rolled his own fags behind the playground fence. He only wore shoes on Sundays till he left school at thirteen and went to work as a cabin boy on the lorries. At fourteen he went for a job as driver with a haulage firm. He'd never driven before, just ridden a horse. The foreman said: skedaddle son, come back when ya c'n shave, ya tit puller. The old man said he did shave and could drive a lorry because he was seventeen. He was chewing tobacco to prove it so the gaffer said get in the seat and prove it then.

For a year the old man had watched his gaffers drive. He knew all the tricks, how engines worked, maintenance, driver's slang. He'd just never tried any of it out. He cranked up the engine with a handle and took the foreman for a faultless spin round Wellington. The foreman didn't even ask to see his licence. I only heard this story once, but year after year it broke through in dreams till it bedded in like genetic memory.

For twenty-five years I drove a dream-car round America. My old man's mimic, his every trick. I'd wake knowing I could drive if I were given a chance because I'd really driven those dream-cars. I built up a driving memory. I drove places I'd never yet been. Places I knew I had to reach.

Two years driving a lorry and dad ran away to sea under a swapped identity, an able-bodied seaman on a merchant ship bound for the world. He became Sandy. Sandy had been a Scot on the SS *Orcadies* who jumped ship in Wellington, on the look-out for a wife to settle with in New Zealand. So the old man swapped his papers and took his place, his real name still out there in some family of half Scots. Likewise our pseudo relations north of the border have never been discovered, or uncovered us. So who do we think we are?

My old woman was working in the Naafi in Gravesend when Sandy courted her. My grandfather was a stoker on the Woolwich tugs but spent his early years in Hollywood, Pearl White's bell-boy. My parents married upriver in Greenwich where a daughter, Lulu, was born just after the war. Sandy worked inner London as a taxi driver, thin pickings even with his vaudeville regulars. When Lulu was born he was still in his demob suit, a pocket full of pawn tickets and coupons. Petrol off spivs. Rations for favours. So he ditched the taxi and bought a 1926 Morris. They loaded up their belongings, strapped the furniture to the roof and set off for East Sussex to seek their fortune. Itinerants, just one step behind the gypsies, hawking their labour from farm to farm. Etchingham, Robertsbridge, Stonegate, Hawkhurst. Spring planting and hop training, fruit picking all summer, autumn apples, hops and spuds and root fodder as the mud turned cold. In winter Sandy fixed vehicles, shot crows and strung them up, poisoned moles, ratted barns, trapped magpies, ferreted rabbits and beat for the guns.

We were liberated from the pestilential farms through the old man's bangers. As they died in quick succession he had to replace them so often he learned all about motor insurance. This hooked him a job collecting house insurance door-to-door for United Friendly. Cars seeped even deeper into family life than the smell of cowpat and hops ever did. When one jalopy went to the breakers another came from the grave. Sandy found them under tarpaulins in barns, dilapidated coach houses, weeded-up yards at the backs of run-down garages, places which became his domain. He smelled out cars like he smelled a rat. His bargaining was shrewd poison. The deal was a handful of change and a few hours clipping the hedge, fixing the gutter, smoking out some wasps. The insurance round widened the field and he came across the real keepers of old bangers – widows and pensioners.

– Whatcha got in that garage then, missus?

Five times out of ten it was her old man's pre-war runabout. One owner, batshit bonnet, sagging on its rims. Hadn't seen daylight since the day Harry passed on or Albert had his accident. Good old Sandy would have it ticking over in the hour. Within a fortnight it became our latest family pukemobile, the nipper prisoned in the back on our way home from a visit to Gravesend, swallowing my dinner mile after mile.

Motoring begat motoring. Sandy soon found a greedy network of enthusiasts to underwrite his motors. He became a *savant* of the rarer eccentric saloons. These he'd insure for himself and we'd spend a few Sundays poodling the lanes and driving above our station till his luck ran out or another took his fancy. A car-sick son must've been a disappointment.

Lulu refused to come in the car with me. Sunday drives, Herod's secret weapon. The Josh family emblem, bangers with old spoked wheels and steaming radiators, recognized from village to village. *Vintage* cars to connoisseurs.

At home the common household vocabulary kept adjunct of maintenance manuals and policy booklets. Aged three I could say *bleed the brakes and spark plugs* to my toy Lanchester. And the passing cars flattened the memory dark too. Those ratty farms; instead of animals I could only remember the grease-coloured muck-ridden doom. I knew there'd been pigs and hens and cows but what remained for me was legs sticking out all hours from under machinery, dad in dungarees, mum in wellies as she carried me up to bed holding a candle.

Then we moved and there were lightbulbs. Dad drove to work in a suit. Mum wore slippers and housecoats. Lulu lived in another room because she was thirteen. It was like the family had split up. The car was still head of household and got all the attention. You just have to wait, hope someone else is on the way. But you look upwards and the sky's like a scrap metal yard full of dream-cars and you'll only gash yourself on the future.

III

*S*now fell at dusk as we drove through Gethsemane, Connecticut. Flakes the size of quarters, slow coins in a wishing well. F said:

– Someone with a lotta bad luck.

It was late March. I was suddenly in America.

– Here we are, F said.

She stopped at the mailbox. The windshield wrinkled in seconds. F came back smothered white, holding a wad of her father's junkmail. This was his house, and he was due up for the weekend mainly because of me. He didn't yet know that the uninvited guest was on his way to a son-in-law entry in the Book of Mayflower Descendants.

F was the daughter of divorced parents. She'd grown up in this house. During the week her father lived with Verity in her New Jersey condo. He was a work junkie and spent all night in his Newark lab. I wasn't afraid of him, not after hearing about his inventions. Electric fish swimming in multi-colour water.

The phone was ringing as F unlocked the back porch door. Yes, she said, her friend from England's here.

– Well, her father said, he better not think of staying too long. Verity's driving herself up this weekend too.

Me and F hoped the snow might pile up and block them off, but the weather reports were good for Friday evening. The highways were salted and the road crews said Route 44 was clear all the way.

The snow in Gethsemane settled as it fell heavier in small flakes. F's father shunted up the drive in one stubborn run, hi-beams blinding the house through curtains of snow. He levelled off and sat with the engine running by the porch steps, lights blazing into our room so we had to throw ourselves against the wall or he'd see us. He clumped up to the workshop door knocking snow off his Bird Boots, thumping overhead; slow, heavy-booted for a slight man.

There was no time to fix a blanket over the window. He was down the steps again, weird shadow lunging across the floor, hauling up another box, dragging furniture across our ceiling to make room for his boxes. Filing cabinets, equipment cases, back and forth, up and down till the car was empty and he didn't need the headlights. F said if he wanted to meet me he'd come and ask. After ten minutes we heard him shout from the back staircase.

– Hell-lo.

F dragged me to the foot of the stairs and introduced me to the back of his retreating legs. His head bobbed into view for a second then he'd gone. That hello had been for both of us even though he hadn't seen F for over a year. She said it was just because *we* were there, his symbolic moving back into his workshop.

We lit a kerosene lamp and unpacked my rucksack of everything I now owned. You can't pack for a new life. You shouldn't know what you'll need. The clothes I'd flown in were a disguise to fool immigration control. This sheeny suit and beige overcoat. In the pocket was a two-week Air India return which didn't completely fool the gatekeeper. A stroke of luck actually got me through.

– Where ya stayin, Mr Josh?

– With The Colour King, I said, handing over The Colour King's calling card.

The Colour King had handed them out on the plane. THOMAS HERDINA FREE ESTIMATES RED HOOK NY AIRLESS SPRAYING **WHEN IT DRIES IT BEAUTIFIES**

Mr Statue of Liberty wet the rubber stamp.

– Any money, Mr Josh?

– Credit card, I said.

He wouldn't know the bank had cancelled it the week it was issued. SPLAT. Three-months' stay.

– Welcome to the USA, Mr Josh. Enjoy your vacation.

F was waiting outside. The Colour Queen in her tie-dye velvet cloakette. F was such a driving certainty it didn't matter we'd only known each other three weeks. All my possessions had become meaningless overnight. I could've dumped them in the trash outside the airport. There was no going back to the people we'd been anyway. We bagged up the suit and overcoat for the thrift shop. That left me some outdoor kit, a couple of books I hadn't read, a bit of irreplaceable fishing tackle. In fact there was nothing to unpack that couldn't stay in the rucksack.

F's father dragged his belongings across the floor till midnight. Must've tried the same box in a hundred places. Then he pottered in the cellar below us, stripping the boiler an hour before dawn. When the birds sang the snow stopped falling.

Their house on Milkweed Lane was built in 1922 on six acres of slope. A long low dark house, shingled roof, pine clapboards, flaking paint. Weeds in all the driveway cracks, chipmunks in the crevices of a low wall. In a back-corner an old New England barn in disrepair where F's father kept his garden tractor and chainsaw and the kerosene for the lamps. In the woods there were deer carcasses scattered into loose bones by turkey buzzards. The deer got hit crossing the highway where they gathered at night to drink from a small pond. Too weak to regain the summit, they collapsed and died among the trees.

The previous owner loathed birds because the dawn chorus woke him up, so he put poison on the bird tables. Then the bullfrogs kept him awake at night so he took his birdgun down the pond. The frogs and birds lived on, so he put the house up for sale and moved back to Brooklyn. Even before F's parents divorced it fell into neglect. The same dust still caked the wooden rooms. The daylight staunched. The paintings always crooked. The pre-war central heating clanked day and night. The woodstove needed bricking, the flue was thick with resin. Each room was lit by kerosene lamps which hung on adjustable chains from the ceiling or stood unpolished on chairside pedestals. There were dim electric bulbs in the corridors and land-ings. No television or other modernities. The cooker ran on bottled gas. Bookcases dominated every room, crammed with generations of books, all handed down. Some wonky chairs in which to read them beside uncur-tained windows you couldn't see through unless you pressed your nose to the glass or took some wire wool to the grime. A grand piano blocked one corner of the living room like a stuffed bear in a clapped-out folk museum. Keys broken into loose shale, wood stained and cracked and faded, varnish peeled. There was a yellow view of the pond across Route 44 through picture windows. Most other rooms were empty and neglected, with small piles of remnants left by former inhabitants who'd fled the divorce. F's mother's perished yellow bath cap. Her brother's World War II bayonets. Her own sophomore legwarmers. Not a place to be uncomfortable with the past. Everything emptied of purpose, except for Verity's mail pile on the hall dresser. Realty guides, with a matching stack opened on the piano top.

Verity was due Saturday morning when the snow turned to slush in the drizzle. The sky lit up the colour of a dead lightbulb as she conked out in her canary yellow Ford Pinto rusting on four sides, trunk held down with string, a big sticker over the pock holes: *I -♥- SPANISH FOOD.*

The house was an unlit box after our sleepless night. The dawn chorus had kept us all awake, that and the scratching in the wainscot, clanking pipes, scuffling racoons knocking the trash and tinderbox inside out. Then the screen door crashed shut behind her. Verity was in, and the house knew it. A second crash on the screen door.

– Oh gee. I hit a skunk someplace near Amenia . . . Oh my it stinks! All over ma car . . . Gee, ain anyone here?

I could hear F's father in his rocking chair upstairs, rocking at the window just above where Verity'd parked. I hurried to the back room with the coffee pot, Verity still yelling down the house and knocking slush crud off her galoshes. F's father was cracking peanut shells into a galvanized pail as he read *Lord Jim*. Verity humped four suitcases down the steps. The screen door crashed four times.

Sigh, crash, oh gee, crash . . .

She dumped three boxes on the dining table. Four carrier bags and the shopping on the floor.

– Well hi . . . Hiiii . . . Gee aren't we all sleepyheads this morning.

The rocking stopped. A door opened and slammed. A slow clump on the staircase like a widower descending with a loaded pistol.

– Oh . . . it's you, he said in his lugubrious voice.

Verity was sarcastic:

– Well hi honey, gee I hope I haven't interrupted anything.

He said nothing.

– Brrrr, she said, I juss doan know how you people can stand the cold up here.

– Hmpphhh, would you like me to, er, build a fire?

– Maybe with the furniture honey. No, I'd just like a teeny weeny bit more help is all. How about the young folk? They around honey?

His hesitating must've been her miming some message to him we shouldn't hear. He must've nodded.

– Okay, she said, I'll go in there an get them out here right now, shall I? I mean gee, this stuff's for all of us to share. Hiiiiyeeeee. Hi Effy. Hi I-doan-know-what-your-friend's-name-is. Come an say hi to Verity. Oh boy, din you hear me about that skunk honey? Yuk! Ain there some stuff fa skunk smell Homer?

Homer Sparrowtree was a Mayflower Descendant in a direct line from the first Governor of Massachusetts.

– Uhmmm I suggest, ah Verity, that you park the ah car . . . away from the house . . .

He spoke reluctantly. Talk was available only if other means were not. Silence spoke the necessary volumes. Most people realized this, but Verity liked getting blood out of stone. Mr Sparrowtree's talk came filtered through excruciating difficulty into excruciating exactitude.

– You might uhm attempt uhm an ablution of . . . tomato juice.

His behaviour was consistent to the core and matched his talk. Each lead-coated word dumped with emphasis where least expected. It was like his consciousness became a mineshaft. You could even see the rusted buckets cross his interface on their way up, hear rusty chains straining under the weight of each word-lump.

– LEAST my FATHER used to bathe ME IN TOMATO JUICE if ahh hah . . . I UNAVOIDABLY TANGLED with a skunk coming THE other way.

He did consider general announcements a necessary practical communication. These followed his habitual fanfare, summoning the listeners from their rooms: AAAHHH or UUHHMMMM or even the first word itself, THHEEEE. We heard it, and waited.

– Ahhhhmmmm WAIT. IF you *pe*ople are planning on putting things away . . . I uh suggest it is BEST DONE . . . in my absence. There may be something to COLLECT at the uhmm dry . . . cleaners.

Verity was irritated. She couldn't believe he'd left something at the dry cleaners up here when they had a perfectly reasonable dry cleaners at the Mall back in Clinton. F told me he just didn't want to be in the house when Verity gave us the third degree. It sounded like he was tearing through his junkmail.

– Which dry cleaners, Homer?

He said the pink building joined to the hardware store. Which reminded him: something had to be done about those racoons. This was our fault.

– You might tell those folk when they appear . . . to take their garbage to the dump.

The screen door slammed. We flattened ourselves against the wall again as he shook on his watch-cap and goose-down parka outside our window then sat in the Subaru letting it idle the exact two minutes. F said when he went in both the dry cleaners and hardware store he moved the car across twenty feet out of decency, even though both stores sat in the same lot.

F threw some clothes on and tied her hair back. Verity was waiting for us in the kitchen. She ran across the floor twisting round obstacles, arms outstretched.

– Effy? Oh my, let me grab ahold of you sweetheart.

F backed against the wall but Verity pulled her off it.

– Oh my, it's been a year too, who'd've thought it'd be so long till you came back to us. An you look just wunnerful in that weird outfit, you know?

F said she looked shit and Verity knew it because Verity had packed all F's clothes away somewhere so she was having to wear a curtain instead of a skirt.

– But oh my, that's so like creative? I'd never've thoughta that.

I could see that myself. Verity was home-spun on drive-ups, the drab flat treeless land of factories and New Jersey suburbs. New England was all right in Fall, cute little villages just to look at and snap some polaroids. But the houses were eerie in winter and in summer you got bit. Her condo in Clinton was worth the rent. Bright green wall-to-wall, frame-to-frame built-ins and sliders.

She'd met Homer at a New England Folk Fayre. Verity was selling muffins and de-caff on the Quaker stall. She was broke, divorced, fifty-four and husband-hunting. Three daughters came to zero so she threw them out and they married firemen. She kept the shades on her eyes all year. Her home knits turned to crochet and rode up at the back as she filled out. Dry black hair touched her shoulder like turn-ups an inch too short. Painted nails, lipstick on her teeth. Community College graduate at forty-five in childcare studies, teaching English to immigrants in NY. She turned on me like I'd farted.

– Oh gee, you mean this is your friend? The one from England who's staying here? Well, hi there, I'm Verity. You know Effy an me're great buddyroos an that, but she didn tell her daddy like how long you was planning to visit us for? Gee, I mean, are you on vacation? Like touring maybe? It's just that I hear, well you know, you haven't actually known Effy like for very long? Shucks, we know how wunnerful an all it is to have contacts in other countries of the world an everythin but . . . huuuuuhhhhhhhh, Effy sweetheart, your daddy an me are real concerned about you right now . . .

– Don't bother yourself, F said.

– Oh but I must Effy. Oh boy yes I must. Gee, you're at a real delicate stage in your life right now, okay? You've had a pretty tricky past young lady . . .

– We have to take the garbage down the dump, Verity.

– Gee you clever Sparrowtrees love your little jokes. I spotted the talent goin on up here first visit, yes indeedy.

She tore off a corner of the *Lakeville Journal* and dug a ballpoint out of her purse. She had a book of names, she said, world names. Little hobby of hers to collect names, look up the meanings and stuff. I let her spring this little trap to catch my surname. I wrote it down and she slipped it between the pages of a Spanish phrase book.

F said we'd better go as the dump closed at one. Verity

stood behind the screen door while we tidied garbage into a sack and put it in the Honda.

– Hey you guys! I'm sorry but gee I think it's real darn wrong of you to scram like this . . .

F slammed the hatch down and we drove off.

The dump was only two minutes out of Gethsemane. The sky hissed grey. Buzzards hopped over mounds like snapped umbrellas blowing inside out. Rats shinnied up after them in half thawed mud, scraping the snow into slush and howking up rot in lumps. The dump warden stood outside his hut checking off dumpstickers on windshields, waving us out with a mittened hand.

– Where do we go now? F said.

Homer Sparrowtree's blue Subaru went by the dump gates as F gave way. She reckoned he'd been out to the Sunrise Diner for breakfast. Being a cafe eater I was now a diner fan, so F took Route 7a to Ashley Falls and picked up 7 out to the Sunrise Diner.

I still couldn't believe I was in America, the way it'd been so unplanned. Instantly America. A few days after we'd met I took F to my room in lodgings. My Finnish landlady called me into the passage.

– Pleash re-moof your starff. It ish infected. You haff a duty not to allow such spreading. You shay it is raining when it is not. I can't haff you in thish house of misery any longer. How dare you bring that . . . *thing* into my housh.

F was sitting on the floor flicking through my paperbacks. I said:

– My landlady's just kicked me out.

F drew her knees up with a grin I couldn't fathom. I said I didn't know where to go or what to actually do about it. F's grin increased my perplexity. I tried taking her hand for the first time but she wouldn't move it away from her knees. Just stuck out one finger so I took that and commenced the recitation of woes but pulled up after a handful. I could see she didn't need anyone who thought their life was finished, so I apologized for being pathetic. No grin but an eye roll. Oh please, she said, and begged me to use the word pathetic properly at least.

In those days she always said, when making a point: *as a matter of fact . . .*

– As a matter of fact, I know where you can go. Come to America, she said.

We left the house and walked round dark streets. She described the house on Milkweed Lane room by room. She said her father was a *savant*. She wasn't afraid of him, but she was afraid of going back to America. America would put her back to where she'd left off, giving her back to what she'd escaped from like she was the loose part in some broken-down machine. Bolted down for good this time. It was her father who'd summoned her home with abnormal urgency.

She flew out a week before me, but her father had stayed away until he knew I'd arrived. F said he'd never issued papal bulls before. It wasn't his way. He only offered suggestions which were measured and never delayed till a matter became urgent. In fact in his mind urgency meant human failure somewhere along the line. He was a scientist. He claimed you couldn't adopt into a system any decision-become-fact arrived at through urgency. Only Verity could do that for him.

The Sunrise Diner was a yellow shed, board and nails, fifties wallpaper, chequered tablecloths. We ordered scrambled eggs, hash browns, wheat toast, jelly and coffee. F said Dad was miserable. He didn't know you could make something go away if you wanted to. Did she mean me or Verity? All of us, she said.

We drove back through Ashley Falls then away from the house past dormant fields skinned grey by grey skies, varicose trees. The landscape F grew up with. Farms and foothills where the snow had thawed. The Housatonic running high and mustard brown in brown light. She said her mother had a good lawyer for the divorce and her father a bad one. She'd forced an agreement thick as the Yellow Pages.

— Verity doesn't have the right to set foot in our driveway without my consent. She doesn't have the right to lay finger one on that screen door if I don't so wish. That's what this is all about. Did you see what she was wearing on that pudgy finger? My grandmother's engagement ring. She thinks she's gonna be my stepmother.

The light culled as she drove and drove. By three the sky had landed across the Northeast Corner and the air turned icy. Frozen lakes. A tiny cemetery with one twisted tree. Bright white barns of the rich weekenders. Empty houses with the TV left on for months on end. We drove into Lakeville for the third time, stopped at the gas station for coffee, parked by Long Pond for a cigarette. WAMC crackled on the FM. Another driven circle in halflight. Whiteboard colonial shining in the wet, deserted make-believe houses. Bartholomew Cobble again, finding ourselves in a steep lane, trees in closed arches, POSTED warnings to TRESPASSERS on every trunk. The place was closing in so we turned again and drove away from the house out towards Twin Lakes across the icy tracks, a bitter wind shrill across the car. Headlights on, we sat and watched iceblown hail off the lake sweep through the beams, crushing warmth back into each others' hands.

At Milkweed Lane we found Beulah Stafford's car parked outside the house. F ran in ahead of me, holding the screen door saying Come-come-come, beckoning. Beulah was standing with her feet apart in the living room, hands in trouser pockets. Verity, caught in the act of talking about us, hugged a cardigan tight across her dugs as F walked in. Beulah straightened, buried her hands in her coat, pulling

the back pleat open, wool crusher hat slipping forward.
Verity broke the ice.

– Hoolah-hoo, back already folks?

Beulah said:

– Oh hi Effy – look Verity, I'll talk with you later
about this, okay? Effy, I gotta run kid.

The lamps rattled as she goose-heeled in her ropers
across the floorboards. F stood aside.

– Beulah? You haven't met my friend.

I was cold, tired, unshaven, jet-lagged, what with
Homer's insomnia and Verity plugging up the house with
threats. The mood was so uncertain and depressing as we
shook hands. I said hello. Beulah snatched back her hand,
snapping out her chin with a HI, peremptory, prejudicial. I
knew all about being put in my place by social superiors.
And I understood from Beulah's presence in F's stories that
Beulah was the most necessary person I had to impress. F's
mental mother, agony aunt, story-maker, refuge after the
divorce, guardian, teacher. Beulah was the talented all-
rounder, the confident, late-thirties heiress with a dying
mother. The ghost-writer, journalist, horse-woman. You
want someone snubbed out, you call in Beulah Stafford.

– Gotta shoot now Effy, okay?

Verity pulled the rocker out the corner and set up a
footstool.

– Gee, there she goes. Beulah. Wow, she's bin a rilly
great friend to me, Effy , since you've been gone. Did you
know that?

Verity gloated my way:

– Did you know, Effy wouldn't've been a goddam thing
without Beulah?

– So what am I now, Verity?

– Oh gee, this is tiresome. Homer's rilly upset with you
two. My, your vibes are just so negative.

She blamed us for bugging her whole day. The rocker
slipped backwards as she plumped in, sneakers scudding,

24

her Spanish phrase book hitting the floor. She thought I at least would be intelligent enough to realize how things were, but she was prepared to try and understand us. She was a Quaker. I asked F what Verity was on about. F said no one ever knew. Verity scrambled up and grabbed her stuff. We'd ruined supper and given Homer a bad turn. Now we were making fun of her instead of being friends.

– You disappoint me, Effy. Your daddy sent you to Europe for culture and you come home a loser.

A throat cleared on the landing

– Ahhhhmmmm you young folk. Do you have ahh any plans for supper?

Verity reminded him of all the spaghetti she got. He said he did not repeat not want spaghetti with his meat. Did we have food? F said we had plenty. That was good, he said. That was okay. He put his steak in the broiler. Verity said why the hell did he think she dragged the goddam microwave up here from Clinton? He had no idea, and went down the cellar.

After supper Verity said F shouldn't be drinking coffee. Even de-caff made you miscarry and she knew F didn't use precautions or know jack-all about Day Care Centres. F rolled her eyes. Mr Sparrowtree's chair scraped backwards at this kind of talk and he left his steak bone unsucked. Verity blew on her microwaved spaghetti and said she'd go wild bananas for real cholupas this minute like – she drubbed the pages of her Spanish phrase book – no mwee pee-KAHN-tay? case she got the runs.

Mr Sparrowtree was tuning up his hammer dulcimer on the piano top. We'd all finished eating. Verity burned her tongue both ends and followed Homer half-way to the piano but stopped when he started up 'The Three Crows'.

Verity hummed, whistled, la-la'd as she edged back into the room with us, sprang forward and had F by the wrists. In this witchy hissper Verity says:

– Sweetheart there's one little bitsy thing your daddy

25

and I have to ask about your friend here, you know? We've gotten a mite anxious in the bench over an *aspect*.

F pulled away:

– You want to know how old he is, yes?

Verity missed this time and clutched at straws.

– Now there ya just damn well go again sweetie, coppin an attitude, tetchy as a goddam lying cat . . .

– Oh for chrissake Verity he's thirty-three.

– Holy shit I knew it, Homer! Homer did you catch that? Didn't I say all along he's just too darn old to be hangin round a young girl?

'The Three Crows' didn't falter. Verity poked about from one room to another. F sang along:

The Third Old Crow his name was Paul
and he was the greediest one of them all
So they all flapped their wings and cried
CAW CAW CAW.

IV

*B*rooksie was the first American I ever met. One day this lady just walked into my old man's office in Rye and said:

– I'm Ruth Brookes Timex and I've got this boy called Brooksie Junior at prep-school near Peasmarsh who doesn't have a place to go for Easter.

The black nameplate screwed to the office door said FISHENDEN, STOVELL & JOSH INSURANCE BROKERS.

– Brooksie Senior insured his underwater cameras here a month back, didn't he tell me, Mr Josh?

– Call me Sandy, Mrs Brooksie.

– Well, hasn't Sandy a twelve-year-old boy too?

That boy stood listening on the landing.

– We'll take li'l Brooksie, I heard my father say.

– Call me Ruth, Sandy, and take this for your trouble.

The office was a short cobbled stroll from where Henry James spent his lonely years at Lamb House. Mr Josh was the third partner and managed his own lonely brokerage.

People mistake Rye for one of the Cinque Ports. The town's now inland from the Sussex coast, but sea once covered the marshes. Fishenden & Stovell had their poky office in Tunbridge Wells and called it the Kent Branch. Come school holidays I was dragged to Rye and banned from mischief. Left to my own devices I taught myself to wog stuff like Avon floats and Batman Rollykins from Woolworth's, hooks to nylon and lead split shot from

Swifty's Tackle. I kept my distance from that office with the dark undertaker's sign, its grave and shabby clients and my old man blotting columned figures in blue Quink.

The afternoon she came I'd been down the harbour brushing off the shit after my first fight over a girl, counting the fishing boats coming up the Rother at high tide. The Quarter Boys struck quarter to five. I was late and legged it up the office. I could smell her perfume on the staircase and heard the door shut. The lino creaked under my eavesdropping, a dead giveaway if this woman hadn't had a voice like a fire-siren.

The Rye office was on a corner off the High Street, through a side-door, up the staircase above a dim low-ceilinged chemist's shop, deep blue jars and dust a fingertip thick on the window shelf. I leaned over the stairwell, wiped a grey hole in the window grime and saw through into the shop below. A lank in a white coat held a shaving brush over the counter. Dust on his voice too.

– Pure badger.

– That's the ticket, the man with a five o'clock face said.

And the woman behind my dad's door:

– Oh Brooksie'll just luv it.

Voice and perfume silted up the stairwell. I tip-toed to the toilet and pegged my nose.

– Okay Sandy, we'll get Brooksie Junior up here no later than three-thirdy Wednesday pee-emma.

– Righty-ho then Ruth.

The threadbare office carpet jammed under the door if I pushed it far enough.

– Who wazzat then dad?

– Where the hell've you bin? It's gorn five o'clock an mind yer own business.

That ear-raking creen of the filing cabinet drawer. Grey United Friendly calendar. Equity & Law thermometer/penstand. A wooden desk with kickmarked legs, drawers jammed tight. The pink blotter furred and fungused with

28

ink rings and varicose doodles. A desktop blight with dead man's cup ring.

This was Easter Week in a month turned sharp and icy. A paraffin fug rose in shimmers from the sea-green Aladdin he'd taken from our kitchen. And standing over it brazing his arse and rubbing ginger fat rooty hands was ol' Ernie Cripps, dad's factotum.

– Y've done a bit o all right there Sandy. Made o brass them Janes is.

– That'll do, Ernie!

– Now now, Sandy.

Ernie came free with the wind-up photostat the dentist two doors down chucked out. Ernie knew how to work it only because it was duff and Ernie had the time and patience and the twelve bottles of chemicals. He sat on his yellow kitchen chair beside the Photo-Matic, waiting his turn. Once an hour he'd pace the carpet edge for his circ-ye-lation. His left eye was glass. Come out from a stuffed fox, he'd said. Dad said nonsense. It were really a cat's eye out the Staplecross road. Poor Ernie was a windy codger, sounding like a steam train shunting up ten stairs in the morning. He drew his pension Mondays and didn't even work for a pittance. Some beer money to spend in The Blue Moon.

The Quarter Boys chimed 5.15. Cat's Eye was ready for his other honorary duty. Posting the envelopes.

– Tootle-pip then nipper Josh, he said. Spec yer dad'll bring yer once more before'm gorn, ay Sandy?

My old man always had an unpaid dog-robber in his numerous self-employments. The imposture worked both ways. Retired or disabled, these gummies called him Sandy in private, Mr Josh in public. They'd pretend to work for him so he could pretend they were his employee. As a bestower of dignity and privilege he demanded awe and loyalty of his staff. Even worship. These old men who'd worked and grumbled through fifty all-weather years at the

29

same gaff and missed both ruddy wars by a hair. Semi-illiterate, they marvelled at his knowledge of the intricacies of Third Party, Fire & Theft, and his black-fingered way with motor cars. Ol' Cat's Eye was genuinely enthralled but once expressed some lingering fascination for Dr Bridgeland the dentist. Mr Josh smacked him down with irritation.

– Dentists aren't doctors. Bridgeland's just a silly old fool. Backed his bloomin Wolsley onta the pavement t'other day an missed me foot by a whisker.

Wednesdays were half closing in Rye but in those days you felt the closure over the whole countryside. In the light, the sky, the absence of people, the crap on Wednesday telly. By mid-afternoon even Sandy Josh packed it in and went home with the Wednesday treat. Three kippers and a jam sponge. My big sister never ate with us, only Sunday dinner when she skinned her peas and excavated the fat fragment by fragment from her one slice of lamb. This Wednesday should've been featureless. Mum paced window to window wringing her hands and twisting her handkerchief. She phoned the office a dozen times and let it ring ten minutes.

– Oh cummon father. Where is e fer Pete's sake? Doesn e know ow worried sick I am? Sick-sick-sick!

I didn't mention the American Jane. In her grief mum still got the tablecloth out and set the tea things. Two hours pacing the windows and my own patience was at its limit. Then:

– Maaaarrrmmmm. Marm 'e's god a boy wiv im.

She flung herself at the window.

– God in heaven father, I dunno. What the ell's that boy doin wiv im?

That boy stood on the garden path looking in at us, the monkey house. A chub-head in prep-school blue, school cap and schooly face. Mum blocked the front door scowling, hands on hips.

30

– Out the way woman, the ol' man said. Let Brooksie in.

No one used the front door in our house unless it was serious.

– E c'n go round the back.

– Don't be daft woman. Now, wipe yer feet Brooksie an leave yer shoes on the mat.

Brooksie stood in the front room. Blue-stockinged, mouth opening to blow pink Bazooka Joe membrane. The ol' man came in rubbing his hands so you could hear the skin whittling.

– Well doan juss stand there boy! This is Brooksie from America so make him feel welcome stead o' gawpin. You too woman.

Mum buttoned her housecoat and nailed her pucker at Brooksie, hands on stout.

– Where in God's name's e gonna sleep then father?

– Oh don't be daft woman, there's plenty of room. What's the matter with you?

His usual clipped impatience was replaced by this acted joviality which I'd learned to dread. It meant Opportunity Knocks. It meant his grammar went all *Ridout Book 2*, sieved through mimped lips with raised eyebrows, a face he never usually brought home with him. Office face.

– Well boy, say howdy to Brooksie then. That's what Americans say to one another isn't it, Brooksie? Howdy?

He didn't like dad calling him Brooksie. The dismay clamped to his face. This was rude. He hadn't known families like ours existed. Red-faced, dumb, like a boy tricked into orphancy.

We lived in a rented pebbledash bungalow clustered with other pokey bungalows round Bodiam village green. Bon Vista, next door to Castle View. The only other boy my age lived at Westward Ho and wasn't allowed to play with me. They sent him up the prow in shorts and magnifying glasses to the curate who instructed sickly specimens. We'd lived in Bodiam once before when mum and dad were in service to Lord Curzon's widow, the Marchioness at the Castle Dower House. I was too young to remember it, but some scrap of atmosphere got passed down to me unintentionally. The fact was they were sacked, turned out on the spot after the drunken cook sabotaged the boilers so Sandy'd get the blame. Lady Curzon discovered the truth sometime later and wrote to my parents, inviting them back. Sandy tore the letter into shreds. Then, when the Marchioness sold up and went back to her seat, we moved into Bon Vista and our family re-lived its bitterness. I dreamed of escape. I dreamed of fishing in America. Even the dream-car had dreams of its own in those days.

The view from our front room was puddles and cinders round the village green, white posts and chain link, some flattened by the coal lorry. The Castle Inn one side. The General Stores & Post Office opposite, summer tea garden at rear. The Tunbridge Wells/Hastings bus stopped hourly. A narrow, sluggish River Rother passed below the village under a hump-back bridge, making its way across the Upper Level to its estuary at Rye. Bodiam Station was closed when Beeching axed the Robertsbridge Branch Line. Guinness owned the hop farms. Old Holborn used a gatepost behind the castle for a magazine ad once. The telly shot a scene for Robin Hood below the castle. Then there were the summer visitors with picnic rugs on sunny days. Their long struggle uphill through sheepshit and thistles. The fourteenth-century castle with its moat and dizzy views, southern towers of real strategic significance. Life in Bodiam. It wasn't really dull for me as I knew no different. Just solitary, with long intervals when time froze solid. Events took place which almost included me and still counted. My sister's boyfriend came seventh in the annual Bodiam Hill Climb. My godfather dug up this Heinkel III in a nearby field, pilot bones still in their flying jacket.

Brooksie would be the great event, the real friend. He'd take me to America. I could live out my life in America . . . Only this false Messiah appears to shame us without opening his gob except to chew. There in our front room, smacking his right fist into his left hand in time with our mantel clock, smack–smack, smack–smack. Me and Brooksie scowling at each other as dad chased mum into the kitchen to square matters unsuccessfully. It was a total lack of symmetry between us all. There was no chance of finding a weak spot in Brooksie. Lady luck made this one. His opening taunt came in a snide undervoice and I fell for it.

– Hey kid, your daddy spent all his wages on my gum.

– E never brought you vat. Me dad ates bubbawl gum.

– Gee, whaddya know.

He squeezed another Bazooka Joe from his blazer pocket, popping the whole wad into his fat face, reading the cartoon wrapper like he hadn't an enemy in the world. He chewed with methodical purpose like running in a new engine, keeping the revs down, field-testing the fresh mix with a bubble blown through a sneer. The puncture made two loud clacks. Mum stomped umbrage into the front room, shaking her head as was her way.

– What's goin on ere then? she said for no particular reason.

The chipped plates were snatched off the table and slammed back in the kitchen cupboard. On went the best china from the sideboard, more bricklaying than table laying. Brooksie pigeoned out noticing this fit ceremony. Dad carried Brooksie's luggage down the hall so Brooksie settled in the master's chair.

Mum snapped:

– Not there mister.

He slid off making a monkey face. I skimmed through the *Angler's Mail Annual*. Brooksie unfolded a *Mad* comic from his inside pocket, laughing loud and chewing to himself till we had to wash our hands for tea. He stowed his gum in a twist of page corner. He wouldn't eat our kipper treat. Said it tasted like an ole burned tyre. For recompense he got a double hunk of sponge. When I complained, dad called me rude.

– Eat up, shuttup.

Brooksie snatched. Dad smiled. Mum tutted artlessly. Brooksie chewed sponge like gum, jam-lipped.

– You'll be sleeping in yer noo friend's bed Brooksie.

– Doan mind.

– Whadda bout me then dad? Where'm oi gonna sleep?

– Doan be s'rude boy – whadda bout me indeed! Y've slept on the camp bed before so what in heaven's name's the matter with you?

– Why carn 'e sleep on it then?

– Just finish yer tea and stop bellyachin lad.

After tea I was ordered to get the draughts out and give Brooksie a game. Checkers, Brooksie insisted. He won hands down, deliberately bored, and quit the second game when I jumped his king. Said he was gonna read a comic.

– Oh? Show Brooksie yer comics boy.

I didn't have comics, just some *Beano*s I'd bought myself from a jumble sale.

– Aw gee, they're kids' stuff.

He fetched me a *Mad* comic and chucked it across with a gloat. He knew I wouldn't get the cartoons, that I'd be shocked by pictures like this vulture throwing up from a dead branch. Mum refused to speak all evening. At bedtime when I was supposed to be brushing my teeth, I eavesdropped outside the front room door.

– Well father, juss what's all this about then ay?

– Oh fer Gawd's sake woman does it matter? The boy's here an he's stayin an that's an end of it.

– Well where's e come from fer the lovva Mike? Outa thin air?

Dad's explanation seemed familiar. Mrs This That &

The Other was the wife of Mr Important Client, hundreds of pounds, a high up, every magazine in America. And between these facts, mum's genetic interventions: pull the other one, it's got bells on, important my foot! Oh e is is e! . . . The Brookes Timexes, flat in London, weekend house in Rye . . .

– . . . and t'other day Ruth . . .

– Oh Ruth now is it?

– . . . came in about insuring a brand new Rover to take li'l Brooksie on a tour of Scotland for his Easter holiday. The poor kid's at boarding school woman, have a heart. He was lookin forward to it.

– S'whass e doin ere then if they're ser high an mighty, eh?

Family trouble in America, dad said. Ruth only come by two days ago. They couldn't take Brooksie to Noo York could they. S'posin our own boy ad nowhere t'go.

– Oh what, when we go t'Noo York yer mean? Nowhere t'go me foot. Tawk about bleedin hearts . . .

– Do shuttit woman! It was the least I could do fer the poor mite. I promised Ruth s'let that be an end of it.

– Ruth-this Ruth-that. She's led you up the gardin path this time. It's always the blessid same. These fellas send their Janes darn an they O Sandy this O Sandy that. Thought you woulda learned be now . . .

– Azzat boy o yawn cleaned is teeth or what? . . .

Just made it to the bathroom as the door flung open and mum shouts, Urry up, taking the ironing board out the shoe cupboard in a right cob.

– Pipe down woman an doan get s'aireated. What's done's done an it's company fer the boy isn' it?

Yeah dad. For Easter my company forced me to desert under fire, *Mad* comic-like spewings, jeerings, tauntings. Inferiority made me submit to my first fag. He made me smoke myself green. The promise of release from worse displeasures made me a smoker, holding down my drag

doggedly while he just pretended. After a smoke he'd
wrestle me knowing I was winded and poisoned, jumping
me from behind, pinning me in the grit the second we
were out of sight, spitting and panting an inch off my face.

– Say mercy. Say MERCY.

– Yeah awlroight oi submit mercy mercy.

– LOUDER.

– MERCY.

– BABY. You're jussa dork, yeah, an ah bet you doan
even know whadda dork is.

– Lemme goo Yankee pants.

– DORK DORK. Repeat after me: I know nothin bout
aeroplanes.

– Oi know nuthin bout planes.

– REPEAT: my dad's car's a heapa jurnk REPEAT my old
lady's ugly as a moose REPEAT I wish I was an American
REPEAT Disneyland's bedder than Bodiam . . .

They'd all been like that. Dead true.

Day three Brooksie had me lob a stone at the pub window
because he'd been refused a packet of fags at the off-sales
counter. Said they were for my old man too. The stone
landed round the back where they stow the empties,
nowhere near a window. But Brooksie went and split on
me, said I was always chucking pebbles at cars too. I
copped a public clip round the back of the leg, and the old
man branded me a big 'eadid show-off.

Brooksie didn't like the countryside because it was
England. It wasn't real countryside where there were
things to do and you could go anywhere and see bigger.
Bodiam was Pumpkin Junction, Rabbit Ridge, Clodville.
The castle was just an ole wigwam. The World War II pill-
boxes were Skunksville. Our food was slop. You couldn't
take a boat out on that crappy creek and most parents he
knew kept a cruiser and lived on lakes bigger than the
whole of Sussex.

– What canya do in a muddy ole creek anyhow dork?

– There's fishin.

– DORK that ain fishin ya do in there. There ain no steelheads in that chuck'ole. 'S jussa dirdy ditch fulla crap fish.

We were in the bedroom.

– You ever shagged a girl dork?

– Course oi ave.

– Yeah? What kinda shag wazzat then dork?

This was my sister's fault. Till she'd stayed in that night she'd not really caught his attention. Lulu Josh was twenty, betrothed to Rob Roy of Newenden who drove her to laybys in his blue souped-up three-wheeler. She worked in Tunbridge Wells and had to get up at six to catch the seven o'clock bus. Rob Roy was three evenings a week and weekends. Thursdays Lulu went home with Anne Foxwell the AA man's daughter to watch Top of the Pops. But come Good Friday she switched hair nights and stayed in for a wash and bath, a get-set for Saturday's Firemen's Easter Ball. She did her hair in the kitchen sink then hogged the chair by the telly, red dressing gown and this Pifco armchair coiffeur kit which was just a box of heating curlers and a perforated balloon which plugged into a dryer and fixed to her head with elastic. Georgette Heyer novel on her knees, tranny ear plugged as she turned shiny pillar box red. Brooksie spied over the top of his *Mad*, contemptuous smirks she soon noticed.

– Mum, avn't they got nuffin else t'do cep sit there gawkin?

In the bedroom Brooksie said Lulu was another moose who should pull that bag down all the way. I couldn't defend her or agree, so neutral because our paths never crossed, not even genetically. She had thick black hair and was taller than any of us. On her window sill were three polystyrene busts. Wig holders. At weekends she wore the curly nylon wig. Brown page boy for work, the spare for specials like weddings and balls. She glued false nails on her fingers and her eyelashes came free with magazines. When Brooksie heard her running her bath he said about the shag, dork. I was so afraid of him I made wild statements, feeling worse each time. The Joshes were just servants in a world of Timexes.

– Oh yeah dork? An whad else dya know Joshstrap haha willy-in-a-Joshstrap never knew what his sexy sister did in the tub rubba-dubba-dubba-doooo.

– Oh yes I do see yankee pants. Oi know what sex is fer a start.

His spittled laugh was so confident of my ignorance. All my school toilet-trained boy-logic went to pieces.

– Me sister told me what it were.

– Dork.

But he was rattled so I took a shot.

– Oi've even godda badge about sex.

True. I'd worn it on the green so Lulu saw it when she stepped off the bus, in a good mood for once.

– Where djew git that badge from, Jewboy? Y'll git arrestid wearin that an doan let mum see it.

Brooksie said there wasn't no badge. I couldn't find it could I. I never understood it anyway.

– Whaddit say then dork?

– *Sex is what yer kerry de coal in.*

– Dork dork dork that ain't sex it's *SACKS*. Anyhow I wouldn shag your sister fra million bucks. Bet she even wears a wig on er pussy. Gee, even my kid sister's godder own pussy.

– Why doanchew shuddup crew-cut. She ain got no pussy. We adda dog but its eye come out . . .

Even Brooksie hadn't taken me for a total dork. I didn't even know what a dork was. He stood open-mouthed on my bed, brain-shaped gum on the palm of his tongue, checking I hadn't made a joke after all. Then he clapped a hand to his face and trampolined on to his back. Above his

38

derisive moaning we heard the bathroom door chaff shut and the bolt clack home. The cold tap came on. We listened dead silent. Cloop, slosh. Lulu settled in.

I kept watch as Brooksie pressed an eye to a crack he'd found in the bathroom door frame. Pipes clunked. Lulu ran a tap now and then. Soaped bum rubbered on enamel. When satiated, Brooksie tip-toed away, jumped face down on the bed gripping the counterpane.

– Your turn dork. Oh boy, juicy blubbers AWWW an a great big fish pond with bushes all round it. Hey, doan forget to pull the chain first coz the floorboards creak.

The day Brooksie left, the old woman warned it were the end of that bloomin ride. Wouldn't get nothing off them you couldn't pull through the eye of a needle. The old man said wait and see before whizling. I knew we were a laughing stock and look who joined in the laughing. Me, planning life after Brooksie. How to get fags. How to get dirty pictures. Make the bathroom crack bigger and try and draw what I'd seen, then get to America armed with this essential knowledge.

We drove Brooksie back to school one evening, spring in the air. Mother stiffly petulant in the front, father so jovial and ridiculous it was obvious he'd something up his sleeve, one transparent hint after another.

– Got the time, Brooksie? Oh no it's not. Yer watch is wrong Brooksie lad.

Then we got a speech about how Brooksie was sure to tell his school chums about the smashing time he'd had. Lucky to have us as friends, his mother was. So how's about a holiday come summer? With us. This caused a shunt up the old woman's throat. He was after driving that Rover to Scotland. He'd do it in a chauffeur's cap, he wasn't proud. We never had holidays. The old man was driving a hand-me-down Austin A10 he'd picked up for a tenner last month. Fumes made us green in the back. Brooksie sulked with his head against the window.

– Tired out Brooksie? What's yer ticker say? All the excitement I expect.

– Huh.

The preps were due back at school for supper. We passed through Northiam, Beckley, Peasmarsh, turning along an unfamiliar lane, coming to a stretch of new orange grit rolled into fresh tar, a gentle hump before the brick pillared gateway. BEWARE OF BOYS. Two iron gates hooked open. The school crest. PEASMARSH COLLEGE INDEPENDENT SCHOOL FOR BOYS 3–18. As we turned in, Brooksie sprang like a dog kicked awake.

– Hey stop willya fer chrissake stop. You can't take me up there! You're not to take me up to the school building ya know!

Was he scared? We'd have to take him home again. His parents would die in a plane crash and no one would want him back. But he was threshing and elbowed the old man out, pushed the seat down, ran round the boot dragging on the handle.

– Juss open the trunk willya Mr Josh. I gotta get my stuff out thanks.

– What's goin on eh Brooksie?

Mum's laugh, nervous-like: oooooooooooooo–eeehhh-hhhhhhh, e's gone over all queer if y'ask me.

– I can walk from here, Brooksie said. It doan madder about drivin me up there thanks. Juss gimme the bags please. You ain ta drive me up there anyhow. Mom said. She did too, she did . . .

Brooksie's face turned to gum, and the gum to stone. In his voice was that bulb which parents plant. In Brooksie it was Spring and due to choke him with growing up. I could see things then, with feelings springing up like weeds. That shame of the Joshes. Nothing a bit of elementary car spotting couldn't explain. A Bentley, a Jaguar, the world of the Vanden Plas, Coupé and Roadster. Those other boys' snobberies wouldn't poke up with a Yankee Pant, an Alien. He'd learned MERCY off *them*. He learned PEASMARCH FLOWER SHOW'S BETTER THAN DISNEYLAND REPEAT MERCY YEAH SUBMIT TWIT off them. Even lonelier than me, his life was total misery. His parents had deserted him and farmed him out to Sandy, Woman, Lulu and Dork. If they saw him turn up with The Dorks now he'd never survive the term. They'd have him by the ankles in the bogs double quick, a swirly for Bilko. Blubbing his lies: My folks' servants had to drive me back in their sardine tin coz we're having a jet engine put in the Rover.

His fists grabbed the luggage as soon as my father lifted it out the boot.

– Yeah yeah that's okay Mr Josh thanks. Thanks I said. Mom juss said ta ditch me here, right? You ask her. So long . . .

– Aren't you forgetting something Brooksie?

– Oh yeah, sure.

And he slammed the boot down so hard it felt like a passing train. The old man was shaking his head and another speech died in the dentures. He held out this white box, enticing Brooksie forward.

– Take it, take it.

– Hey, whassis about? Ah doan wannit Mr Josh. Ah gotta go to supper.

Uncle Jovial's face flattened. Auntie Well-I-Never squirmed on her arse.

– Whaddizit whaddizit? Brooksie was frantic. The box was in his ball–mitt palm, nesting. It wouldn't hatch. The old man's impatience made a grab.

– Look, it's a pocket watch lad. Make yer pals sit up this will.

– Oh gee sir, I gotta watch. Dad got me this Rolex from Geneva. Give it to your own son, Mr Josh.

– But wait till yer see this Brooksie. There, look at the name of the make, son. Ain't that somethin?

41

Brooksie just shrugged. Submit.

– Oh yeah. I guess so. I mean . . .

– Whassit say? I shouted. Whassit say on the watch?

– It sez Timex, dork. Guess it's the name of some crummy clock company. I gotta go now.

Slow the first few yards, like waiting for the hand to fall, the trip wire. A spurt, and he runs up the drive. Behind us a chauffeur beeped politely. Our car blocked the entrance. As we backed out, two boys spied on us from the back seat with periscopes.

V

My second week in America and F went blind at the wheel driving back from New Jersey at dusk on the Taconic Parkway out of New York. She nearly passed out but managed to swing into a dirt lot behind a diner. We were thirty miles from Gethsemane. I was the runt who'd never learned to drive. F'd been driving since High School and I didn't even know how to tilt the seat forward or work the tape or pull the fuckin ashtray out. I couldn't even unlock the door and she slumps sideways saying you drive, you drive, you gotta drive us. All I could do was curse Rabbi Jake who'd obviously just tried to kill us. And Beulah Stafford who'd fixed up the treatment.

F had acne and a lazy eye. Homer Sparrowtree said he didn't want F driving till she'd done something about that eye. Verity got Beulah to make the appointment. Dr Jake used vitamin treatments and claimed to cure anything. He kept a faceful of stubble right up to his eyes. F said he played his guitar between patients and named all eight of his children after famous racehorses.

It was a routine appointment, 2 pm at The Tabernacle Clinic. The receptionist handed F a questionnaire. Other patients sat in the waiting room trying to fill in the 260 questions. This 180-year-old woman with wrinkled bones. A mad girl with her mother. A man with a boiler suit on back-to-front. You ringed either TRUE or FALSE.

ANIMALS JEER AT ME. SOMEONE MAY WANT TO BITE OFF MY GENITALS. I FEEL OLD NOW. I WANT TO MUTILATE A MAN'S GENITALS. STAIRS SEEM STEEP TO ME NOW. PEOPLE STARE AT MY GENITALS, and so on, 260 like that.

F said she was definitely not filling this crap in after the drive down had been such shit. Four and a half hours on packed highways.

– That right, honey? the receptionist said. Ah'll tell the doctor. This'll interest him ... Hello Doctor. The Sparrowtree girl refuses to co-operate ...

Dr Jake's message was: no questionnaire no appointment, surcharge for wasting time. The old woman and the mad girl were having their questions read out loud.

– PEOPLE SPEAK TO ME FROM A LONG WAY OFF, TRUE OR FALSE.

– What dear? Are what false?

– I said can you hear people from a distance, mum?

– No, not very well.

– True then.

– WALLS SEEM TO CLOSE IN ON ME NOW, TRUE OR FALSE.

– I SEE MYSELF IN SHOP WINDOWS, TRUE OR FALSE

– I WANT TO MUTILATE MY GENITALS, TRUE OR FALSE.

F said the poor Doc had fallen under another new influence but he usually grew out of them once Beulah got around to ghosting his next book. She'd just done *Cure Your Schizoid Kid in 60 Days for under $100*. The problem was, F said, he was actually very sound on vitamins and got greedy after easy success.

To save time F didn't read the last 250 questions. She ringed them all TRUE at speed, but even that took over five minutes.

The first sign something was wrong on the Taconic Parkway was F suddenly saying:

– I've lost touch with the car ...

Jake'd called her in after ten minutes checking her questionnaire. He took a blood sample and cut a blade's worth of hair from her nape, talked about God then hit a button on the desk.

– This is the girl, Jake said to the thin man who came through the back door. They kicked off with the newscaster routine.

– Everyone has this itsy bit of psychosis in em, Jake said.

– That's right Ben, no need to be alarmed, usually . . .

– But we're alarmed girl . . .

– That's right, alarmed . . .

– Why Ben?

– Yes, we ask ourselves why?

– Well, we'll tell you why. Your Experiential World Inventory Test . . .

– Exactly, your EWIT is WAY OUT girl. I had Rudi here . . .

– I'm Dr Rudi Backwater the clinical psychiatrist . . .

– . . . check it over for me. Now, you want the resta the treatment, so you come back and meet with Rudi in two days from now . . .

F said no way because psychiatrists make you feel evil and she didn't want to feel evil right then, thanks. And as for the EWIT, well that was a joke. She'd filled it in as a joke.

– Okay, Jake said. I'll give you your Vitamin B12 injection now, kid. The rest you come back for.

– That's right Ben. Ben's right kid. You should be on Prolixin.

– Hear that kid? Rudi's an authority ya know. Howabout some Prolixin?

F said:

– No way, what is this?

In the car I ripped open the envelope addressed to F's father. We'd thought it was just a bill and the insurance form. There was a facsimile of the prescription sheet. The Rabbi had spiked her with a huge dose of IM PROLIXIN *with parental consent*. Diagnosis: *schizophrenia*. Signed by the psychiatrist. Treatment proposal: *Long Term Psychiatric Supervision in an institution*. Fee: $120,000.

I was shaky on American law but knew you could be over the age of consent and still a legal minor. If me and F were married, could they still do this till she was twenty-one? Could they even consider her unfit to marry of her own free will?

In front of the diner there was one truck and a police car. Half an acre of vacant grass straggling beyond us bounded by provincial highway at the intersection. Fumes blew across the verge and a dead ball of filthy New York sun dipped under the tip of the bare trees. I took F's arm and walked her to and fro across the grass. We stumbled in circles over hidden ruts as she gulped the foul air, collapsed on the third press-up, cried as she jumped on the spot. Back in the car she just lolled forward again over the steering wheel and dribbled in her lap, half asleep, eyes like glazed eggshell. At one point she snapped to, a dying fish. She beat her fists and cried out against the Prolixin as it dug in like a saboteur. The air turned grey in the dusk. No buses, no railway line. Hitching was illegal. F wouldn't leave the car in any case. She would have to try and drive it. I still couldn't even work the air thing, open the glove-box or adjust the seat belt, me.

We started out dual control. I held the wheel with my left hand from the passenger seat to keep us on the road. My first touch of a car in motion in America, but the responsibility was too great to bear. F tried 30mph alone and had me read the road signs aloud, judge the distances and do a running commentary, like: You've increased speed to 35 – you're doing 35 steady, empty road, repeat after me my description of . . . But the normal everyday world of the habitual driver was for me a random, sudden threat, like everyone else was exaggerating and out of control and predatory. TRAFFIC. THE ROAD AHEAD. DISTANCES. F visualized. I even did LICENCE PLATES till it grew too dark and I picked out any detail from the gloom. I calmed in this halflight as the threats dissolved. I tried to recreate the way I drove the dream-car, the way the dream-car always drove itself, my participation child's play, sensory and passive, a means of conveyance through the imagery. It was like the way F made the car drive itself.

F knew where she was from my commentary now: INTERSECTION ROUTE SIGN MILEPOST DINER CARPOOL NUMBER GAS STATION, so familiar with the road her confidence increased. In complete darkness we pushed up to 40, UNDIPPED HIGHBEAMS burned into her, slowing her, crying out: *I can't see I can't see.* DON'T REST, I said. HIGHWAY PATROL shit, turned and passed a second time pulling over SOME JAILBAIT walking across the MERIDIAN in high heels. F said she'd have to change lanes and overtake at 45 or they'd pull us in for slow driving. A full half mile with her eyes closed forehead touching the windshield: *I can see as far as the edge of the hood where the lights start.* I couldn't see a way out of this. We couldn't stop, and her worst moments never coincided with the safe pull-ins TRUCKS loomed in the rear view LIGHTS CHANGING RED 100 YARDS, she changes down and THEY'RE GREEN NOW change up again lurch FUCKIN TRUCK blaring klaxons up our arse. Things I'd never reacted to before. Never drove the dream-car up the Taconic Parkway after falling asleep, such unfamiliar motion, my inability to co-ordinate instinct and reaction.

The dream-car broke down. We couldn't wake. We were in different cars anyway. My frustration, which under control might've been a contribution, tended to veer off course.

– I DONT KNOW WHAT THESE FUCKIN ROAD SIGNS MEAN DO I! Sorry . . .

So I described them in an inarticulate rush instead of naming them and added a curse for ignorance. F ended up calming me instead.

– Just roll some cigarettes and calm down. Even if we hit anything I'm not going fast enough to kill us.

So I rolled cigarettes and all the windows were down to keep the air cold and we were going fine again. First thing I'll do, she says, is teach you to drive. And I noticed that what passed between her and the Honda Wagon was so different from what had passed between my old man and his bangers. The way he drove them with too much knowledge of their mechanical fallibility, every cycle of the pistons meant a potential of 4,000 types of breakdown. Like I suddenly knew that F driving this Honda would get us home.

Coming off the highway onto Route 44 we drove in the real dark on an empty road which silenced us at last. Home stretch, and the car working itself because F knew both perfectly and she even made out the nearside yellow line making commentary useless till a lone vehicle struck us with glare leaving undissolved panic once the dark resumed. We raised the question we hadn't dared yet, like it was some truck looming on us, some deliberate malice from the opposition which'd gathered this first week. Sullen malice over our engagement which had turned septic.

– HEY, LOOK WHAT IT SAYS, WELCOME TO THE NORTHEAST CORNER OF CONNECTICUT. We're here . . .

Facing that last bend before the house scared us. By now F's mouth had dried up and she could hardly talk for coagulated saliva. She'd never had to think about this corner before, she'd done it hundreds of times. Left into Milkweed Lane across the tip of a snake bend . . .

– Okay, here's the flashing light, I said. A hundred yards now.

Three vehicles slipped from nowhere. Slight rise thirty yards. She changed down to coast. A thing she never did. I could see us missing the bend. I didn't have the dream-car memory of the exact reflex action to correct F's closing trajectory.

– Now, I said, CROSS, expecting her to shove it into third and accelerate. But my sight's nerve was crap. And when it came to it the dream-car was often a thing with no relation to a real car. Once it was a flying slipper and had a spare bobble sewn on the bonnet. Another time I just skidded along the road on my trousers miming gear changes all the way down the A21 to Sedlescombe. So I thought F had clipped the wrong angle. I forgot she wasn't driving a pair of Honda pants. Instead of correcting it with my hand gently, I yelled: Go right, confusing her. What else could she do but touch the brake to gain time to figure out my ignorance, letting me see she was exactly where she was meant to be, inch perfect but ramming it into third underpowered. We gargled across as this row of searchlights flew round the bend and took a paint scratch off our rear. F hit the floor, pulled the tit in second and we ruddered into Milkweed Lane, snagging on a verge in a retch of overrun and stalled. Lights off. We hid in the dark. F pitched forward, out cold. I struggled through doors and locks and seatbelts to pull her free like we'd pitched into ten feet of creek water. She came to and puked a lot of drive-up french fries down the fender. It wasn't the end yet. We dumped the car and I gave F a piggy-back the last 200 yards. She'd just flaked on the bed when the phone rang.

– Oh, her father said. Is F there?

His voice clumped up the line dragging unpacked wordage.

– Oh . . . well . . . in eh that case, I believe she should eh . . . be told . . . uhm sometime before tomorrow if eh that is possible hhhrrrmphhh. She should not drive . . . the Honda. Uhm the eh prevailing opinion, Verity informs me, is that eh F is not ahhhh . . . fit to . . .

– I know the prevailing opinion, I said. It's wrong. In the meantime *I'll* be driving the Honda.

VI

*E*ven aged five I knew dad was no fisherman before
I'd seen him fish. The way he toe-punted the football and called it footer. The way he'd no relatives
and my mum had dozens. He fetched the fishing rod from
the village shop when the kerbs were like breakers shifting
in the heat and fatted caterpillars gorged through the cab-
bages. The heat out front was like a hand smack on the
back of my legs. I swung half-way up the garden gate
watching out for the rod, already sensing family limits.

Every two swings I ran round the back to the wasp-trap
on the coal bunker. I'd shift deliciously in my skin as
trapped wasps cruzzed on sugar water, the sound dying in a
jamjar as the heat came down and the house shadow
moved off the bunker on to the path. There was no shame
in running from that, diving at the gate to swing hard at
the catch and quiver the box hedge. Dad's head bobbed
over the lavenders two doors up, his winter Blakeys silent
on the melting pavement.

The way he carried the rod gave him away. Uncertain,
hand too far along it, walking-sticky, a switch from a
hedgerow. And he was no fisherman most of all because
he'd had to go buy the rod from a sweetshop just to fish
with Uncle Bruce sometime. Nothin fancy Sandy, he'd
said. Cheaper the better really, case fishin's not your
cuppa tea.

Uncle Bruce took us down his garden shed to show off

his own half dozen rods for all occasions, hanging in their brown cloth bags from a neat row of nails. Our rod wasn't for any occasion. Old Pullin who kept the sweetshop only had the one rod in stock. A boy's rod he called it. Well, for coarse fishing in 1960 Mr Crabtree was telling boys to begin with a good whole cane rod with split cane tip. Ours didn't have the split cane tip. They'd whipped a curtain ring for a top eye to the middle joint leaving us with a seven-foot billiard cue for yanking pike out of meres, pike for pot and cat. And we were going roach fishing with Uncle Bruce.

He wasn't really my uncle. False uncles came and went like false Messiahs, never heard of again. But our boy's poker did look nice in the sunlight with its red silk whippings, mottled tonkin smooth under yacht varnish, bottle-green wood handle, brass fittings and a rubber button.

First outing was down the Rother at Etchingham, a nat-ural stream till they dredged it into a flood-relief channel. We'd been to these winter floods, an annual sight-see. You stood in the lane of a Sunday afternoon gazing over the flats with plastic telescopes and Brownie cameras, guessing where the true line of the river was. All the family cars per-fumed and Turtle Waxed in a row along the hedge. People waded across or swooped down on bikes through an open gate into the brown water which came over welly tops. In nightmares I stand alone in those fields of flat calm shallow water on all sides. In one unknown direction I'll drown in the river, no warning line of bankside trees.

We tackled up beside a five-bar gate. Uncle Bruce with his swanky three-piece float rod, long handle of smooth Spanish cork, ferrule stoppers like Taj Mahals. Showing off got up the old man's nose. Uncle Bruce must've been a vengeful prongo. On went his Nottingham centre-pin with its brass starback, spinning like a top at the slightest touch, fine line carried away like cobweb.

– There y'are Sandy, abracadabra.

I was spellbound, the way magic Bruce looked down the eyes to line them up, flicking his rod to check it was tight. Sergeant Bruce examined his platoon of attentive floats, all with names and numbers, sitting in a polished wooden box. He chose an orange-tipped porcupine quill. The hooks were in a leather wallet, tiny gold spade-ends which flashed.

– Haven't got all day Bruce, dad said wandering off, bored already.

Bruce pinched his split shot on below the float and leaned his tackled rod against the gate, quill ticking on the cane. Dad was away up the lane poking something black and shredded with his toe. Bruce called him over and said he'd show us how to tackle up the billiard cue. Dad punted the shredded object towards us.

– Someone's gorn an lost their fanbelt I'll be bound.

He took our rodbag out of the car and tipped it upside down. Two pieces fell out on the verge.

– I wanna do it dad.

But he was shoving them together like home-made chimney rods. Bruce just took the mickey and said he'd fix us up for catching old boots.

– Caw-haw, you wanna take this rod up the Legion Sandy, 'ang it over the bar.

And when he saw dad's tackle in a brown paper bag, PC Bruce said there was a law against kit like ours.

As the men fished I looked down the windswept river from a high bank throwing shadow on the water. Dad fished standing up, rod skyward, trying to grab his hook as the wind sent it whiplashing out of reach. The Compleat Angler sat downstream on his wicker basket, stock still beside an alder, orange quill riding the current. Black fingers Sandy couldn't get his bread to stay on the hook so he pinched a sultana out of our scones and nicked that on the point. It fooled a roach.

– Abracadabra eh, he said and started shouting, Bruce ee yare Bruce.

He swam-dangled the roach up into Bruce's pitch.

– Oh bloody Nora, Sandy. Y've sent em packing now inya.

Our last trip was in November. The Hexden Channel down from Newenden. Cold dark green grass, first thick winter muds, the hewing wind across our bobble hats. Dad tried two half-hearted casts then handed me the rod with no instruction. I'd never been allowed to touch it. A wind knot in the line kinked into a bird's nest. The rod blew out my clutches before the float came out the sky.

– Nay goot, he said. Pack it in.

Bruce stayed catching livebait for jack pike. Back home our gear was dumped under the bench behind the dog box in the shed and forgotten.

Five years later Lanky stepped off the 84 bus outside the village shop and lanked down to the bridge. A sight to stop me bouncing the wonky sheath knife off a tree. He might've been the grocer's boy or a fifth-year up Swattenden. He was tall and pale even from a distance, rubbing his eyes on the bridge and peering about. I followed him down to spy on his cargo. The fishing rod in a khaki wrapper, the gas mask bag slung over his shoulder. He scanned the upstream banks making downwind eyes to read the old metal sign, BODIAM ANGLING CLUB DAY TICKETS ON BANK. I was ten, and waking: this was *that* River Rother, that roach, that old cane fishing rod still dumped behind the lawnmower, primus, shoe-polish, cobbler's anvil and this cannonball, least m'dad said it were a cannonball. He said that about the meteorite so I took it to school. Mr Mills shattered that illusion with a hammer.

From the bridge I watched Lanky kneel well away from the water's edge twenty yards upstream. Half ten and the weak sun blots through a thin rag of cloud. You could drop a feather in the air. The Castle car park was empty. Old Ted walked out his hut and leaned on the fence smoking a roll up, watching the mallards clap and duck in the shallows. The pub landlord propped his blackboard against a barrel. OPEN FOR MORNING COFFEE PLOUGHMANS & PASTIES. I leaned over the parapet and stared in the river, flicking grit. Lanky gave me this look and stopped his busying. Anxious, not unfriendly. Jaw set white as he continued to tackle up. This patience was exciting, slow and riverlike. Had to stay and watch him catch his fish.

Something about Lanky was embarrassing. His stealth, or the poverty of his grey jacket. Bet he didn't know you catch roach with sultanas. That might be cheating. Bet *his* dad cheated too.

Most boys biked to Bodiam. Poor Lanky had to catch the bus. Poverty, the way my parents said our poverty was better than them Palmers' sort of poverty.

– Please don't do that mate . . .

The voice was nearly pleading me. He'd crept up unnoticed.

– Do what?

– That, flicking grit in the river.

Lanky leaned over, grasshopper arms.

– Look, I'm after those chub, that's why. Chub spook easily, see.

I couldn't see no chub even when I shinnied up on my stomach and leaned over. A car honked over the bridge, children in the back singing wwweeeeeeeeeeeeeeeeeeee as their stomachs jumped. I'd done that loads of times.

– Whossa chub then?

Lanky said there were three of them in the streamer weed just inside the bridge. Them blue-grey shapes.

– Nah.

Couldn't see them. I was scared of water anyway and coudn't swim. I followed Lanky down through the iron

54

gate and along the bank to his pitch. Lanky stroked and pinched his chin looking downstream at the bridge.

– Know what I am? he said like you tell a joke and grin first. I'm an ebberman.

From Lanky's pitch I could see the hop gardens where we'd lived in a concrete hut. Dad had driven the tractor and we'd washed in this river. Perhaps we'd eaten chub too. Was Lanky hungry? He was threading a queer-looking thing on the line.

– Whassat?

– Coffin–lead.

It was a lead coffin, size of a thumbnail. I wanted to be in Lanky's life, but I couldn't tell if I wasn't just afraid of hating him. I was used to this puzzle, bailing out the good in me so's not to sink from the weight of it. Lanky smelled of camphor and hard green kitchens like my gran's.

– What was it you said you was?

– You'll see, he said.

He mixed breadcrumbs and water into groundbait, snipped a few lobworms into lengths of slug with nail scissors, pressing these morsels into the groundbait, kneading two palm–sized balls and creeping sideways down the bank, tossing well upstream of the chub. Lanky wasn't like he looked. He spoke his words without damaging them. Whole words like teachers said.

– What school jew go to? I said.

– Kingston-on-Thames Grammar. Near London.

– You ever bin to America?

– Yes.

– Jew catch chub in America?

– I'm sure I could have . . .

Should I run home and tell them? Nope. I knew to keep it to myself. When the bottle didn't have a tight cap and I let something slip down the glass, it dried up in their breath. *Doan be s'daft boy. Doan shriek so.* Lanky would just

55

catch his bus back to London, so there was no point telling him either.

He bit a split shot on to his line and moulded a gobstopper lump of cheese paste on the hook, measured his cast with an underarm swing, a delicate flick. The coffin plipped in just under the bridge, bait bouncing off the dark wet sandstone.

– See, he said. I'm an ebberman. I fish under bridges.

Tucking his rod under his right arm the ebberman sat hunched forward telling me to sit. He held the line between his fingers, tight to the coffin.

– You can feel a fish blink with your fingers.

No waiting. He tensed as a chub blinked at the bait and the rod top knocked. Yyyesss as the tip arched in a whipped swish, rod and ebberman leaning sideways, a windbent tree. A commotion of boils under the bridge echoed flat. Something bronze jack-knifed in the ructioned water, walloped it to foam and set off after two fleeing companions. The ebberman was on one knee, silent with concentration.

– Cawww, I said, view goddim, zadda chub mate?

His rod kept up its swaying curve, line cutting to and fro the water. Where he gained, the line above the water hung with streamer weed like ensigns, the dogged, tired fish rolled upstream against the pull, then into the net without another say. He carried his chub up the bank to the softest grass, laying it gently, two shaking hands parting the mesh and extracting the hook with a swift two-fingered tuck. The chub's fixed cold eye was on us. Heaving gills sucked air. I pretended I'd caught it. It looked at me, blamed me for this. I nodded, touched its tail, smelled my finger. Me and the ebberman had something people didn't usually see. He weighed our chub on a little spring balance hooked to a netbag.

– Two pounds two ounces, not bad.

He stooped for a picture with his Instamatic then we

sidled together down the bank, chub in the dripping net. Ebberman slipped his chub back two-handed, a kick of its tail as it glided from sight.

Curious answers to my string of questions. Lanky said he lived in Wimbledon. His father played the clarinet in an orchestra. You can sometimes catch chub on floating breadcrust. His aunt was a smashing lady, she lived a few miles away in Hawkhurst. Lanky was staying there, only his step-uncle was dodgy and beat him with a hairbrush. What he really wanted to catch wasn't chub, but a carp. Were there any ponds in Bodiam? I said The Castle had a moat. Really deep with lily pads and reeds. He whistled and said his name was Bob.

I took him up the moat. He said there were carp in ponds all over Kent and Sussex. Old wild carp he'd read about. Been there since 1066. Long dark bronze and mud-green fish shaped like torpedoes what broke your line like cotton.

Next morning I was at the bus stop as the sun rose on the dew and the empties on doorsteps. My kit rattling in an Oxo tin. Gas mask bag, bottle of squash, two jam sandwiches and the old cane rod dusted off and leaning on the fence. Bob stepped off the early bus grinning with his rotten teeth. For the first time I looked at the moat as a fisherman. It was a breakthrough. My parents' authority didn't stretch this far. In a corner by the outflow Bob set me up, showed me how to bait a hook with a worm. The dumpy float cocked like a railway signal. A few seconds and it was jigging, plucked under and popping up. A top-heavy flick and Bob hooked a fish, a gurgling perch swung in on old Cumbersome. Spines up, fat worm thumbing in perchy's throat. He left me to them and moved fifty yards up the bank to catch a carp. I was sorry for him. He'd told me about the cunning of the carp. Walton had called it a stately, a good and very subtle fish – hard to be caught –

the river fox for cunning. How did Bob know if carp lived
in the moat? His dough bobbin didn't move. When he
reeled in the bait was gone. Knees drawn, long white
wrists, troubled over his failure.

VII

.

*B*eulah Stafford called me a *clochard* in her letter to F.
– That's French for tramp, F said.

Her letter came in the mail. Easter week, with everything bad. The letter summed up her opinion of me based on our one split-second meeting. It was well written. Authority, perfect pitch, the right three-page length not to weary of its subject and go flat in the middle. In fact the letter was that good I felt defeated, wiped out. It was that wrong in being so right (because she knew nothing), I never stood a chance.

Beulah said she just couldn't flog herself into getting to know me. That floundery handshake just wasn't pleasant enough to make the whole thing more than an onerous chore. I depressed her too. And F dressing like an old hippy and romantically eschewing the world was not a real answer for a real person. I wasn't worthy of F's talents and potential. Yeah, and I'd better clean up my act instead of looking like some street person from Haight-Ashbury on a time walk. I was probably after a Green Card. People in real life didn't marry after three weeks. Babies didn't heal broken hearts. The solution wasn't to marry the first man you meet then play wife to a misfit. F had to be real and setting up a pseudo home with that *clochard* was not the way . . . And so on . . .

F was transfixed and incoherent at the mailbox. She was going up there. Was a mistake. Phone. The letter furled

59

over the yard. I capered after it as F ran in the house. She'd tried phoning Beulah the last three weeks already. First few times Beulah wriggled off the hook. Couldn't talk. Dinner guests. Packing for New York. Gotta deadline. F never got her word in. Then Beulah plugged the answerphone on twenty-four hours a day and never called back.

Spring was early, which made it worse. The bank was dry enough to sit on, the choke cherry in blossom, bullfrogs hornblowing every dusk in company with the peepers' million whistles. Beulah's letter was even more cunt-hooks on the second reading. So published, seminal, concrete, so well crafted on a word processor, so engraved across my prospects. Then I saw the handwritten *post scriptum*. Most of us put PS and use the same plate for our cheese. Beulah's black scratch like flawed cut glass: *Don't take him anywhere near the house while I'm away because I don't trust him . . .*

Back from the phone F was inconsolable. Beulah'd gone to Canada for four weeks, least according to her answerphone. I suggested she was lurking in the woods with a shotgun waiting for me to turn up. F said, rather illogically I thought, that Beulah was not that kind of woman.

– She hasn't exactly left our dinner in the oven, I said, or left the key under her mat.

F said Beulah never locked her doors.

– Jesus, I said, I'll use my influence with the committee and make sure Beulah gets the Nobel Peace Prize, man.

F said this wasn't the time for sarcasm. I reminded her it wasn't the best time for Beulah to slag me down and send her protégée the bum's rush.

At least the Prolixin had worn thin by then. For the first few days I'd dragged F out of bed at 7 am, half pint of mineral water then straight outside to kick the football round the field. Bare feet, freezing dew, get the blood pumping for half an hour, chase the glaze off her eyeballs, the yellow white out of her skin. After black coffee and yoghurt she'd run the mile up the lane and back. She still flaked through the afternoons with a headache, dry mouth, handshakes, clumps of hair coming out in her brush, but she'd fought her way back to clarity by the end of the week. She could see again and wanted to read. Mr Sparrowtree and Verity were due up this weekend. We hadn't seen them since the first time. Okay, I said. It seemed the time had come for F to teach me to drive. In two days I'd better be on the road.

Beulah had taught F to drive when she was fourteen so F could take her into Salisbury when she'd run out of cocaine, when Beulah was too polluted to drive. Then she'd drive Beulah into New York City just to park on Madison Avenue so Beulah could spy on the Goldfish apartment. Goldfish was this seventy-year-old lawyer who lavished her, to her amusement. Once he got Beulah a $1,000 Western saddle. Beulah rides English so she threw it on the dump. Another time he sent her a $10,000 cheque because some shyster had paid him a fee he didn't want on the books in case Mrs Goldfish saw who paid it. Beulah called him cheap and fed the cheque to her cat. Goldfish said forget it, a cheque's only paper. As recompense he gave her his Shih-tzu because it'd just chewed up his $8,000 Mafia shoes hand stitched by angels. The dog cost twice that, he said.

F and Beulah'd sit there in the car on Madison Avenue till Mrs Goldfish had their inferior bring the limo round. This was F's cue to run up to the apartment, $10 bill for the doorman, a white box tied with pink ribbon, *Zed Goldfish III* scrawled in red ink. F had to hang the packet on the door, ring the bell and beat it. Beulah said Goldy screwed the maid soon as Mrs G took off to the beauty parlour for her sexy massage. This little packet would interrupt the randy old squirrel. Beulah never said what was in these boxes, so one evening F had a peek and found a pile of clippings. She told Beulah it was disgusting.

Beulah said: So Goldy likes chewing my off-cuts, okay? What's wrong with that? But Beulah, F said, you don't paint your nails blue. Okay, so some are my mother's. He only likes toenails anyhow, he trashes the rest. But Beulah, your mother's got Alzheimer's, she's in a hospice. Beulah said: Okay, so they're not all my mother's. They keep Goldy happy. Till mother dies believe me it's worth keeping him happy. After that he can chew on her corpse, see if I care.

I telephoned Jake the day after our Parkway drive nightmare. He refused to come on the line so I jammed the switchboard all morning, hitting the re-dial button time after time till he gave in.

– Hey, what's the big problem? he said. I do not like sieges.

He sounded like he looked, a pig-eyed, soft grey moccasin man, a bunch of idle fats. F said a few years back he'd been a lean idealist who made you feel unique if you had parents who hated each other enough to divorce. In other words, anything was better than what you wanted him to treat. Now he slumped all day in his swivel chair making phone calls in the middle of your conversation, usually to ad firms about his TV commercial, or the pet store to see if they had anything cute and cuddly which wouldn't live too long. Next day he sent out his bill in triplicate along with a wad of order forms for his books, $30 each.

– Your girlfriend not doin s'good, that right? Can't expect miracles to stick these days, you oughta know that. You've been around some.

I said F was my fiancée and Prolixin wasn't a miracle. Didn't he think we might get killed on the motorway?

– Excuse me, friend? On the what?

– The highway. The road. You knew she was driving.

– Did I? Did I know she was driving? I don't think so.

We batted this particular ball between us till it split. He couldn't see the connection. I asked what acne had to do with schizophrenia. He got shitty and said he was prepared for this, so let's straighten it out, friend. F came to him with acne *and* schizophrenia. He'd already known it. He'd had reports, trusted judgements, concerned parents.

– What have I got here? I ask myself. One alienated family, for instance, disturbed by their daughter's derailed behaviour, okay? Facts, friend. Big loud facts. I've done a lot of family analysis.

– By the way, I asked, what family are you talking about?

– What family? *Her* family. What goddam family dya think I mean Mr uhm, what *is* your name?

I said he knew perfectly well what my name was. I'd given it to his secretary about a hundred times.

– Okay then Mr Josh, let's keep it that way. So what else dya wanna know?

I said he hadn't answered my question: Who authorized Prolixin and why?

– Uh-huh. You wanna know who and why eh? Well, let's see. Your girlfriend's real sick, one real sick palooka. You want to know how sick maybe? Well, there's evidence friend and we got it all. Take the EWIT Test. Worst I've ever checked off and I've seen thousands . . .

– Don't make me laugh. She filled that in as a fuckin joke. She didn't even read the questions they're so ludicrous. If you're so experienced you'd realize . . .

– Realize? Listen bud. We're dealing in impulse here. She shows impulse to effect her score on the EWIT and zap! We got her. The picture stays the same, you understand?

No. I didn't understand. I told Jake he was out of his depth and knew it. What qualifications did he have to practise psychiatry?

That's when he hit the wall and said he had some pretty

influential patients when it came to dealing with critics and my ass was verging on the unclean.

– Okay, I said. Back to facts. What facts do you have?

– Fact One all emotional stuff with F is irresponsible right now. Fact Two she needs constant supervision in a controlled environment. Fact Three she's in no fit state to get married or make intellectual decisions for another three years. Fact Four drug poisoning means her whole persona's out of control. The way she relates now to the world is schizoid. She may believe she loves someone like you but the truth is she's so confused her reactions are one hundred per cent escapist. She just failed to adjust after the divorce. Understand now? She's not real. She's quit. Go home mister. Okay?

– No, I said. Did Beulah Stafford ghostwrite this little phantasy? I mean, when's the musical coming out Doc? Eh? Is she paying you to set this up?

– Look friend, schizo-girl was pretty high and pretty damn weird in my clinic, so I took a hair sample. Shall I tell you why? I'll tell you why, okay? This is why. We can identify every substance she's fed her bloodstream in the last five years. You with me friend?

Yeah, I said. He'd find no substance in her bloodstream he hadn't put there himself. *He* was the fuckin schizo.

– Yeah friend, Mrs Stafford's about summed you up. There's one astute lady. Lotta friends. You'll be hearin from some of em.

He hung up. F was still more upset about Beulah's letter than anything that fat shrink said. It was Beulah who'd lined up the shrinks in any case. Mr Sparrowtree's health insurance'd had a turbo fitted after the divorce. All F saw was a string of nuts milking the policy. You consult the next nut to undo the previous nut. Beulah claimed Jake was the unrecognized genius. Professional jealousy. Anti-semites. All out to get him.

F showed me the result of American health insurance.

$3,000 worth of tubs, bottles, packs, phials, capsules, liquids, syrups, pills, creams. Jake's prescriptions started at $50 a piece. Who was using who? Where did F fit into the experiment?

She said she'd been Beulah's tame stray really, her gamine. All fine and dandy if you don't actually bite the feeder. The thing was, Beulah had been trying to have a baby for years with this prick she'd married. She'd just dried up. Couldn't write a novel, couldn't have a baby. Anyone's guess which one of them lied about F being pregnant. Verity or Beulah, a connivance of the two? Fact One Beulah was out of a job. One dotty old ga-ga mother sitting on a fortune, a $16,000 dog with an expensive taste in footwear and a slob she cheats on. Trouble was she had the kind of influence a $16,000 dollar dog gets you.

VIII

*D*ad's cars gave us nothing back till I was six and Lulubelle swept us off our feet and put motoring in the family way again. Lulubelle was a white Austin 7 Tourer built in 1930. Long bonnet, chrome head-lamps you could cradle in your arms like geese, wings swept down onto a running-board where two brass-capped Redline cans painted blue were strapped with buckled leather tack. The flat glass windscreen opened out-wards. A velvet blind with silk tassels pulled down over the oval back window. The seats were like deep green leather armchairs. Onlookers clapped when we drove by. A rook and caw from the hooter made them cheer. Through Lulubelle's mediation family life was sacrificed, dedicated to the motor. Dad spent every evening under Lulubelle, on top of Lulubelle, hours after dark with an old headlamp rigged to a car battery. Weekends were spent touring breakers' yards or chasing up enthusiasts from their adverts. Eccentric men in leather caps and goggles came and went. Men with long smelly names which sent our dog into a frenzy. Their low resonant voices made the windows rattle. Silk cravats and red necks which made mum tut and scorn. They all turned up in some Austin Splendour. Beauties, they called them. Fancy a spin in the beauty, Sandy? Leaving mum indoors to moan and moan about the blessid beauties making our lives another blessid misery.

★

Lulubelle was taking us on holiday, dad hinting at a mystery miles and miles away. The great canvas army tent was strapped to the roof with four camp beds, billy cans, buckets, blankets, wooden ammo boxes full of special equipment wrapped in newspaper. The villagers stopped to watch us go like they did back then, dad honking as they waved.

We spent the first night in a field where a cow demolished the tent. Dad went down the farmhouse at breakfast to cadge milk but the farmer told us to clear off his land. In Wiltshire we got some toffees with a picture on the tin. We picnicked in the exact spot on the picture. Mum was edgy with dad.

– Hurry hurry hurry, it's always hurry with you.

The tomatoes in Lulu's bag fell through the bottom and rolled down the bank into the river. She called our holiday stewpitt and doubled her sulking. Couldn't camp here, couldn't camp there . . .

We arrived at night and pitched the tent in the light of the headlamps with the engine running. They made me stay in the car while dad bossed the tent inside out.

In the morning sun we looked across the bombsite. Flint glass thistles, tangled metal, rubble, a high razor-wire fence protecting several acres of tarmac the other side. A factory. Outbuildings the size of our village. And parked on the strip in long black ranks were the latest Austins straight off the assembly lines. Birmingham. Birthplace of Lulubelle.

First kick my football punctured on a rusty spike. Dad set off alone on foot and stayed away all day. Lulubelle reeked of sun-baked sick. Lulu gave me Chinese burns when Mum wasn't looking.

On the Big Day dad drove Lulubelle in the procession. The Mayor of Birmingham stuck a rosette in her grille. Bicentennial meant sweet Fanny Adam to me. Trapped in a forest of legs, the sky blocked in with umbrellas as the drizzle soaked in and the unreliable cameras clunked. They gave me the empty toffee tin. Birmingham's pride chugged by amid the cheering. The picture on the toffee tin was blue sky, a bridge over the River Kennet, dark green trees. I was lifted in the air between the brollies and the last toffee fell out my mouth.

– Quick boy look! Mum said. Ere goes yer father in Lulubelle.

Lulubelle made her final run that winter. The Annual London to Brighton Car Run was for Veteran Cars. Lulubelle was Vintage. We didn't start in London with the official competitors. We picked up the run in Bolney and drove the last twelve miles like a wolf among sheep. Crowds whistled and cheered. Flash guns popped. Dad waved back and honked, lapping it up. We cruised by conked-out Edwardian motor cars, goggled owners in blue cravats clutching filthy rags, cranking handles, wiping oily brows in despair or dropping red hot radiator caps as steam gushed skyward. Didn't Sandy feel ashamed of this superiority? Those fallen men in ulsters and the women buttoned onto their seats in canvas wigwams looked so authentic and crestfallen, their machines adventurous and authorized.

We looked out for dad's new cronies among the casualties but they all made it through the drizzles and fogs to the finish. Dicky Fawkes-Gun'arde was a pudgy toff in patched-up tweeds. He ushered us into the official paddock. Lulubelle got an honorary pass.

– Marv'luth ruddy sthplendid run down, Sandy.

Dicky's Victorian villa in Crowborough was now and then our Sunday pilgrimage, a brick edifice amid this rhododendron jungle. Dozens of eccentric pre-war motors strewn in various restorative stages. Eight Bugatti on the tennis court. Two Bentleys blocking the front porch. I'd counted thirty chimney pots. It took 1,001 strides to get round the outside walls. Dicky had a million pounds in a teapot. For the run he'd driven his Royal French bleu 1904 Peugeot. We stood and patted it in the paddock.

– Fanthy a thit in her young'n?

Hoisted in, I car-sat for the grownups while they went off for the ceremonies. An old woman in a purple cloak made her way from car to car, leaving something on the drivers' seats. She stopped at the Peugeot and held up a green velvet bag.

– What year is your car boy?

– 1904.

She fetched out a black penny and pressed it into my hand. A smooth date: 1904. Then a princess came by. Princess Grace of Monaco walking with Prince Michael after making the presentations. Delighted with the little blue French car and me sitting at the wheel in my school anorak. She polished the brass lamp with her hanky and kissed me on the cheek.

By next winter Lulubelle was sold on and it was like the dog had died, there was nothing to talk about. Hard times again, what with the old man scratching at insurance on a rat's ramble. The daily mileage was practical motoring. Mum called it trapesing for a crust and it obliterated Lulubelle's memory. For a while we were like everyone else, then worse. Sandy was back under the old bangers. His colleagues evolved from florid chumps in flying scarves to pasty, seedy twerps in stained suits who grunted, stank, bluffed and earned no praise. Sour-voiced with tea-stained whiskers they drove Morris Minors or Rileys like school-masters. There were always piles of little grey account books and elastic bands on the front-room table. No time to read his *Exchange & Mart* or *Motorsport*. It was all dormant. All bitter. The void which Lanky filled.

But even Old Cumbersome the cane rod soon warped and split down its middle, so they forked out for a new rod and reel but never wondered what fishing actually meant to me. It was all I did then, my fortress against them. It kept me away from the house in all weathers, in times and places otherwise out of bounds. I lived in a parallel world.

Brooksie came and went. The Wednesday treats died out and we got a council house in Hawkhurst. Ends never met. All downhill, going short. Sick-sick-sick of it, Mum was. Even the dream-car couldn't get up hills any more, and once it was a piece of wood nailed to four cotton reels which only went a yard at a time under the influence of telekinesis from which I woke exhausted on the edge of nightmares. Something would surely come along that empty lane where the trees met in the middle and blocked out the sky.

One morning we all drove to Rye with our belongings and valuables jugged and boxed and wrapped in newspaper. Dad parked outside Septimus Quayle's Emporium and went in alone. Septimus took everything. Mum sat crying in the car. She knew Septimus Quayle's sort, getting his clutches on our antiques. Most of our stuff came out the big houses they closed down in the war. Come Armistice the contents went to auction. Local junk dealers got the leftovers which in those days meant anything after 1850, furniture and knick-knacks. You paid a tenner and the junk man came and furnished every room complete, knick-knacks, pictures and all. Dad said this friend of his in Rye had an antique shop and owed him some generosity. Mum said why's it called a Bric-à-Brac Emporium then?

She nagged him all the way home, nagged his nailed face.

– Ow much'd e rob yer for then? I've a right to know, father!

He never said, but he was just as disappointed. Wished he'd never met the ruddy bloke. All those objects I'd considered organic family attachments were gone and the house was even more a prison without them. Old brass, silver spoons, three watercolours 1790, a little servant's bell from India, two Swiss Army dolls, lampshades from parchment wills, ship's tobacco jar, all dad's war souvenirs, other funny medals and weird coins, 6,000 matchbox labels, brass fishing reel, leather book, best suit, a sword, the cannonball, my Egyptian penny, an everlasting brass calendar. All the vases, tea trays, bone china, salad dishes, fruit bowls, kettle, drinking glasses, the tin I kept my brass tacks in, a tooth my sister dug up in the garden, and my clockwork tin car dad said had come from America, an off-white thirties saloon with a rubber wheel on the bottom which stopped it falling over the table edge, sending it to all four corners before it ran out of spring and cogs . . .

The paint peeled off the walls about then and the money went on coal and rent. The only furniture left in the kitchen was a fold-up ironing board. The Rye office folded up too. Dad got a job as a council rent collector and said he needed a decent car which wouldn't cause no bother. Out of nothing came this Jowett Javelin, reg. number HNJ 8.

We were away again and it heralded change and division in the family too. Lulu was engaged and driving her own banger to work. Snapped your head off too if you called her Lulu. As a matter of fact none of us needed each other. We hated our household duties and lived only for our escapes. Dad eloped with the Jowett, a severely elegant car from the dark fifties. Swept back, shrewd windowed, cold metallic green with a cream interior, buff leather seats, white steering wheel. She drove him straight to Nick Stripe who lived with his mother in this thirty-roomed house called Highgates out by the new golf course. Slumped in Nick's gravel drive were half a dozen Jowett Javelins, part-built, stripped or rolling chassis. Nick got one up and running once, drove it to work up the A21 and broke down near Green Street Green in one of those knuckle-skinning cold spells when it's dark by 4 pm. The phone rang in the middle of tea. Nick's SOS. *Rescue Nick* became a regular chore at winter teatimes, so did jokes like beatnick and sputnick. Mum said God almighty every time Nick rang. Another burnt tea. Eccentric wasn't the word for Nick. *Savant* with a touch of autism. Oily black hair flipped like a lid up and down his face. One lens of his gigs cracked from lying under Jowetts. Sticking plasters on the frames, his fingers, his face. He spoke like a ventriloquist and wore mechanic's overalls day and night.

Nick and Ma Stripe occupied three rooms on the second floor of the back wing overlooking the kitchen garden, a jungle of ten-foot nettles breaking through rows of glasshouse roofs. Old Ma Stripe'd once owned the entire view across the fields but she'd sold it to the golf course developers. One massive pine tree dead centre of the back lawn kept the house in shade. The brick walls were slimy under the windows and weeds sprouted from the cracks, moss and ferns carpeted the steps and paths. Ma Stripe never left her room, knobbing her Peking Lawyer on the floor all day or clanging on the servants' bell for Nick to scurry up half rotten staircases. Black handprints on all the doors, cups, walls round switches. Twenty-seven rooms were uninhabitable. One was full of rotting apples from the orchard the golf course grubbed up years before. All these brown shrunken Coxes boxed and stacked up to the ceiling. Nick scooped me up a jamjar full of maggots for fishing, thin-skinned juicy whippets useless on the hooks I used. In one room you could look up three floors and out through the roof, or drop a spanner down through the floor to the cellar. In another room he'd dumped his hoard of owners' manuals, every make, model and year of motor car ever built or imported to England, one giant mound like a silo you had to clamber over on all fours.

Nick's failure was contagious. We became not a two-car but a one-car/one-chassis family. A sudden run of minor automobiles came and disintegrated. We disintegrated. My sister despised us all and only came home to wash her hair.

Her only porcupine response to any of us was STEWpitt and a loud TUTT. She'd trawl her sulk up and down the stairs then slam the front door behind her. The rest of us used the back door.

Mum was drawn into middle age like a slow puncture overnight. An *Exchange & Mart* widow. She joined the Wednesday night Social and walked down the Institute with women she'd never deigned to notice before. The Social was a council tenants' downshoot of the snobby WI who didn't mix with us Hawkers, Palmers and Joshes. I was usually down the pond, up the field, along the stream, driving round America.

We came home one day and caught the old man in bed with another car. The 1938 Rover was gangster-fantasy-black, long, fast and loose. So loose it rattled mysteriously and had to be dismantled every weekend. The old windscreen stars were the best. Mounted winglamps big as cauldrons. A hump in the boot for the spare. Spoked wheels and painted wing nuts. Brass instruments in an oak and walnut dash. Flying lady on the radiator cap. The few times she ran we glimpsed speed and dominion. Like everything, it wasn't there next day. I never knew where they went or even why.

The Renault Florida was a flarsky one, odd but with distinguished provenance. Reg. BVB 7. In the logbook the original owner was Baron von Brabazon the 7th. He'd sold it to Richard Todd the film actor. A gold convertible, the Florida lasted a whole summer, mostly with its top down. Placid, elegant, it bit when roused, but it was a queer car to see parked outside a council house. White-wall tyres, pull-out vanity mirror on the glove box . . . this wasn't *au bord de la mer à Nice* down All Saints Road. Come September she was scrapped for the metal. Fifty quid for the number plate. After that he bought winter cars. Black sky-green puke boxes which always died after dark.

It was Nick Stripe's turn to ferry a wrench that winter.

Operations which turned to autopsies. These were winters when the only heat was a one-bar electric fire in the whole house. I washed every three days shivering in the kitchen sink. Hot water out the copper tank on Saturdays. Last-straw vocabulary at the tea table: *distributor, piston ring, bearings, sump, choke, gasket.* Sinking doom-laden words. Words that ruin a week and put the kybosh on routine. And when Nick's machines fell oil-side-down they debited the labour between them. Whole winters with mum's marriage under a tarpaulin and dad wasting his life on one perishing dud after another.

Kids at school'd say to me:

– Chroist Josh, whoy doan your ol man git imself a fuckin secon' and car loike everyone else?

– Year, ow many cars your ol man ad?

– Ere why carn e afford a fuckin Consul then? They're crap in they?

Teatimes were mum's limit. The bread and jam stuck in our throats while the old man bolted his down and kept up this dirge on having the clutch out before News At Ten, nothin else for it woman! Should get it back in before the Cassius Clay fight in Las Vegas comes on the radio at three in the morning. He moved like a blizzard. *Out the way boy!* Brisking himself into two pairs of old grey office trousers, ripped anorak with the stuffing hanging out, setting off in the dark with his hefty metal torch, farewells like chilblains.

– Right then, right then oh bother! Bloody torch. Ah good, that's fixed it.

SMACK.

– Right then, I'm orff. Sees yer when I sees yer.

Mum stands in the kitchen as the back door slams, shuffling her face.

– I dunno boy, when's it gonna end ay? I'm fed up to the back teeth with it I really am.

For the next four hours he's lying on some old bit of sack

and underlay up the cinders behind the bungalows even though old Stemp's complained to the council umpteen times about that Sandy Josh's wrecks taking up parking space. Got it near the streetlamp too the cheeky sod.

He's back for News At Ten and a cuppa cha ma. Barked shin, skinned knuckles, a moan like the wind and sleeting. You'd think the car'd pulled a knife on him. Burst gasket, sheared nut, shattered clutch, knocked it out with a wrench. The car lying there in pieces in a pool of wretched weather and oil.

My own immunity was breaking down. Fishing only liberated 6/12ths of my year. The unchallenged ritual was that in winter Sunday drives took preference. No ifs nor buts. One Sunday morning Nick didn't like the sound of the Morris either. Over dinner the old man said:

– How's about a shufty up The Downs for a look-see.

The old lady scoffed.

– Oh yeah? Pull the other one.

At Cross-in-Hand we parked in a breaker's yard.

– I knewwit! she toothed up.

Me and her sat in the Morris all afternoon. Our cars never had radios and we were morose company. The scenery didn't help either. Sumped on ruts of metal-mud, oil-green weeds, broken shards of orange sidelight. The daylight faded into gloom. Floodlights glamoured on the chrome blades of Zephyr and winter Anglia poking out the sludge. The old lady opened the door to stretch her legs and blow off. A pack of Alsatians grinned in wait and sent her slamming back in. Smelling mum's blood they roamed on fifty-yard chains, climbed on crushed jagged heaps of ex-family cars like ours. You'd think the little Sunday boys like me were still in the back if you saw the blaggers who did the crushing. The dogs haunched and whimpered when the blaggers swore and hauled doors out the wreckage for baying greasers. The old lady tutted every time she saw one.

– That's the likes of who yer father spends is Sundiz wiv!

Other blokes parked up, went in, came out, skidded off.

– Where the bloomin ell is e? I'm fed up with all these yobs.

The yobs peeled fins off Rapiers, wings off Zodiacs like fishmongers and butchers. Must've pranged their motors Saturday night. Blokes like them still came round our house for covernotes. Sandy did armchair insurance. Cheap, quick and handy for the frequent car changers. His experience cornered the Come-Cheap Go-Fast market. Hardnuts getting flashy motors and crunching them in burn ups. Oak & Ivy to The White Dog in under five minutes. Oak & Ivy to The Shades in twenty seconds. They'd all come round, Borstal boys, both Chapman brothers, that Larkin fella, Goddard, Gunn and Kirby, Dousty till he was banned for life, Don Ham the ex-boxer with his stock cars, even Pratt before he hit the monkey puzzle doing a ton, Oak & Ivy to The Shades in ten seconds. They found his head two days later over the bus station wall.

The trouble was, my old man the pragmatic motorist despised the lot of them, what with their Ford Consuls, Zodiacs, Anglias, Cortinas.

– Flashy bloomin rubbish. Only driving about for a fight.

After they'd left with their covernotes, you could hear the old man's motor neurones humming louder than our telly. I believed it all too. All that *no more sense than in my big toe rrrrrrrrrrrrrrr. Have to take the engine out to fix the clutch* . . . So why didn't I dream of revving up my own Anglia on the front lawn just to make him pop his lid? I could never look at a frigging Anglia myself without saying: *look at that cory in that poxy pile-o-junk you aff ta take the clutch out juss ta fix the wiper*.

No, mine was the clean dream. I wouldn't be a teenage driver. I'd have to bide my time because I was heading for open highways in a wagon that fixed itself like those self-clean ovens . . .

But that Sunday-bloody-Junkyard-Sunday. That was the first turning point. Me and the old lady'd had enough. Dad came back after darkrot smearing his hands in Swarfega at the standpipe, rubbing off with an old Y-front vest. He wrapped some prehistoric metal bone out this four-wheeled Morris Shakespeare Junkosaurus in the Y-fronts. Slamming the boot sent the cold wind through us. I jump-started right off:

– Oi'm gooin fishin nex Sundie idd ain fair oi ain allowed no fishin on Sundiz . . .

Sarcasm on the back of his hand. The old lady said:

– Shuddup the paira yer.

She wanted her tea but got more frostbite from the heart of darkness.

– Wouldn be no tea without a blessed car woman. Let's have some respect round ere an stop bellyachin like a paira goats. I got the clutch cylinder didn I? What more dyer want, a bloomin Jag an chauffeur?

I burnt some more rubber about fishin and got nubbed on the bonnet.

– Oh let the boy go fishin fer Pete's sake father or we'll never get no peace, all this car nonsense every Sundiz drivin me crackers, an look at yer blinkin cloze man. Wors'n a blinking tramp.

The Lanchester came with Spring when the trees were still bare and there was sleet all Easter. Lulu chose a good time to leave home. Broke off her engagement with that Rob Roy fella and then wrote the Standard off on the A21 at Flimwell. Her ex bought himself this Triumph Spitfire out of spite with his half of their six-year bottom drawer, then drove round the village pubs with a new blonde bird. Lulu was fed up with Hawkhurst. London for her. Earls Court. Or Ell's Court as mum told the neighbours. Rob Roy joined the Navy and took blondie down to Portsmouth. Three of us left at no. 51. Just suited us then, the Lanchester 14 Roadrider Deluxe.

The old man let them laugh. Who else had a wooden car built in the thirties? Exactly. It breaks down and you call out Rentokil. I called it Aero. With its grey balsam paste livery, Aero encapsulated drab, plummeting spirit. Some element of Welfare in the little saloon, though it was actually a luxury cart for them with only a little extra to spend doing A to B between the wars. All the Philistines down All Saints Road were jeering again: Oh-ho, stand back, anuvver Josh banger going off.

The old man tried to use the Lanchester to win me over too. I was thirteen or fourteen when one Sunday morning he says: Wanna drive the Lanchester? He'd taught all the spinsters and widows, the quiet footbound wives to drive, had Sandy. Queenie Miller, Edith, Mrs Baxter. Sunday mornings up Bedgebury Pinetum. They'd passed their tests and bought a Morris Minor, one of Sandy's archaeologies, but still, it made you wonder.

He took me up Flimwell, this field behind some sheds, a sharp slope with a dirt track where he said some boys he knew rode scramblers. He wouldn't let me drive it myself. I held the wheel but he selected first gear. 3mph, his fist doing all the actual steering and steadying. At the slope's foot he let me make the turn unaided. I stepped on it and swung. We stumbled and the engine let out a yelp. A red light popped up on the dashboard. I'd unbalanced to port and the old man took evasive action and ordered me out and told me to walk up the shed and wait there while he parked the car and went for a word with Ken. Half the shed was open barn. I pulled out a drawer in an old table and discovered treasure. Naturist magazines, *Health & Efficiency*. Noods. I shoved one down my trousers for later and flicked through the others, knob straight in the pocket. The leaky roof had crinkled the pictures but who cared!

There was this game of tennis, mixed doubles in the birth-day suits, plastic jocks on the birds and blank-outs over the blokes.

– Put that back my lad! I've a good mind to . . .

But he didn't. His hand fell loose. We both knew my childhood was over. It was why he'd put me in the driver's seat. That part of me which had no past was gone. Now I had a past.

Till then I'd even had to share his bath. Saturday evenings he'd bang on the floor with the Vosene bottle to signal he'd washed his hair.

– Right boy, mum'd say, git up them stairs and leave yer dirty pants out.

I'd squeeze in one end of the bath. Dad would have his back against the taps and scour it with a flannel. His scummy water lapped my ribs.

– You c'n bath on yer own tonight, he said as we got back in the Lanchester.

IX

*W*e were sitting in the garden as the dusk turned chilly. Spring peepers rose up from their winter mud, pea-whistling. Separate cars appeared in the drive. F's father just nodded our way and shut himself up in his shop. Verity Keffelk unloaded her Bible and a white greenhouse orchid like we didn't exist. We stayed in the garden to await events, moving up under the trees. Homer and Verity acted their parts like nothing had happened, no phone call about the car, no schizo-conspiracy. They moved in separate rooms and the Honda sat there for all to see, facing the road, ready to roll.

I was a driver now, with two days' experience. F had taught me to drive in an hour. She'd driven us into the forest, a clearing in the spruce, learners' leap. A hallowed place. There she'd taught me to dream, dream through the gears, the semi-telepathic exchange between driver and car. She was teaching me to drive the dream-car. I could already drive the Honda. Instead of waking with a mind in motion, I had clutch foot, gear changer's cramp, steering muscle fatigue.

It grew dark and Verity's patience broke first. She opened the screen door and yelled into the rapid chill for us to come in. The porchlight came on. Mr Sparrowtree had settled in his rocker with a book. Verity stayed downstairs flitting from window to window till she pulled the rocker out and put her specs on. F sneaked in and got our coats and the car keys. It was time I learned to drive in the dark. When I started up the Wagon, Mr Sparrowtree hardly glanced up. F showed me how the lights worked. Verity rushed to the screen door but I was away.

We drove round the lanes, criss-crossing highways, stopping for coffee and potato chips and microwaved crap at gas stations. I learned how to fill up with unleaded, first time I'd ever touched a pump. I learned to see in the dark all over again, driving like you'd tap a white stick along the kerb. At 1 am we found Verity waiting up for us, mumbling over her phrase-book Spanish, right hand stuck in a tub of deep-fried nut mix.

– Kwan-doh sah-lay el prohk-see-mo bar-ko?

Her orchid was skunking us out.

– Hey you guys don't ah ah ven-gah oos-ted ah vayr-may ah-mee-gohs oh boy yeah, whata language.

We stayed in the passage. Verity looked at me like I was Barabbas. We let her in one ear and out the other, but some words stuck in the wax. Easter, spiritchewell, Jesus . . . She supposed the presence of her Bible in the house would offend us. We went to our room singing *Michael Row the Boat Ashore*.

– You're ducks outa water Effy, gee, ahss-ta la prohk-see-mavess . . .

Midday Good Friday she came back from church in her flowery bonnet and pale blue chinos, pink lace-up cardigan and vinyl sneakers. Mr Sparrowtree was tipping junkmail in the bucket. Me and Effy in the kitchenette tried to make a run for it. Mr Sparrowtree made his announcement.

– Aahhmmm will you folk ah pay attention one moment . . .

– Homer, why don't you just come in here now and let me handle this. Effy, your daddy wants to clear things up sweetheart, so you just step out into the kitchen with me for our little chat . . .

Their plan was simultaneous interrogations in separate rooms. F and Verity, me and Homer. Me and Verity, F and her daddy. Me and F, Verity and Homer. Then all of us together again. Homer was facing the wall on the far side, nose-on to an oil painting of a fallen tree. I sat quietly scratching while he tried to straighten the painting. I could see he thought the fallen tree had caused the angle.

– Just ahh, how long do you eh intend, exactly, to eh . . . stay . . . here uhm in America?

We listened to Verity telling F she was irresponsible.

– Don't you even wanna *know* about contraception?

Mr Sparrowtree's hands tightened behind his back, shoulders knitted. Verity was shouting.

– Don't you even know fa chrissake how Day Care Cenners screw up a kid and exploit mothers, gee? Holy shit!

F said:

– Why should I want to know that?

– Why? Gee Effy you're gonna be a dangerous mother to that poor child. You thoughta that? You thoughta anyone but Big Liddle Me!

F said she was going to the bathroom. Miscarriage of justice. One baby round here's enough.

Verity yelled through the bathroom door about this an that. Above the noise I said to Mr Sparrowtree:

– I really don't know how long *we'll* be staying.

– Oh, he says, oh oh, well, uhm, hrruuhh, in that case would you mind eh telling me how er how uhm you manage to uh support yourself?

Verity was knocking on the bathroom door.

– You answer me, Effy. Let's have lessa that dirty comeback okay?

– Well, I said to Mr Sparrowtree, I'm a rod builder. That stumped him. Fishing rods. Fishing poles. He saw.

– Ahhh, you mean . . .? Yes. No.

He didn't see really. Hand-built, custom-made, specialist, traditional. Alien concepts. And he could see I wasn't doing this in his house, and that Americans wouldn't want this kind of stuff anyway. I said there might be other ways, that in England I took in home-work from tackle makers, whipping rod rings, two quid a rod, ten rods a day. He'd probably read about it in a Dickens novel. No, that was a new one on him. Well, I said, his mechanical fish was a new one on me.

– Oh, he says, you know about that? Hah. Electronic fish are not mechanical fish. Ahhm, let's get that straight between us please.

F sat in on this brushing her hair and the chats were abandoned by the three of us, so Mr Sparrowtree asked if she remembered his technician, Ted Climo, because Ted Climo was dead and . . .

– Homer, what is goin on fa chrissake? Ted goddam Climo, goddammit! Does she or does she not go see your specialist up here as we planned? Have you told *him* how sick she is?

She pointed at me. F said: what about Ted Climo, dad?

– Uhm, well, Ted Climo died a few weeks back which left me in a fix . . .

Verity went upstairs and slammed a door. Mr Sparrowtree moved to the passage so she'd hear his proposal to adjourn the uhm, theeeeee . . .

Homer and Verity were late back from the Meeting House. Verity slipped straight upstairs, Mr Sparrowtree tinkered in the workshop turning his lights off at midnight. Me and F had napped till early evening so we were wide awake at 2 am. We went to the kitchen and started to cook. Toast, grilled cheese, scrambled eggs, fried onions, coffee. We talked low and shared a cigarette. The landing light snapped on. A door prised open. The stairs creaked under slippers.

– Oh, he said. It's you folk. Well, okay.

Verity scuffed down behind him in a pink bathrobe.

– Homer? Homer? Is it a fire Homer? Is the house alight?

She clutched her purse and an overnight bag, her car keys pinched between free fingers. Hope more than fear. Mr Sparrowtree's face was puffed red from sleep blisters. He didn't often sleep so early.

– Oh-kay, he said. Verity claimed she could smell smoke.

– Gee Homer, I doan know what's wrong with your noses, I can smell it from here.

She took two steps down and touched him on the shoulder. He disengaged himself like someone'd cracked a raw egg down his neck. He came into the passageway and straightened a picture. Verity blew off:

– That's not the only crooked thing round here, Homer. Eh?

She laughed at her own joke and threw her bag down in the living room.

– I'm not going back up them wooden stairs till you find the smoke. This whole fuckin house is made o' wood and I don't intend to cook in my sleep.

F said she'd just burned the toast fer chrissake and we were smoking a cigarette.

Mr Sparrowtree fetched a flashlight from the drawer and had us search the house while Verity sat on the piano stool. Her elbow sent a wrong note whining through the house.

– I do *not* imagine things, Verity said.

– Exactly, F said.

Verity left her overnight bag downstairs and went back to bed. Mr Sparrowtree said he might as well stay downstairs and *do* things, he guessed. He sat at his desk with a lamp on, a rigid frown over a yard of computer print-out, the solemn pulling of files from his briefcase. His face didn't change. His breathing came in heavy clots through his nostrils. We watched him as we reheated the food. F whispered that Verity had really pissed him off this time.

At 3.30 am he drove off without a word. F guessed he'd gone down Colin's Diner, two minutes away in Gethsemane. His briefcase sat on the floor gaping open, files exposed. The computer print-out was in a file marked *JOINT PERSONAL V & H* headed *VARIOUS TOPICS AND THE VIEWS HELD THEREON BY VERITY KEFFELK AND HOMER SPARROWTREE AS COMPILED BY THE LATTER at The Red Barn Meeting House, Massachusetts.* This was a long set of questions on personality and opinion from Religion to Finances. The document concluded that *without fundamental compromise the relationship would be placed in jeopardy.* It was signed by a counsellor and dated yesterday.

In the file with our initials on we found scraps of paper, messages on legal pad in both their hands. One sheet headed *Tues A.M.* said: *Homer, Beulah called again, has consulted friends and all are concerned about packing the guy into a car − could he charge you with kidnapping? Beulah says we need crisis intervention, which is when a group of professionals come to the house to force a coming to terms between the guy and F with the guy present.*

On other sheets were telephone numbers of lawyers and psychiatrists with rough notes appended, like: *Nunley Kellington, position at closing − subject has no standing in house − can order him out and if he returns call police. I have no control over him once out of the house but since he then has nothing to do I can offer him a lift to the airport. If he refuses to leave the house CALL THE POLICE.*

Like all good page-turners there were some evil characters too. *Jake was with patient − call him 5.30 today, at home.* He must've done that because F found a note written at 6.00 pm in her father's automatic writing. *F is 'sicotic' and the situation looks bad and from what somebody has said about this guy he is unfit too. F said he told her he hadn't spoken to anyone in a year!* Another phone call, from Beulah, as reported by Verity: *F looks awful and tried to cash a check at the drugstore. They called Beulah up and said F was on drugs is why.*

Verity's pneumatic writing bounced off the paper: *Beulah said F accused several older men of sexual assault in Paris! She agrees we have to get ahold of F — she is disturbed thru sex and it is her desire to be molested by older men. Beulah agrees she must go into therapy because she has a history of bad behaviour since age nine.*

Verity's final note was a wall of victory capitals, a calligraphic fly-past dated two days ago: *HAVE HEARD FROM B. THE GUY WAS UNEMPLOYED ON WELFARE AND HAS NEGATIVE CREDIT RATING. WITH OUTSTANDING LITIGATION. GET THIS HOMER — HE'S AN EX-MENTAL INMATE.*

I said we'd better clear out, they couldn't stop us. They could turn me over to immigration. Anyhow, they wanted us gone didn't they? How much cash could we grab? Better slash their tyres so they couldn't come after us. What was so funny? Had F gone bonkers? Come here, let the psycho-bankrupt clochard disturb you thru sex . . . The files slid all over the floor . . . we were laughing on our backs, two drug-crazed lovers on angel dust whom nine good bullets wouldn't stop. Let's set light to this fuckin wooden house.

X

The second American I ever met was in the mental hospital. I was seventeen, acne, deep in unrequited love with Sarah. I smelled bad too. Sarah told me to stop leaving her 200 self-pity poems a week in her mother's milk crate. Poems about my craving for TB and wishing I'd been born middle class like her. Sarah had been in Bethlem Royal for depression she'd said was caused by writing poetry and reading T.S. Eliot aged fourteen. After she rejected me I spent days on the bed acting doomed with T.S. Eliot. I was accidentally at college doing English and Art A Level. So I became a Pre-Raphaelite and grew my hair, skipped lectures, sat all day by the River Medway. Fishing had evaporated at adolescence. Rivers weren't for bream and eels any more. You drowned sorrows in their melancholy flow.

The village doctor gave me the latest anti-depressants. Dr Lewis, oddly enough, lived in Bodiam behind the Manor which had become the Manor Hotel. Dr Lewis wore the sports jacket with the leather elbows and drove his blood-sample-colour MG open-top on house calls. A smoker, he always had a Guards pluming in the Roche ashtray during check-ups. A pocketful of fountain pens leaked inkblains on the tweed. Always asked how yer mother was. As a boy I'd watched him play cricket with the shopkeepers for the Wednesday XI. A nippy bat. He did what he could for me and dithyrambulism, as I named my melancholy. A fortnight on the pink things and I couldn't tell Keats from Shelley, didn't know yon sootys loft's penumbran dark from heaven's diurnal fireball XL5's glim. I slept through class, dribbled on the bus home, then paced the night away circling an easel in my bedroom. The old man jawed wearily across the landing in the deads before dawn.

– Will you pack it in and get to bed!

– I'm only paintin.

– Only paintin my foot! Yer ma 'n' me can't sleep with you scufflin about. Now do as yer told or do I aff ter come in there.

Ah, you couldn't blame him. He had to get up at 6.30 am to work at the Esso Garage in a grey storeman's coat. His gaffer was yet another big-headed fool who made his life a misery. We heard about it every teatime. And our car was back to a face-grey Austin Square 1 with gearbox disease. Things couldn't get worse. The paint had now peeled off the kitchen wall and the bills were stacked against us. What could I do but sneak out the back door when they were asleep and sit up the churchyard? This scared the tongues off them.

Without shame Dr Lewis referred me to an expert on haunted dithyrambulism. No need to tell my parents, he said. It was June by then and my general malaise became specific, even if I hadn't named it scientifically. My low ebb had the whole summer to flood Hawkhurst. How could I face that in a village where they never bothered changing the Almshouse clock to summertime? No girls'd look at a working-class freak in any case.

So late one afternoon I walked from college down to the Outpatients' Clinic in Tonbridge. The expert on poetical youth came straight out with it first question.

– Do you masturbate? . . . Oh come on, we all do!

Next question was trickier.

– Do you hear voices?

I said yes.

★

Unprepared for the destination of his next Sunday drive, the chauffeur said:

– This is a blow, son.

My mother bit her knuckles through a handkerchief.

– Why carntyer stay at ome where yer belong?

Till the morning of my departure it was never mentioned. In the event, like Brooksie had been, I wished he'd dropped me at the foot of the hospital drive, only I'd packed too much to carry. My entire belongings as a matter of fact. That is, all except my fishing gear. I crammed that bubble car up with boxes of books, two easels, my 78s of Adrian Mitchell reading his ancient polemies; some weird sculptures I'd put up on the front lawn which'd embarrassed our next-door neighbour and which the council had asked my old man to remove; my bottle and bones collection; all my paintings which had sandwiches and anti-depressants glued to them, and two goldfish in a bowl. One was dead on arrival.

We might've been prouder failures if the old man had the 1956 Sunbeam Alpine Mk III Roadster chugging up the beech-lined asylum drive instead of that Austin A to B, but she was still dismantled. When I admitted myself into Oakwood County Asylum, Barming, she was 7/10ths rebuilt.

The expert had called Farm Villa his *unit in the country for people like yourself*. It turned out to be a snake pit. Unpredictable, action-packed one minute, somnambulant and post-ECT the next. Frustration exploded in full view. Misery was turned inside out. Dirty linen day was every day. For the village boy in need of all the modern forms of self-pity this was Treasure Island. It was literally an island too. The main wall sat firmly in Barming, a Maidstone suburb. There was no back wall. The grounds just faded into fields. Farm Villa was the old TB Unit slap in the middle, half a mile from the Barming Wall. I could come and go in my own clothes. Three meals a day. Landscape painting.

So one June evening I was still a new patient standing among the pines with my easel set up in view of the occupational therapy sunlounge. I stepped back to admire another scalded-in pine tree done in a streaked whip of headache green. Someone stopped behind me. Two snicks of a disposable lighter. A sip of smoke. An outburst. Seeing as Oakwood was a mental hospital with hundreds of free roaming lunatics, I construed the outburst accordingly.

– AWOH. HOWA. WAOHHHWWW.

I suppose it could've been My Cat Jeoffry with a baked bean tin tied on his tail but I prepared to leg it. The nut could have my painting. Some of the long-stay blocks were dumps for mad Polish demobs from World War II. This was obviously a shell-shocked Pole. I'd seen them in work parties up the Pig Farm and in the gardening gangs, shuffling men with lumps big as oranges on their foreheads. Then I'd sometimes drunk tea with this bearded woman in the patients' canteen who said she'd split her mother's skull in two with an axe in 1937. On second thoughts I grabbed the easel to defend myself and spun round to face the monster. Atlanta Stixel Fairservice-Frost. Just her name was like a convoy of Black Marias on the way to Broadmoor. She was making faces like she'd poisoned herself. My painting was going to finish her off. She already looked deadly in that same daily knee-length grey wool skirt, slapping the midges off bare legs, skating out of wooden Scholls, long arm dangling when not in use, dangling from a rugby shirt this evening, the mustard yellow cardy hitched permanently round her shoulders. She dropped a bomb of a carpet bag to the ground, tucked a long strand of sparrow hair behind one ear, cocked her face, eased a top lip back from a full set of gelastic, smoker's-yellow teeth under a broken nose and said:

– AWW OHAWAH WAHOWAHHAAOW.

I warned her off:

– Don't come any nearer, the paint's still wet.

Words emerged from the honking.

– This is oh wonderfawwllll, so-so-so wonderfawl oohhaw do you know? Do you know where this reminds me of? No? New Hampshire. New Hampshire in Spring, Fall, Winter and Summer. The Four Seasons. Oh my Goooooooorrrdddd The Four Seasons, I can just *feel* that tree from here.

Atlanta jabbed her finger at the painting and finished her cough.

– I *must* have that, aw I won't sleep nights till it's mine you hear?

It was a deal. I let her have it for a King Size Dunhill. I was already in the Players No. 10/Sovereign Alliance chain-smoking gang so popular on the ward. This was 1972. Skinhead fags for the mean cupped-hand smoke. The pincer drag for nicotine tattoos. But in Farm Villa you also found the likes of Atlanta who owned bulk cartons of Dunhills and Chesterfields. Half the poke, twice the smoke.

My parents' first visit began in silence. They both lit up. The old lady on the Embassies while he rolled a fat light-it-again-Sam out of Old Holborn. I'd never told them I smoked. She'd never said much if I nicked an Embassy out her milk-book drawer. So on we sat, the isosceles triangle. She kissed out her smoke. He nose-leaked it. I sighed thin air.

– Well boy, she said. Dyer smoke or doancha?

– Eh, well, I mean sort of a bit I suppose, why?

She opens her plastic handbag and showed me the top half of a packet of twenty Bensons.

– Dyer wannem or doancha?

– Well, doan mind.

They watched me light up in front of them for the first time. This was the closest moment in family history. We all three smoked down to the butts in the sunlounge while nurses prowled up to the door now and then to check on the family bliss. I smoked three that visit and discovered that twenty Bensons lasted a normal day. That made a weekly deficit of 120. Atlanta's husband convoyed her supplies up twice a week, 200 at a time. She'd done me over that painting all right. Especially as I found out she gave them free to half the ward. That way she could blame our sore throats on her husband.

His visits were models of punctuality. Wednesday evenings and weekends. On Sundays he brought Ashley, their nine-year-old son who boarded at Marlborough House Prep in Hawkhurst, just up from Nick Stripe's. James Fairservice-Frost said to me especially:

– How awfully kind of you to make a gift to my wife of such an interesting painting. It is so fine. I'm having it framed for her study, for when she comes home, you understand.

I understood. Pulled my chin, acted with the authentic sosphistication of a fine artist. This club was *the* place to be that summer. I didn't actually understand the honoured guest, or why Atlanta couldn't be better off at home with him right there and then. I thought give me that impeccability any day. Or was it just wealth or manners or the mid-forties New England bulk and full Russian beard? Or was he European, the member of some intelligentsia gang? And why did he wear that drab wool suit even in the hottest weather? He was a smoothy though. He spoke the Harvard King's English to us all without condescension. A great mistake on an acute admissions ward. His patience embedded like a fossil, probably an evil thing in anyone else. Heavens, listen to me! What a jumpstart! But he was all that, and bore it on his face like it was all a hopeless tragic prefiguration.

But on the outside he was a draughtsman, an architect. On the inside, at night, in real life, he was a musicologist. He'd just uncovered a fraud after five years' research into the cataloguing of Bach's sonatas. Even to me, his social inferior cum-man-of-the-world all of a sudden, he was bowed under the weight and magnitude of Atlanta's trouble. She'd told me about their lonely oast-house in Sandhurst. I knew where she meant too, near this pond I used to fish, ten minutes on the bus from Hawkhurst, a thousand rungs up the social ladder. And another American at last.

– You really must visit us someday, he said, laying a quiet hand on my arm. I *mean* that *sincerely*.

He put up with a half dozen of Atlanta's favourites pulling up chairs and joining in for coffee. Such tireless trouble to understand our batty projects and appalling problems. He gave advice when asked. Shook hands in turn with everyone else's visitors. Even put up with Basher puking chips on him and calling him *Fuck May It's Gunga Din* every twenty minutes. Only once about every ten visits did he say:

– Would you all excuse us a minute to allow me a few moments' private discussion with Atlanta.

– Cor, we'd say, what's up wiv im today?

During the week Atlanta would conduct inconvenient phone calls home just after night medication. The patients' payphone was in the dining room with its lino acoustics. It was actually screwed on to the wall the other side of the male dormitory. Atlanta screamed at James till midnight, cursing him blue till the night nurse came and tripled her Mogadon.

Lunchtime performances were compulsory too. Mr Fairservice-Frost lunched in his office in case Atlanta needed to talk. Even she recognized etiquette and never called him during work hours. So in front of the entire gobble she'd accuse him of today's special, some over-boiled emotional crime or proofless pudding. Poor Chinese Suzie-nurse had to quit ladling our cod 'n' mush to lead her away to the medication room. An hour later she'd appear with bogged red eyes, a plate of scrambled eggs and a dozen schemes for cheering us up.

For weeks I believed I was her right-hand patient, one of the war council, my antenna alert for revelations. I found out nothing even though she dissected every feeling she'd had in her thirty-eight years. So I asked her straight:

– Why are you in Farm Villa under Section 28?

She blew the roof off.

– Heeee put me in here the bastard.

– Who?

– James the bloody first put his own wife in the bloody tower hawhawhaw.

I didn't get it. Even the nurses told *her* everything, all their affairs and betrayals, hospital gossip, rumours, professional gripes, which male charge nurse wore women's knickers, who was smuggling out barbiturates. Juicy snippets from the patients' files. She was popular but it wasn't popularity by trust. I was getting edgy. Her women's nicotines were wearing me. My application for a ticket to America with them at Christmas was turned down.

She stood out so, all six foot. You could hear her coming a mile off, smoker's snort, gluthering sinus, each journey a cluff-cloff of wooden Scholls. You could follow her trail marked in acrid plumes rising from ashtrays. Her filter tips weren't like ours. Hers had the tar honed to a single thickened point, the mark of a crack suck. Her ashtray fires were cunning incendiaries and had to be doused by coffee. Officials would run through the foyer with handkerchiefs over their nose, but Atlanta's ocean slapped every shore on the ward, all the key recreational points were moulded to her social shapes. Wandering cubs just homed in on her snide cackling signals.

– Oh my gawd did you know what Dawn just did? Oh Jeezuz she only got her *you know* stuck and sister had to aaww put a rubber glove on and fish for it oh my gawwdd.

Her time came. She was unmasked in the daily course of events as we all were. It was psychiatric tradition but Atlanta was the first I'd seen and it put the wind up me. It was treatment and you learned to live with it. You called it experience and lit up, sat down and blew it out, just keeping an eye out for a while. No one guessed Atlanta's problem. What a fool I was. Hadn't even seriously wondered why she was never in group therapy with the majority of us. She'd always mentioned her illness in the Farm Villa way, the obstacle to responsibility, the vague born-to-endure-it like half a thumb or sciatica. That doesn't leave a lot to ask. It was all so normal after a week. The ward didn't even have a cat-flap in case My Cat Jeoffry needed a home.

So how come I knew she was so doomed? An instinct you picked up for health and safety reasons. It was why we didn't criticize her emotive contradictions. Didn't object to her stammering rage, the door-slamming inbursts. You let them go like trapped birds flying into the glass.

One Monday morning in August everything was in its proper place. Atlanta the centre of attention. James due Wednesday. We were lounging in the foyer armchairs after breakfast like fish in tanks, waiting for group therapy. Not a care in the world. Jeoffry on my lap, and if Atlanta had snakes coming out her vagina like someone said, I wasn't dippy enough to see them.

– Morning Kay, morning Bert. The cleaners, hoover and lino polisher making Farm Villa nice. Unlucky were the patients on the washing-up rota that day. Dr Corky's secretary wasn't in yet. The ward clerk was just parking her car. Sister Mona Macreedy came like a streak of bleach out the office for a showdown.

– Atlanta! Come along now please. Stand up! I think the charade's gone on long enough, don't you?

Charge Nurse Paddy charged Atlanta from behind and grabbed her wrists, jabbing her cigarette out on the ashtray.

Half a dozen heads collided under the table because we all ducked under for the cigarette holder which flipped on to the carpet, already a martyr's relic, Saint Atlanta's sword. She was snatched from us, frogged into the corner lock-up right outside the TV lounge. Bare brick walls painted yellow. Green door, sliding peep-hole. Bars on the tiny window. Single iron bed. Concrete floor. Slop bucket under a chair.

We sat like worms chopped in half, twenty feet from the lock-up. We knew it was staged but we hadn't known Atlanta was sicker than the six we'd given her on our scale. She was yelling and swearing as Sister held her down on the bed. Paddy trundled out this hospital trolley, a bottle crate on wheels, across the foyer under our noses. Booze. Paddy had to kick Basher off.

– You'll be next Basher me boy.

Pimms No.1. Gordon's Gin. Cinzano Bianco. Fuckin Dubonnet too. Paddy left the door ajar. Wing Wong went in with a kidney tray and the paraphernalia. Atlanta's screaming turned fiendish.

– You just dare stick that fuckin needle in me you slit-eyed bitch and I'll slit six more eyes in ya.

She was strapped to the bed then Sister came and packed us off to Group. We were back in our seats for morning coffee listening to Atlanta's soft crooning. Christ I was thick. I thought maybe she'd had a baby or an abortion. No one was talking about it except Basher who reckoned she was boozing with Paddy and Mona. More attacks ripped through the wall without warning.

NNNaaaaaAAAAAAWWWWWPLEEEAASSSEAAAAWWW WeeeNUFF STOP.

Puke puke puke retch puke puke and they forced it down till she puked blue murder, at James for signing his consent, at us bastards too. This went on all week, 9 am to midday. No James Wednesday. No fags. Gasping we were.

Good old Sister Macreedy chucked us a pack of Dunhills

through the lock-up door to stem a mutiny. The second week, plan B. Random and unpredictable. They'd wake Atlanta at midnight or 5 am. We'd lie in bed listening to the dawn chorus, Atlanta's Pimms trilling in her throat. Or the Midnight Horror, Spew From The Tomb. She was locked in day and night and we were banned. Atlanta was banned. The peep-hole bolted. Mr Fairservice-Frost never set foot inside Farm Villa again.

One morning as Atlanta let go a plume of acrid groans, Sister made an announcement in the foyer: Atlanta wasn't our friend. Alcoholics didn't have friends. They didn't know the meaning of loyalty. Atlanta would sell her own son for a bottle of booze. She was a liar. James hadn't driven her to drink. He didn't keep her in Farm Villa. He was at home grieving for nine dead sons miscarried from boozing. Five years' boozing, folks. Nothing apomorphine treatment can't shift — aversion therapy to us. Unless she's incurable. You can't cure the unashamed boozers because they thrive on shame. No, you can't stop a drink driver before it's too late . . .

Friday afternoon Mr Fairservice-Frost pulled up in the car outside and sat there. A nurse humped Atlanta's baggage to the boot. Atlanta was conducted past us, travel blanket over her head, flanked by the Nursing Police. Mr Fairservice-Frost held the car door open and she was bundled in and driven home.

Late August Paddy evicted me from Farm Villa saying I was a con and had never fooled him for one minute. A half hour in Hawkhurst and I phoned Atlanta to suggest we had a nutter's reunion at her place. She said she missed the old gang and supposing she got up a Sunday lunch?

James Fairservice-Frost picked me up from outside no. 51. I'd be their only guest that day, a social experiment to get Atlanta back on her feet gradually. He drove the way they play the piano in concertos. Abnormal concentration on the steering wheel and windscreen, a crouching pause at the junction.

James only relaxed once inside his oast-house, calling out:

– Aaart-laantaah.

She'd locked herself in the kitchen to roast a side of beef, so James sat me in the drawing room with a dry sherry and explained the rise of classicism in nineteenth-century Russian music. Oh, I said, because he made it sound like bad behaviour. He illustrated the talk with a few bars and phrases on the grand piano. I was conned into sophistication, the most pleasantly cultured Sunday I'd ever spent. James wanted to be my dad. He might let me live there. Yes. It wouldn't matter about Atlanta having another miscarriage. Better still, just dump her in the long-stay ward and take me home to Boston . . . I sank into the grand tartan-rugged armchair, twiddling the cut-glass stem of my sherry glass, James working the piano keys like musical massage. I needed a name. I was Dick Fairservice-Josh, just back from a spot of the ole Varsity cricket practice.

– Where's the au pair, dad?

Pater quit tinkling a minute.

– I'm afraid Atlanta sacked the poor girl within minutes of arriving home. You understand, I'm sure, that she has . . . she feels . . . to prove her capability once more.

Already, Atlanta was an obstacle to my new life. I took a thoughtful sip. Perhaps we *should* put her back in Farm Villa at least. I could see Ashley now, beyond the open French windows, standing under an apple tree, squashing air from a burst football. He took a swipe at a dragonfly while scowling at what was probably the kitchen window. Play on, James, a Bach errr ditty . . .

But there'd been a change. I'd got too close. He could see his nine dead sons in me. His piano eyes were like stitched-up button holes, teeth clenched, exhalations through his nose. He was playing an overture to the next scene, the one where something dead, heavy, glass, hit the kitchen wall. Shards hailed on to the quarry floor followed by the old Farm Villa war cry DAAAAAAAAAAAAAAMMMMM- MMMN. About the loudest I'd ever heard. Fists drummed on the cupboard doors. Several wet squeals descended into final moans.

Ashley ran off through the orchard. Mr Fairservice-Frost played out the phrase to perfection, tapping his fingers twice on the still-humming piano before rising like a man in a club lounge who needs to go 'wash his hands'. The key was in his back pocket. He entered the kitchen through another door, closing it behind him with a smooth oiled click. A few seconds later he re-appeared, shutting the door behind him again.

– If you wouldn't mind, please wait outside at the orchard table.

This put me at an acute angle to the house, away from earshot. Ashley was nowhere in sight. After fifteen minutes Mr Fairservice-Frost came and stood with me.

– Ashley, he summoned. Ashley, there's a good boy.

We scanned about. No Ashley. He wasn't surprised or worried.

– I'm very much afraid, he began in slow drumbeats, and I cannot honestly say it was unexpected, and that I was unprepared for this eventuality . . .

This was Henry James now. A pompous git in a waist-coat. Dignity and understatement couldn't admit that the treatment never worked and that Sister Macreedy was right. Atlanta just wasn't herself yet, not quite up to company today. He knew I understood these things, perhaps better than he did himself. The strain of returning home. Time for adjustment. It affected us all. He was most ashamed about lunch. Invite a hungry chap like me who's had to put up with hospital swill for three months. Sorrow and apologies.

– Ashley. Ashley, here at once please.

The three of us drove back to Hawkhurst. He dropped me off at the top of the road. I cadged enough tin for ten No. 6 out the bus station machine.

I was lying on my bed Wednesday dinner time when the phone rang and the old lady shouted upstairs: You're wantid. Atlanta was in a phonebox in Hawkhurst, out shopping on her own. Said she'd pick me up outside The Library if I liked, pronto. As we drove out to Sandhurst I could hear muted bottles rattling in the back under a travel rug. Ashley was standing in the driveway sucking his thumb. Atlanta wound the window down.

– Darling, go count ten minutes right down the bottom of the orchard, honey.

He stooped away in silence. There were two crates of booze in the back. She told me to carry them upstairs to the top landing then go wait for Ashley:

– I gotta hide these bottles now and he only counts five, the liddle shit.

Ashley hadn't even bothered counting five. He was standing on the back lawn wringing his hands. Atlanta came right down.

– Shove Ashley, like I toldya, okay?

We watched him walk all the way to the bottom of the orchard.

– Doesn't he know? I asked.

– Who, *him?* Ashley?

– No, yes. I mean anyone . . .

– Neither of em know. You don't mean James fa chrissake? Haw, my husband, James. Christ! Doan leddit getya down. Listen, my vintner keeps his mouth shut, right? I pay. *I* pay. Pay pay pay pay. So you-know-who ain gonna know. It easy comes out the nine dollars housekeeping.

– What? Nine quid? Nine quid a week?

– No goddammit. You think we starve? I doan know how much. Nine quid a stinkin day, what else?

I said my old man only earned £40 a week.

Atlanta said:

– Well ya gotta drink honey if it takes nine quid a day! Gotta live dammit.

She finished a cigarette at the orchard table then went upstairs to take her Valium. She came down half an hour later with a glazed face and Hardy's poems, slumping against the table sweating yellow.

– Here. Readem loud t'me willya.

Folded between every other page was a sheet of lined foolscap, well pressed, faded and suffocated.

– My anthology, she said. Me an Hardy. You read my half t'yaself.

The two I read were handwritten, blue ink, looped sloping letters in neat ranks about New England glades, sunsets in fall, that old white wooden house by the pond up a dirt track through half blue hills she'd never see again it was all so, so lost. She rhymed Boston with lost'em, deep blue hills with keep new pills. As I read she kept interrupting saying:

– Well? Well? Well? Yeah, poetess me, hey. Ya know, I put maself somewhere between Liz Browning and Emily D . . .

Eyelids dropping, jaw hanging open, her arm fell over her foot like a baboon. I thought she was dead. But she'd only passed out and slipped off the bench in a crumpled twist, both legs trapped under the table, her face upside down on the sharp yellow grass. Thinking of Mr Fairservice-Frost on the piano, I finished off the verse aloud, you know, hanging on to that final note while you've got it.

> The ancient pulse of germ and birth
> Was shrunken hard and dry
> And every spirit upon the earth
> Seem'd fervourless as I . . .

Ashley helped me drag her like a hammock into the house. He was a massive build for his age, fisty, sullen, rock silent. His characteristic movement was a scowled head-shake to flick the heavy black fringe from his eyes. Hair which made him look fifteen, a good man in school mud. We anchored her to the sofa. Ashley was used to her dropping on to the floor, the way he chocked her up with cushions, positioning her head so it was face down. She snored and horsed her teeth each snarl. I found her sandals in the orchard and took some air. She'd made me feel sick. Just the sight of her hammer toes and the hair stuck to the sweat on her face. Then Ashley wedged her sandals back on and she pissed herself. He turned away, both fists tight. Her piss sounded like a leaking hose. The hurt and shame on Ashley's face needed comforting, but I failed him. All I could say was:

– What about you?

– Oh I'll be all right, he said. I don't mind if you want to go home. I know what she is . . .

A week later Mr Fairservice-Frost phoned me from his London office. He was in a meeting and couldn't get away, you understand. He just wanted me to run over to The Oast and check on Ashley. The poor lad had sounded upset on the phone and Atlanta wasn't available. She'd not been well of late, he said. He wouldn't presume like this unless . . . well, Ashley liked me and I sort of knew the situation.

I couldn't just run over to The Oast, as he put it. It took an hour and a half. I tried hitching but no one stopped. The road ran out of verges at Four Throws and I was stumbling up narrow banks on thin bends avoiding hay lorries and delivery vans. Finally the Bodiam bus came along but it turned off at Sandhurst and dropped me a mile short. I ran it in a smoker's record and found Ashley waiting for me at the top of the lane, eggbox grey, fists on both thighs.

– Mum's locked herself in, he said.

In fact she'd bolted every door and window. She'd done it before too. Ashley had hidden the spare backdoor key once but she found him out and this time bolted it on the inside. He'd gone up the pub to use the phone, having memorized his father's number.

We fetched a ladder from the orchard and broke in through an upstairs window. Ashley pointed out Atlanta's room then stumped down each stair like a ballbearing. From the landing window I watched him emerge and resume his apple picking down the bottom of the orchard. Atlanta's was one of the round-walled rooms. The keyhole was blocked. She wouldn't answer my knocking. I put my ear to the door and heard the clump of a dropped bottle. A bleak lowing from Atlanta's throat. I tried the door and it opened slowly against a thick carpet till it jammed, wide enough to get my head in. I made out the dark brown of closed curtains and smelt vile puke. Booze, sweat, ashtray. And she'd cacked herself or cacked in the room. Then from this muddiness she emerged like a new-born pit pony, on her knees, a pink crochet blanket slipping off her hind. I recognized the striped shirt and brown shorts as she crawled towards me, otherwise I wouldn't've known her. She picked up a bottle. I ducked out and pulled the door with me. The bottle crumped into the plywood and she started screaming at me. She didn't know who I was.

– Ged outowtowowowowowow ouutttt.

We wanted to get away from her so me and Ashley walked out to the Newenden junction and Ashley phoned from there. We settled on the bankside verge to wait but shit, no fags. I ran back to The Oast and ransacked all the rooms, stuffing about 200 Dunhills in my pockets made up from half-smoked packets everywhere you could think. She wouldn't need them. We waited hours at the junction, chewing straw, blowing smoke, chucking grit at a road sign. About tea time Mr Fairservice-Frost drove up from the station.

– Here's the bus fare, he said. Here's a bit extra. I'm awfully sorry we can't take you home this time.

She didn't even make that Friday's *Kent & Sussex Courier* because her death missed the deadline. The following week it was old news buried on page 9: OVERDOSE OF DRINK KILLED WOMAN. *A verdict of misadventure has been recorded at Tonbridge Coroner's Court on the 38-year-old woman who died after drinking a large amount of alcohol.* The plain facts were more explicit. He'd spared me any inclusion. The husband of the deceased had driven home from the junction and found his wife's bedroom door jammed shut by her body. He'd heard her snoring so he assumed she'd drunk herself into another stupor. Her doctor advised him to leave her be. At 6 am she was dead. The doctor said she was in daytime clothing. The pathologist gave the cause of death as suffocation associated with acute alcohol poisoning. 406 milligrams of booze per 100 millilitres of blood. PC Rhoades told the court he'd found an empty bottle of Dubonnet and a half full bottle of Pimms No.1 in the bedroom. There were no suspicious circumstances or evidence of foul play.

This was mid-September now. I never went back to college. The Sunbeam went under winter wraps. I tried hard on Atlanta's behalf but felt zero. I hoped I was wrong about that, thought it might even be a species of grief itself. But I was even unmoved by the self-disgust I lived with over my own Atlantic loneliness. All those falling leaves and the mist round streetlamps made me write a sympathy letter to the widower. I said I hoped he'd come to see Atlanta's passing as a release for him and Ashley from the fruitlessness of it all. His quiet reply said she'd been buried in a sloping, shady corner of Sandhurst churchyard. Of course he still regarded me as a friend, only because I'd witnessed Atlanta's suffering at close quarters. So under the sad circumstances it might be wiser if I kept away.

The old man struggled on with the Sunbeam till it was complete, while my own life had a loose connection and flickered on and off. The ex-mental patient was reluctant to rejoin the community. My old man's therapy was a Provisional Driving Licence. So one Sunday morning in May off we went, bucklegged into the Standard and up Bedgebury Forest for Lesson 1: The tying of the L Plates. An introductory lecture on the function of the clutch and its place in the modern combustion engine. To include gears, pistons and revolutions. Lesson 2 followed a successful lecture. I shunted. Back and forth, first, reverse, first, reverse . . . An hour later I was crawling in first towards the dual carriageway at Flimwell.

– Right, he said. Off we go. Increase yer speed. Clutch out and change up, which is down, into second gear. Remember yer rhymes: If In Doubt, Both Feet Out.

I hadn't changed into second before. My left hand sweated on the gear stick. My right was a dead weight and the car started to veer into the oncoming lane.

– Are you dense lad! Use yer savvy an swing to port! Both feet out both feet out.

My feet danced a mazurka on the pedals and every living thing in me gave up. The old man banned me from motoring, but the dreams continued, dream after dream on the long wide empty American roads, twisting overhung lanes, deserted city thoroughfares, silent forest tracks. And I always woke fascinated by the sensation I'd felt while driving. Movement and gear change were keys which cracked codes and meant freedom. You could only drive like that in America. But the come-down was instantaneous. Depression that I could never drive because I hated cars and guess why. I never even bothered to pack the fishing rods in the back of the dream-car after that.

When the Sunbeam was unveiled it won honours galore. My parents' outings became ceremonial occasions. Identical leather caps, letting the handstitched soft-top down, motoring the byways of Kent & Sussex to the admiration of all. There were the weekly events on the Sunbeam Club's Calendar. Assembly at Sir Philip Sidney's Penshurst Place or Lord Montagu's Beaulieu. The old man became a *concours d'elegance* judge. Honorary radiator badges polished up with the Silver Wedding Plates. Contestant's rosettes. Mentions in the Newsletter. Mr Josh of Hawkhurst carried Miss Bexhill at the head of the Easter Parade in a 1956 Sunbeam Alpine . . . Special Pictures in the Gala Edition of the Hastings *Observer*. That year was the pinnacle of a life's motoring. My mother finally accepting with grudgy pride a permanent place in the leather passenger seat, prouder and haughtier than him as they posed for tourists outside Olde Devonian Tea Shoppes.

XI

*W*e sat up till dawn planning to elope in the Wagon. F was sure her father had left his files out deliberately, giving us a chance to read them, giving us fair warning and revealing to F the impossibility of his position. He stayed out the rest of the night too and we fell into exhausted sleep before his return.

It was mid-morning, Easter Sunday, when Mr Sparrowtree woke us with a shout from the end of the passage. F panicked. She'd only left the spare Honda keys in the desk. She didn't have her lenses in so I went over to the window. The Wagon was gone. Mr Sparrowtree was still yelling down the passage.

– Will you folk respond please?

F opened the door an inch and responded. He gave us fifteen minutes. Verity was wearing red velour slacks and a blue running-top. She'd knocked some grape soda down the back of the stove and couldn't get the mop in. F asked where her car was. Verity asked where the Handy Wipes were.

– Where's my car? F pinched her lip with her teeth.

– Gee Effy, I just spent two hours prayin for you. Two goddam hours. You might pick up some glass and act less hysterical. You've been spoiled honey. The car's mine now. Your daddy's handing me the keys next week. Gee, you folk give me the runs, you know?

Mr Sparrowtree parked the Honda, locked its doors and

stood there squinting at the house, putting the keys in his pocket like something he'd picked out the garbage. Verity fussed in her purse when he came in.

– I was just telling your daughter how I was planning on having the Pinto recycled . . .

– Is she having the Honda or not dad?

– Ahhh . . . that's a separate issue . . . ah . . .

Verity butted in:

– Now we're all gathered Homer don't you think it's time we had our little heart-to-heart once and for all?

We had no choice. We needed the car. We all shunted into the living room where the sun had broken through already then fled. Verity headed straight for the rocker. F kept a fixed but distant grin in contrast to her father's toothache face. Verity told him to sit because heart-to-hearts go better sitting down. I perched on the arm of F's chair. Verity's hands floated round the room describing how the pretty patterns our chats'll take were gonna suck out the nature of the problem we were causing her and Homer . . .

– What problem? F asked.

Verity had her notebook out and scratched a thigh with an Arny's Arco Bic.

– Acting dumb won't answer that Effy. You're the god-dam problem.

– What problem? she asked again.

– Boy Effy, you're so immature about personal communication.

We knew what was coming. F wasn't scared of her, so I said:

– Just give us the facts, ask us some questions, tell us what's bothering you.

She sighed, pitied us and said:

– In your shoes I'd be afraid of the facts.

I said:

– I give up, just call the police.

Mr Sparrowtree drove a plough through his throat to clear the phlegm suggesting that Verity made a more concrete statement because this didn't appear to be leading anywhere. She slipped forward on the rocker to help ease her cramps, face like a rock-cake, staring at F through two dry currants.

– You're daddy 'n' me're gettin married and we're gonna sell the house.

The smile of triumph on the stepmother's lipstick.

– Is it true dad? You're gonna sell the house?

He managed to stand, sit down again, legs apart, hands dangling like a man peeped at through a slit in the door.

– Ahhmmm yes, it is ah true . . . it seemed the ah lesser of two evils. That uhm is the why of it . . . you know it's too far for me to commute . . .

F said it was wrong to sell the house and didn't believe he wanted to, or even could. Verity folded her arms and hung onto them like safety bars.

– Juss what is it you're aimin at Effy? I mean, gee, the law's pretty clear to me. My happiness wouldn't occur to you would it? My-my, I shouldn't have to spell this one out, but we're getting married and that's that. You might be sweeter steada thinkin of little me me me me. Gee I get fidgety vibes off you. Your daddy is not interested in what you think about the house because what you think isn't worth a hill of beans. You don't seem to have understood much: I'm gonna be your stepmother.

– Gee momma, F said, where'd yer keep your eye-teeth?

– Homer, damn you. Tell Effy how much her worthless education's cost the value of this house, okay?

He was too slow, so Verity said it wasn't worth Jack Shit because Effy's school fees and stuff had ate up and sucked dry every last nickel. She'd dragged twelve real estate dudes through this dump.

– Every Joe Shack of em, that's OO-no thru OHN-say,

said spend 100k on the dump now or it'll rot under your feet. It goes.

By then the kerosene lamps were rattling and the house was rotting under our feet. We bathed in Verity's smugness till her fiancé took himself under the chin and asked us folk what our plans might be. F started to say that depended on the Honda, but Verity tore up the charts with another Looney Tune:

– Are you two planning on getting married?

She was real-real concerned about that. I said:

– Oh, is there a deal in this? She ignored me and said if F was thinking of marriage she should not.

– Bad bad bad. Homer thinks so too.

I said in my best English noise:

– We are getting married, like axh'lly.

Verity didn't think so. That would be big serious trouble. Someone not 100 miles away had a secret he might not want to reveal to the authorities in a hurry. I said true, I was pretty sick of my own past too. Hadn't she considered that? Wasn't America the land of . . . of . . .

F rolled her eyes and said:

– Mechanical fish.

Mr Sparrowtree let off a big ha. This stung Verity up the arse.

– Goddammit Homer you're the only man I know who'd sit there making cracks when every John 'n' Jane Doe in the Northeast Corner but you thinks your own liddle girlio's pregnant from a thirty-three-year-old dough-nut-hippy.

I felt old and dirty again. That it didn't matter made no difference. Her just knowing about me and a mental hospital made me scum in everyone's mind, and my own mind. I had no insight to offer them. Nothing about me would ever change their opinions. No matter what I did or had done. Yeah, what had I done anyway? I didn't even dare get angry in case they'd think I was going berserk. How did I know the crisis squad weren't at action stations under the window? There was nothing I could deny and this gave me no access to logic. We just wanted the car back so we could fuck off, but this B-52 QUAN-do PROX-ima BARK-O wanted us obliterated. I had to get off the chair and go slash like an old man. And they probably thought I'd climb out the toilet window and make a run for it with whatever I could snatch out the fridge.

I came out the bog and tried to straighten a picture but the wire unhitched. Mr Sparrowtree came out to look. Oh, he said, and took it upstairs to the workshop. The three of us listened to the toilet cistern fill. Me and F held hands. Verity smirked. The landscape was bulging off the canvas, its river bursting the banks.

F told her father she was *not* pregnant. This was Verity's fantasy. Neither did she wish to be. The word pregnant was a welcome threat. Mr Sparrowtree could settle this one with his mind. It wasn't a family word. Verity tried saying it, hoping it would stick but it clotted up the place, joining the thick pumping swarths coming from her sickly orchid on the piano top.

– Ahhh . . . good, Mr Sparrowtree said.

– And I'm not a doughnut-hippy, sir.

I had to deny something myself. Verity was off her rocker, coming across the floor like a conger eel looking for a wreck, stopping inches from my sinking face.

– You an me're pretty much of an age, Mr Josh. We oughta be capable to understand each other, uh huh? We're gonna go for that now. Effy, this is hard for me but I want you to just trust your friends. We've all been cutting corners to help you outa this mess honey. I got daughters of m'own, remember? Now then, Mr Josh, we've got just one question for you: just what is your game with my step-daughter?

It was like I went into decompression, or into the dream-car, or I was cashing in my last wish. I needed

111

insight. I had to know the real answer to this question. I had to leave my body. My mind had to know how, if just for one second, to read the future. It's just survival. It's that seven-foot fence you jump when the bull charges. The inhuman strength we have to pull ourselves from the wreckage without feeling pain. It was all right. The answer came: I loved F. It was real. I wasn't conning anyone . . . I looked about, floated off, floated in, Mr Sparrowtree mowing the lawn or chopping the wood. He wasn't here. I had nothing to say. I was fishing in America at last. I came back and . . . washed the Honda – I didn't think we'd ever axshly wash the Honda, F said. I was floating round the room again. Old Sparrowtree had his specs off now, rubbin the cud with a handkerchief. Below the window this big shiny metal truck rumbles through Gethsemane on Route 44 and the house shakes under us.

Verity did concede I was doing it to myself too and maybe needed help. She wasn't accusing me of doing it on purpose to her and Homer and F, or of not loving Effy none. She was sure I thought I loved her, but they were kind of scared. She started quoting Beulah inaccurately and with no effect. What kind of love could a disturbed man like me fill a young heart with? Thank Christ F was making all the right shapes at this and doing all my fending for me.

– You think I'm bullshittin, Effy? This man is a weirdo honey. A con-man. He did three years in a state institution. I mean he ain't exactly gonna be no handy stepson-in-law about the house for me neither.

I suppose I got a bit interested then. At least they'd run it through their minds, but no, I was a chiseller, driftwood, been on state benefit for years . . . Alarm bells went off then. How did they know any of this? They thought they needed protecting from me. Verity was on her way over to the trash can to see if she could fit my clothes in it.

112

– Dad, F said, do we have to listen to this?

– Ahhhmmm . . . no. No, on reflection no, you do not
. . .

Verity's Bic flew across the floor. Effy was brainwashed,
drugged, seduced.

– Yeah, I said, by you and Beulah and Doctor Crippen.

F hit her on the head with deduction:

– Now I get it, you're selling the Pinto to pay off the
cheap private detective . . .

Mr Sparrowtree called over the recriminations for some
attention, to make inquiry. Did us folk intend, in the foreseeable future, to get married?

F said:

– Yes we do, as foreseeable as June. The Judge in Sharon
agreed to officiate on the twelfth when he gets back from
Toronto.

Verity looked skunked, hands like treble hooks on a Big
Charlie Brown Mugger. Mr Sparrowtree said the wisest
course, right now that is, seemed to be a practical one, in
his opinion. We might discuss things to more effect when
we'd all calmed down a little. Verity was breathing like a
bike pump.

– I might've guessed. Gee. I wished we'd gone thru with
that Crisis stuff instead of listening to your rational advice.
Hear what they had to say my ass. Holy shit you've upset
me.

She was slamming suitcases against the wall upstairs. Me
and F wandered off into the woods. An hour later the
Pinto was gone and Mr Sparrowtree was out back mowing
the grass on his mini tractor. F said her father just wasn't
reacting yet. Sitting out there on his tractor made the grass
more important than all of us, he could deal with that.
There was a machine for reducing its growth.

XII

I was twelve when I began to notice Mr Chittenden. The Chittendens lived next door in no. 49. Both three-bedroomed, only their house was raised on a steep elevation which made their front door almost level with my parents' bedroom window. Their back path went past our toilet window upstairs. And this wall towered over our back door and cut out the light and kept the Chittendens' house and garden from coming down on us.

Bill Chittenden rode a BSA Bantam 125 with a leopard-skin saddle cover. He'd had the gear change converted because his leg was tin up to the thigh. He lost the real one in a motorcycle crash, Army Dispatch. After the war the old-style gamekeepers like him died out when the estates were dismantled. He and Pearl had three sons and a cocker spaniel which he trained as a gun dog. Even All Saints Road was built on an old Victorian Estate, Copt Hall. It was parcelled off, auctioned, and the mansion demolished. Mr Chittenden hung his sign on the pea-green front door with its view across the Weald:

CHITTENDEN PRODUCTS
Leather Goods
Shooting & Fishing Accessories

Because of his tin leg, they'd shifted rooms and lived

upside down. The workshop downstairs, where the front room should be. Telly and tea upstairs. Dinner in the kitchen. The council didn't like it. Every Spring he turned no. 49 into a trout and salmon hatchery. The bathroom was put out of bounds and several thousand trout and salmon eggs hatched in the bath, from fry tank to stock pond size, the bathroom rigged out with longitudinal flow, regulated temperature, water circulation, corrected oxygenation, a system of trays, tanks, tubes and overflows. And in the backyard under the kitchen window he built a three-foot-deep pond, lined it with blue polythene and connected it to the overflow pipe and circulating pump. In went the fingerlings, dry-fed, wired-over. He released the rainbow trout yearlings a brace at a time into Slip Mill Lake and Riseden Lake. From Slip Mill they leaked into the stream and we caught them on worms as far down as Ockley Pool. They only weighed 4 oz. Wayne Pope said the bigguns stayed in Slip Mill. He'd poached it once, said he'd caught a one and a half pounder on maggots.

Lord and Lady Millais resided at Slip Mill House. I walked up the drive to get permission but the gardener barred my way with a dripping fork. I stated my business.

– Come to see the Lord 'n Lady bout fishin.

Got the cheeky nipper treatment so I poached it. The only way to crack it from the lane was casting uphill over the dam wall. The chute full of nothing but green slime ran under the road and into the mill. You had to use a heavy float too and if it never went in the tree you speared your armpit on the railings and everything tumbled into the chute and came back covered in snot. That old gardener was a bastard too if he was working round the front and saw us. He whipped old Gibbon round the ear and bent his tank aerial in half. Then I caught one, 8", swung it out through the railings and took it home wrapped in a dock-leaf. The idea was to hang about the front garden till Mr

Chittenden came down his garden path. He didn't know I went fishing yet.

He winked at me and clicked his tongue like he was calling a spaniel.

– Ello, bin fish'n tharn? Any joy?

– Yeah, cawt this.

I put the trout on the hedge and he creaked down for a butcher's. Shook his head.

– Tut tut, shouldna killed that. Way undersized, and I'm sure it's one o' me rainbers. Where dyer ketchit?

– Down the dump, I said.

He knew a fisherman's lie when he heard one.

I spent months trying to worm my way back to his attention, convinced he would like me and take me fishing if he saw I wasn't just next door's kid who poached one of his rainbows. I spread my fishing gear all over the lawn, hung my net to dry in the ivy, dug worms all day, put them back and dug them up again. He just ignored me.

As Mr Chittenden was a fly fisherman I decided the best thing was to pretend I was too, so I swished my rod about in the back garden to see if it could do as a fly rod. The tip flew off and put a crack in the Chittendens' kitchen window. I gave him up and got on with the actual fishing. The tench down All Saints Pond were bigger than his trout in any case. We were in different worlds, especially after *Trout & Salmon* magazine did a centre-page feature on no. 49: COUNCIL HOUSE TROUT – SALMON IN THE BATH.

He gave up the breeding not long after that, keeping a few rainbows and one brown trout in his garden pond. From my bedroom I heard him feed them at night. 10.30 pm, their backdoor creaked open. He called his spaniel click-click-click with his tongue. His tin leg creaked and the steel tips of his Veldtschoens rang on the concrete path as he took his usual turn, sniffed the air, looked at the sky, pulled the cover over his Bantam. The warm still nights were best. I'd sneak to the window. He had his blood-wet

116

polythene bag of defrosted liver chunks. He'd clear his throat like kick-starting the Bantam. Then he flipped the liver chunk by chunk on the water. A mashing lash of trout foam as they ripped it with their needle teeth, gorging swirls like a Piranha monsoon. The spaniel whined at heel. Man and beast, the way they slowed the world and gave my imagination the slip. These were sacred minutes for which I'd stay awake to share with them. I'd kneel at the window in the dark trying to see what they were doing. Why so still, so silent? What was I craving for in that nothingness? It was all beyond me so I just decided they were lingering out there with the six fish circling each other in the liver oil slicks, the bare lightbulb from old Hop-along's window, and then his bulky shadow limping over the water a fraction before the light was extinguished. I couldn't fall asleep till then. And when I did, the dream-car took me to unknown lakes packed with rainbows.

One night I thought I'd go out there and capture the moment myself, be Mr Chittenden, steal the secret. Mum thought I was washing in the kitchen sink before bed. In fact I'd snipped the corner off tomorrow's liver and crept up the back garden in the dark, lobbing it over the hedge at Hop-along's pond. No splash, nothing. I had no dog. There was no moon. It was a chilly autumn evening. I'd forgotten about the chicken wire pond cover which stopped falling leaves fouling the clear water. The liver must've stuck on it. Then some bloody water dripped off the liver I supposed. There was one listless swirl, then another until they were lashing at the wire, half a dozen trout about 2 lb each throwing themselves at the mesh right under the Chittendens' kitchen window. I wrote the dream-car off that night.

One night that October there was a knock at the door and the youngest Chittenden asked for me.

– Me dad said jew wanna see a fish eez caught?

117

This was out the blue and I thought it was me he was aiming to catch. But the fish was slumped on their kitchen table like someone in the family had died it was so huge.

– Well, he said winking, dyer know what she is then?

– Big trout, I said.

– Sea trout lad, sea trout. Nine and a half pound she is. Caughter down Udj'm, in the Rother there. Isn she a beauty?

My parents pronounced it Ewedium. The Rother at Udiam was just a small brown trickle under an old bridge.

– Ow did I ketcher? he said. Oorn a spinner. Sawer goo whoosh a coupla toimes. She grabbed it first chuck . . .

And then another slow winter and I'm not the wink in his eye again. He's off on his Bantam with his gun, Chittenden Products game bag and Lady his spaniel sitting upright in a green wooden pillion box. Next day a brace of pheasant hung outside their back door. Or duck or rabbit. Come spring and off he went with his trout rod tied to his back with hop string, and the smell of baking trout rises over the hedge, game bag hanging out to air on that nail by their back door. Not so many trout in Ockley Pool any more. Not so many worms in the front garden either.

Next door was always busy, they kept their front door open all day and the smell of leather and dog and trout pellets always worked its way across our hedge. The sound of growing lads thumping up and downstairs, the treadles in the workshop, Mr Chittenden clearing his throat. It was like they threw their house open for an illustration in a school encyclopaedia, a cutaway drawing with all the rooms inside out and everything labelled. The rest of All Saints Road was parlours and net curtains and not a peep from the Josh Chapel of Rest in case it gave mum a headache. And all the while up and down the Chittendens' front path went all these kids and women with handbags, belts, watchstraps and satchels to mend. Or tall countrymen in Norfolk Jackets with gunbags and rod cases. Then one day mum sent me.

Pearl came to the door.

– Me mum said c'n Mr Chittenden mend'er ambag fr'er?

She was always jaunty and he was in his sea trout mood.

– That Sandy's lad, Pell? Bring im in.

He was dressing flies and said I wouldn't be a fisherman until I could tie one. I learned quickly under his tuition. After an hour I could tie a plausible nymph, March Brown, Greenwell's Glory. He gave me an old fly tying vice, a cardboard box of assorted dressings, even a very used wet fly line to be going on with. I already had this two-in-one rod. Split cane, 30/- down Pullins. The five-foot pike section converted into a nine-foot fly rod. So I asked the question I'd saved up all winter:

– Can I come fishin wiv you up Riseden?

– No, he said.

I was thirteen so Darwell Reservoir was like a sea to me, even the calm patches big as any pond I knew of. The flies hatched in the May afternoon. Mr Chittenden really wanted to go out in the boat but for my benefit we flogged nymphs off the East bank a hundred yards apart. He was wading up to his thighs down the concrete slope. Fly fishing! Gave me the spice really, it did. Didn't even see a trout. Every cast I hooked this pair of eyes with perch fins. Their first meal, my nymph. Hop-along said to kill them but I slipped them back on the sly. Then about four o'clock there was a yelling. I threw the rod down and legged it along the bank thinking he'd hooked a big one. He'd only got his tin leg wader firmly wedged in a crevice, water up to his pockets, and he was a stout heavy man not used to nimble ease and balancing acts.

– Run down the weighin hut, he said. Fetch Ted or Sammy up here, doan be long.

They both held Hop-along under the arms so he could unstrap his leg then hauled him up the bank and hoiked his leg out with a boat hook. I carried on flogging for perch as he sat on his jacket and dried his empty trouser.

Some evenings later he came down the front path with his fly rod, bound for the evening rise up Riseden. I was that kid next door again who caught blunt smelly roach from russet farm ponds. He winked and swung his head, only his square face stayed impassive, hard lines, fissures in a drought. Perhaps his leg was rubbing his stump. Perhaps hair turning steel-grey hurt as it turned. He stood by his Bantam talking to himself in that burred throtteral voice:

– Oh dear, he said. Oh dear oh dear oh dear.

Then the Bantam was kick-started and wheeled to the kerb, everything on course again like he'd never said those words. I went down the pond with some stale bread and no heart in it. Riseden: I'd seen it on the Ordnance Survey and had a blank page reserved for it in my Fishing Log Book. But me and Hop-along weren't in sympathy. There was something about him coming through like a weak signal. I was more reluctant to attract his attention. When I asked him what he'd caught up Riseden he cupped his hand over one ear and said:

– Hmmmm? Rizden? Come again lad? You carn goo up Rizden, no. It's private.

One morning up the shops mum bumped into Lanky Bob's aunty. Lanky Bob, the carp fisherman who made an angler of me. He'd said his aunty lived in Hawkhurst. He'd remembered me from Bodiam, she said, and Bob was coming down for August and did I want to go fishing with him. Well, I decided, I'd tell him about Riseden, see what he thought, and have another go at Hop-along. I must've watched Hop-along scrape up and down that path a hundred times, brogue and Blakey, wader and cleat, buff cords, oilskin leggings, stump-ache face, the sigh of a man who couldn't rest on the other leg, who hoarded Riseden to himself.

– You sid there w'z tench in Rizden.

– Oh? he said, did I? Well, less there's some big ole fellas bin there donkey's years I shouldn think they goo more'n two pound.

– Whadda bout carp then? I said like a thief. Any o'them?

– Carp . . . ooh I should say, cor-haw, lunkin great fellas. You c'n ear'm suckin under the lily pads of an evening ssshhhhhlllluckkk, great big ole mouths opening . . .

His face closed like a door. He lost interest, he wasn't there. He'd best be gett'n orn with things and he only just remembered my name.

August. Bob lanked up the front path.

Mum said:

– Chroist all-bloomin-mighty. You talk to im darn be the gate boy.

Bob had gone weird all right. Pimply bumfluff, six feet of knee and elbow, hair down his shoulders. Slapped his knee and said:

– Hi maaaannnnn, you've grown. Booked me a kipper?

We toured the village ponds. Bob did guitar sounds with his mouth, strumming the air round his jacket pocket and telling exotic tales about his life. He'd taken up the guitar and didn't live at home any more because his old man was a straight and had gone in his room and smashed up all his progressive sounds. His dad had wanted him playing chaconnes not riffs. So he lived, oh wow, with this Indian Prince called Bubs and his brother Sunny. They were going to drive to India.

– Hey Mandrick, where's this Rizden Pool? He slapped me on the back. Mandrick, Mancub, The Quest for the Carp Beast.

We looked at the map.

– Wow, serious estate lake, perfection.

So we went on a spy. Took an hour and a half to walk there. Bob dawdled over leaves with amazing patterns, filling his pockets with magic stones and freak acorns. At Field Green he leapt the five-bar gate and started to sprint across the middle of the field. I shouted at him to keep a lookout and creep round the edge. He waited, panting at the stile on the other side, lighting up a numby, finger to his lips now we were almost there. The fence ran along the foot of pine trees. A nye of pheasant fretted away. Wood pigeons cluttered through the trees. Bob's flares were yellow with pollen and covered in burrs and spears.

– Creatures everywhere, man. Hey, look at me, The Green Giant ho ho ho.

We climbed the stile and thrashed about in the undergrowth. Bob thought no one had ever set foot in there but he just didn't have the lore. There was even a sign. KEEP OUT. NO FISHING. It rotted sideways. One push and it was on its back in the brambles.

– Hey, Bob said. Beware of Victorian anglers.

I said:

– They do come ere yer know. Pikeys do coz they poach it fer trout an eels. Op-along said so.

Bob didn't think much of the country code.

– Land belongs to the people Mandrake. This lake is not fished, if there's a bloody lake still in there. Let's bash a way onward.

We took up sticks and cleared a path through the nettles. It was obvious Hop-along hadn't been up here so where was he fishing? Where did he go? Bob was saying we'd respect the gentlemen's trout and eels. We were after their carp. And there it was: Riseden Pool like an ambush. We were in one corner where the path emerged on to the dam. The most beautiful lake we'd seen.

– Fucking Paradise, I said.

– The dream lake, Bob said.

It was, so why wasn't Hop-along up there? You could see no one had been there all year, not even the pikeys. Instinct overtook us now and we kept low and crept a circuit, through tunnels in the rhododendrons, twisting into gaps, coming to the shallows where the spring ran in through bog and great sedge, rush beds shirring in the wind, clishing in the back breeze. Here the water rippled in sunlight. Elsewhere it stayed black and still. The other bank was open but for one toppled beech tree with its limbs lopped, the grass shin high, a gently sloping barley field pushing up to the fence. Back to the dam on the south bank where the overflow shoggled through a leaf grate and down the steep embankment into the chestnut wood below.

– Bout three acres, Bob said. You on, Mandrake?

No second thoughts. It wasn't Hop-along's lake anyway. We were on a farm now, not a grand estate. Everyone poached farm ponds, the farmers didn't care. You could get permission. You didn't even need permission if you were from Hawkhurst. I'd seen stuff about old Riseden in that local history booklet mum got out Piper's. This French family had the country house for three generations. Ended its days housing troops in World War II then stood empty till demolition in 1956. The stable block remained, saved by a preservation order. Somewhere over the brow was the farmyard. No one could see us from there. Any doubt vanished when this carp came out of nowhere, hanging in mid air close off the bushes. It set the water rocking, a slap which ripped feathers off beating wings, a ridged half circle swelling like a black eye across the whole pool.

Bob kipped in a tent in his aunt's garden because his step-uncle wouldn't let him in the house. Bob didn't care. Soon as the old sod went to work his Aunty Jean called Bob in for some mollycoddle. Nice hot bath because he stank, breakfast and a yarn. Fabulous lady. She let him have some blue cheese for the carp baits. She made me sandwiches and said for Bob to share his bottle of squash. We set off for Riseden mid afternoon, Bob keeping up the reminiscences. How he started fishing when they went to Italy with his dad and the Philharmonic. Bob saw *Moby Dick* on telly in the hotel. Gregory Peck was in it. So Bob bought this three-foot plastic rod from a toyshop. The reel was moulded on to it with twenty feet of crummy string tangled round paper clip rings. He crossed the piazza and saw this huge barbel swimming in a marble trough. He just had to catch it, man. Moby Woppa wasn't it, the sacred barbel. Three old men ran out the caff and kicked him across the piazza. Tried the plastic out on Lake Lucerne next. Useless crap snapped in the wind so he chucked it in.

We made our first casts teatime, Bob along the bushes where the carp had jumped, Mandrake in the corner by the dam, fishing paste on the ledger and worm on the float, a good striped brandling from the old sod's compost. Tench and rudd went berserk. Bit of a laugh when I hooked one of Hop-along's rainbers. Float dipped again, felt like a tree stump, then I'm yelling for Bob as the line pissed out. Bob couldn't talk me through it quick enough. A tangle jams the rod straight and I open the bail arm like a right cunt. Bob shouts, no no man, and the line cut clean on the trip lever of my cranky Intrepid de Luxe. Bob grabbed the line but the fish had gone. Forty yards he wrapped round his arm. The hook had straightened into a spear. The power and size of the carp were so frightening it made us think we'd lost everything still to come in life.

XIII

The house was dark and empty. The Honda sat in the drive with a shift lock fitted. Mr Sparrowtree had left a note on the kitchen table. He was willing to strike a deal if F saw a specialist on Wednesday (he'd agree to Kelly), so he could get some kind of assessment he could trust. He'd be driving up Wednesday himself to take her there. I was shaking my head at this when the phone rang.

– Where's Homer? Verity said.

F said he could be anywhere.

– Indeedy? Well I should puke. He's on his way home to *me*. He's half an hour late. Say, you're pretty dumb Effy for all that expensive education. You think I'm gonna stand by and see you marry that flunk? Honey, I don't want to flam you over this but get it straight kiddo: from this day on your daddy-o is not giving you nickel one, okay? Know why? You are not gonna need nickel one where you're going. Doctor Jake's givin me the key an I'm chuckin it down the sewer . . .

I dialled her back.

– Why're you doing this? I said.

She wasn't doing anything. I was destroying their whole life. Things were fine till I came along. Her and Effy'd seen eye to eye fine in the past. If we'd just shacked up together somewhere it might've been different. I saw a crack here and said hang on, what's the difference?

– Oh, she said, you are just the most unpleasant, arrogant, sly, hateful and . . . you know you have driven me out of my house. Your presence in that house is . . . well I'm not setting foot in there again till you've gone.

– That suits me you old cow. We don't wanna stay in this crummy old house with you anyway so just give us the car and we'll go tomorrow. I don't see why you can't wish us well and wave us goodbye, you know, nickel nothin and quits . . .

– Because I do not wish you well and I will never wish you well . . .

The phone rang again half an hour later. F picked it up and said it was for me.

– This is Homer Sparrowtree here. I wish ahh I wish to say ahh that I have been watching you this weekend and ahh I do not consider you to be ehhhh in any fit state to marry anybody ah least of all my own daughter . . . Sss . . . so why don't you ah ggg . . . gooohhh and ah have some success . . . ah somewhere else . . .

– Hey, I said, hang on. Why . . .?

He'd nothing more to say to me. The phone was snatched away and the line snapped.

F had to talk me out of despondency. She kept saying:

– I know my father better than you, please!

– How can you think of eating? I'd say, as she cut a wedge of brie and stuck a pickle on it, hot black coffee all over the floor and she just laughed. I thought I'd lost her, that *we'd* lost. She was cracking bad jokes that weren't funny at any time. And this specialist Kelly she was supposed to see.

– Trust me, F said. Kelly isn't afraid of Verity.

By Wednesday I was more convinced we stood a chance, in the sense that I'd survived those phone calls like I had Beulah's letter. I mean I'd not lived with F for as long as I'd lived with myself. I mean the fact that I woke up every morning must've worried people, or amazed them so much they became more powerless. The way to remove me would necessitate becoming obsessed with me, and they wouldn't want that. So I thought they'd backed off. I thought we'd slip through on the blind side.

Mr Sparrowtree arrived late afternoon and went straight down the cellar to tinker with his wires and connections. He came up to tie more junkmail into bundles and stacked them in a garbage sack. At 5.30 pm he shouted from his desk to be ready in ten minutes. Me and F sat on the wall outside. Like Disney Time with chipmunks skipping through the crevices, a woodchuck poking its head through the barn window, chickadees skiffling in the blue spruce, me and F holding hands. Then the maiden's father slammed the screen door and walked out to the car scattering the animals. He didn't lock the house. He frowned because we'd both got our coats on. He held the car door open like a walking frame, twisting away from us. F said he obviously didn't expect me to go with them. He let the engine idle, unrolling the window.

– Oh-kay.

But he only unlocked the passenger door as we both walked over to the car still holding hands, which disturbed him. His neck turned red.

– Beautiful evening, I said, tugging a few times at the locked back door. Will you unlock the door please?

His woodchopper voice said:

– Are *you* coming?

– Yes, I said, I am coming.

F's look said calm down. A second's hesitation and he unlocked the door, telling F to go lock up the house then. We drove over the state line into Massachusetts in silence, making our way along dark, overhung forest roads. It even felt like an inward journey. I'd been here in the dream-car too, when it was the tap end of the bath, cold tap steered to port, hot tap to starboard. The bath-car was powered by light in those dreams. The darker the sky, the slower the car. And I'd be naked, waiting for whatever it was to come round the bend. Atlanta's husband had gone back to Massachusetts. So in the back of Mr Sparrowtree's Subaru, I was watching out for James Fairservice-Frost to come by at the wheel of a hearse.

Kelly Kimberkick's house stood alone in a clearing amid spruce and larches beside a calm yellow pond, an old green punt moored to the jetty. Mallards scootered across the shallows as the car pulled up on the gravel. No breeze ever touched that water. Even the rain bubbles were preserved, skin intact where they'd fallen. White featherdown was becalmed, bowsprits up. Trees dripped in silence on the forest floor. I couldn't believe that anyone who lived here so deliberately wasn't balanced enough to see through Verity and all the others responsible for this evening's drive. But then Beulah Stafford lived in identical surroundings, a model of ecology.

Kelly Kimberkick said she'd see F first. She said she was glad I'd come. Mr Sparrowtree said he'd wait outside, so I had the cushioned nook-room to myself. One of those regress-the-psycho-while-he-waits rooms. All lacquered pine, picture window and self-help books. Pink fluffy brown bears, draught snakes, cushion cats with stripes and painted whiskers. I started reading a novel with blue stripes down the cover but I couldn't finish a sentence. I shoved it deep into my pocket and had one of those *well this is it* turns. Time to pace the cage.

Somewhere in the house there was a television on. Someone's dream house too. All those split levels and polished beams, balconies and skylights. A house where solar panels even power the armoured window shutters. The satellite disc was like an airport radar . . . Then I knew I was being tracked. The concealed camera, Mr Sparrowtree conveniently waiting outside, standing down there I saw, beside the car watching the ducks. I mean, they didn't want the unemployed psycho-clochard roaming about their pine dream home untracked. There'd be a red panic button somewhere. TV screens. An air raid siren. A central locking system. A Crisis Control team sat out there in the forest playing cards in the back of a Wingdale Asylum truck.

The more I thought it through, the more obvious it seemed. A wealthy female psycho-therapist living in a forest had to protect herself. Wasn't she buddyroos with Beulah Stafford? Didn't they lunch with Meryl Streep? I even thought I found the camera, deep in a pine-knot on a joist. Or was it a magic eye?

I heard it coming, the springing trap, and that bastard Sparrowtree going outside to block his ears and make the ducks quack so he didn't have to listen to his own daughter screaming as they dragged her towards the service exit in a Wingdale laundry basket. Somewhere deep inside this pine monkey house she was going: no no no no. I heard it rationally the first time for what it was. The television. But irrationally the second. Because she wasn't with me I thought they'd got her. Verity, Beulah, Jake . . .

I wrenched open the cupboard door and a load of paper fell out. Very clever, decoy door. I found the real door and set off after the screams. Stairways, landings, catwalks. The gunshots didn't surprise me. More gunshots than screams now. I could just imagine F grabbing the little snub-nose out of Kelly's secret drawer. I shouted for her, a throatful of dry rats instead of words. It was probably a panic attack. I was even ready to snap a piece of banister off and charge the kidnappers. But I was stopped in time. The Police sirens faded into a well-known tune. Hawaii Five-0. The commercial break. A Beach Boys jingle.

I'm drinkin up good vibrations

Sunkist Orange Soda sensations . . .

I was back in the waiting room. Mr Sparrowtree came in with a dog he couldn't shake off, a typical pine house dog.

– You saw me outside, dog, he said and for one split second I loved him for that, the total restitution of normality, my whole mental world exposed as imaginary, the hope that flooded in for the first time in weeks.

Then F was standing there with a big grin on her face. Kelly Kimberkick had changed into this sweatshirt. ZORBA THE PSYCHE. I must've missed that joke. Someone turned the TV off at the next commercial break as I followed Kelly up a pine ladder to her consulting room.

She asked me about Homer and Verity. This was her problem, how they'd behaved, communicated, how I'd felt in their presence. She was fascinated about the night Verity smelled the house burn down. We went over that twice. It only took ten minutes. Then it was Homer Sparrowtree's turn. He was in there forty-five minutes. Kelly came down alone and said to me and F:

– Don't look so glum you guys. Homer has something to tell you so come on up.

He sat in the centre of the room. We took up stations on three sides. Low, deep padded armchairs didn't suit him. He was trying to write a cheque, screwing up one after the other and stuffing them into his pocket.

– Aah . . . oh I ah seem to err, no, there is one left . . .

Kelly prompted him:

– I think you have something to say to F and her *fiancé*.

This time he finished the cheque and flapped the ink dry. He tested the ink with several fingers then held it out for Kelly. I watched him and thought he was in no fit state to be my father-in-law. The man was a wreck. Kelly was impatient with him but not unpleasantly. She suggested he might like to repeat to *us* what he told *her*. His voice staggered into confession.

– I have come toooo . . . theee conclusion . . . that I have ah nothing in common with errr Verity, hah . . . but the ahhh. We don't get along. Uh therefore we shall not marry. Oh, an er I shan't be selling the house . . . Oh yes, I hrrmm do wish you two well, myself.

He told all this to the floor, not us, but you could see it'd cost him, that he meant it. Extracting our joy from his collapse was like a chemical experiment. It could've burned a hole in the floor if it had gone wrong so we muffled it and simply breathed fresh air. One evil stepmother poisoned off. Why did we feel so bad? All three of us managed to express that without needing to look at each other. And we waved aside his only stipulation, some evidence that we could make a financial go of it.

We drove to Great Barrington for a pizza. The peepers were so loud that Mr Sparrowtree stopped the car in the dark and made us listen. Further on he pointed out a white colonial barn. The Folk Hut where they had musical gatherings which he'd stopped going to after Verity had come along. He didn't mention her by name. Now he had the time again, he said, he'd like to come back here and get involved. At Manhattan Pizza he ordered a beer, something else he was picking up again. Verity had banned alcohol. He poured it slow, holding up the glass to look, smacking his lips. F went to the bathroom. He leant across and said he was giving F the car back.

It was a dumb, chewy meal. None of us toasted our luck. F's cramps were snarling so we went outside for a smoke in the parking lot. Mr Sparrowtree stayed to finish his beer, drinking with his eyes. We could see him through the window, looking like a jilted man. He was the only customer left, and they put a CLOSED sign on the door.

One evening a month later the three of us were sitting outside after supper, drinking coffee in the twilight, a Skeeter Beater alight on the table between us. By then Homer Sparrowtree was living in a room outside Clinton, but even F didn't know exactly where. He spent Wednesdays and weekends up at Milkweed Lane. So me and F were talking about food when he said:

– Hah, a woman I once knew, who err humphhh, is

outa the picture altogether now, by the way ... used to put spaghetti with my chop ... doesn't work, that.

That was the only time he ever mentioned Verity. He didn't attend our wedding. He didn't mention that either, so we didn't invite him actually, which we regretted, but he did give us a wedding present: he paid for our gas across America.

XIV

*M*y lost carp killed Riseden that afternoon. It took Bob like nerve gas. He dropped his tackle box upside down in the mud then fell in. I couldn't stop trembling. I hooked a swan, snapped my reel handle, saw a rat disappear with my sandwiches. It was like we'd polluted the dream lake. We felt like the poachers we were. Then some plogger on a tractor appeared on the ridge and said we'd better scat or he was off to fetch his twelve-bore.

Bob went to India with Bubs and Sunny to become an addict. We all entered the seventies together. Plastic handbags, plastic belts, plastic fishing bags. That was the end of Chittenden Products. Mr Chittenden had to register as disabled and put REMPLOY labels on his handbags like prisoners and mental patients did. The smell of leather was gone. A van came once a month to take his gear to a warehouse. It ended up in Snobs Gift Shops. The Bantam was replaced. The spaniel wasn't. You'd think he'd hung a NO FISHING sign on his heart. He took up things he wasn't any good at, like painting by numbers, scenes of rural life, gundogs, shire horses, a rising trout. Just paint squeezed from a tube and moved into contortions on a bit of hardboard. Then there were Nature Notes from Bill in the Free Ads paper. Words squeezed into more contortions, rural idylls dreamed up in a rundown workshop, the wildlife notes of fields and streams which didn't exist any more except as the names of more Barratt's Homes.

Pearl took up driving now the boys had passed their tests, taking her 'disabled' passenger up Bedgebury car park or the Rother Flats on outings. By 1972 it was like we'd never known each other. We never spoke. Two ex-fishermen who gave up at the same time and stayed indoors now.

Did he ever wonder how come I went to hospital? And what was the use of that experience if I couldn't spot a genuine sadness under my nose. Not a fragment of empathy, not the ghost of a clue. Not at the time.

I don't know how my parents explained my hospitalization to Bill and Pearl over the fence. If he ever thought I'd laid out my fishing tackle on the front lawn all those times for his attention, brother anglers, why did he think I constructed my forest of crucified villagers along his hedge? All done with coffin makers' off-cuts bummed from the undertaker's chippie. Giant matchstick figures dying on the cross and facing no. 49. The council suggested I take them down. Next month I was in Farm Villa.

After Atlanta's death, I really felt I had no past which wasn't just effluent, pollution. I slept all day, a dreamless sleep. I was re-admitted in the Spring with some justification this time. They set me weekly motivation targets. I went to work in the Industrial Huts, packing plasticine strips and tying REMPLOY labels onto three-pin plugs.

They smartened me up too. Haircut, fresh clothes. I had my first ever shave with The Farm Villa Electric Shaver. The man who spent all day on the end bed outside the bogs saw my new hideous face and interrupted his monologue, about how he couldn't wank any more because of the medication, to laugh his head off because I'd cut myself all over with an electric razor. I'd joined the ranks of the female patients who get their tampons stuck and have to call a nurse with a rubber glove. It got worse: that time half of Hawkhurst was in Farm Villa.

Group therapy was like the village fête. Even that bloke who washed the buses and his mate Lez who made the tent pegs for our holiday in Lulubelle to Birmingham were in there. Wormhole was following me about and getting on my tits with his bleeding from his arse again thing. His origami was vandalized by Basher whose mum went down The Social with my mum, so she was asking after me without too much shame. There were two boys I'd fights with down All Saints Road. Basher was one. The other one came in shouting and crying and saying he'd kill himself if they didn't change him into a woman. His girlfriend had chucked him.

I couldn't explain why, on June 15th, I had to get out of Farm Villa for the night. The fishing season began at midnight. I wanted to go up Riseden. Perhaps in a lucid moment I couldn't give up the dream. I thought Riseden was inviting me back for a second chance.

The bus arrived in Hawkhurst at teatime. My parents were more worried by my arrival home than my re-admission. The old man phoned the hospital to check I had overnight leave. They kept saying:

– You all right boy? You sure, in yerself, like?

I was regretting it by then. The line on my reels was rotten. My tackle box hinges had rusted away. There was no time to sort it out. Bolted my tea and took the lot. Flask of Typhoo, three cream crackers and a lump of cheese. I ran for the bus, sweating in a pair of light baggy flares, old football socks, nylon shirt, tank top and spare V-neck. The outdoor gear made all the difference: desert boots and dad's old anorak. Two irritated parents washed up the silence I'd left behind. Bit queer, they thought.

– Bit queer this sudden fishin, the old man had said. There's no need to go fishin of a sudden an addin to needless worry.

135

The last no. 84 dropped me at Field Green. I waded in twilight across the field, plunging into thick darkness under the trees. This wasn't the picture I'd had of it in Farm Villa. Getting the cycle lamp out the bottom of my haversack was a Lucky Dip. It squeaked on, went bright if I smacked it twice, and half the cracked glass fell out. I could smell myself, the sweat and effort of tackling up on my knees with cramp and twitching eyes from the anti-depressants. Withdrawal symptoms too because I should've taken my night medication an hour ago.

I got the legered worm out about midnight. The old lady only had a farmhouse crust to spare for bread paste, but I did manage to get a float out without the bait flying off, and for half a minute the old excitement gripped, the float danced in the lamplight. Even kidded myself I'd land a carp, settle old scores, take my gear back to Farm Villa and have a crack at the Medway. At one minute past midnight I took in the surroundings. I thought of the long night to come. I felt the cold now, the cold of being alone. Quick cup of tea, stale thermos, stomach-churning grey tea. I'd never land a carp in the dark, it would pull me in, the snapping line would take an eye out. The torchbeam would give me away and the pikeys would come. My parents would tell Mr Chittenden, and there'd be shame both sides of the fence . . .

I was wobbling on a fold-up garden chair, bright orange flowers all over the rent nylon. The cycle lamp scared off the fish, making us blind. I wouldn't know I was surrounded by pikeys and farmers. Three fags left and the hair stood up under my shirt when a badger screamed. I bashed the lamp off. A bite on the leger, something tugged on it like a poltergeist. I whimpered at it: get lost, so I can scarper from that crashing in the woods. I went to grab the cycle lamp but kicked it in the lake. The beam flickered back on a second to light its way down till silt snuffed it out. An air bubble. I slung the leger in the grass, left the bail arm open. The tench could swim about all night if it had to. Sod the float rod.

I got the real thrill from escape, walk-racing to the open field, a cold sea in the half moon. Ankle-snagging brambles and face-high scratches across my new tilled skin. Tired and cold I curled up in the middle of the field and smoked two Sovereigns tip to tip. Didn't have the guts to fetch the flask. I woke at 4 am, teeth chattering, tiny spiders up my nose. Last fag as I stamped up and down to get rid of cold numbness.

You could stuff fishing. Back at the lake I found they'd nicked one of the reels, the bastards. Emptied my tackle-box over the ground just to show contempt for my crappy gear. They didn't want any of it. The reel was missing off the leger rod. Poor tench. I was back in Farm Villa by din-ner-time. They all said, didn know you was a fisherman.

When I heard about Mr Chittenden, I said: didn't know he was depressed.

It was the way he planned it, first task for Monday morning. He'd learned to drive from Pearl and took deliv-ery of a new car the previous week. His sons and daughters-in-law and grandchildren came for the week-end. Then Sunday night he took his usual turn round the back, dogless by the empty pond, down the path, out to the car. Only this time he took a shotgun wrapped in a travel rug and locked it in the boot. In the morning he drove out to Bedgebury Forest and parked in a clearing under the trees. Took the shotgun out the boot and . . . walked away from the car. His leg was made of modern fibreglass by then but he still had to rig up some one-foot method of kick-starting the trigger, sitting down, stiff leg out, back against a tree. He didn't die in one perfect cast, one magnificent shot under the sacred tree. He just scared a load of squirrels, just alerted the Forestry Commission that some nutcase was blasting a shotgun illegally. The grim gamekeeper, poaching his own life under the keeper's nose. But what was up next? He wasn't still alive? Surely not bleeding to death? He staggered back to the car, the new car. He knew it was bad, just too bad, just dear oh dear oh dear. All the kennel dogs a mile off made such a din, such a to-do. There was the shotgun, the car keys, the slippery seat and poor Pearl's steering wheel and now he'd got to *live* with what he'd just done. He could clear up, but they'd have to know. That might be good now. He'd have to go to Farm Villa. But he could drive away from that tree so there'd be no need to show them where he had the accident. Dear oh dear oh dear. Just had to weep, he really had. I mean look at him, driving a car, that was the miracle. Or did he learn to drive just to do this? All those dreams of driving a car to suicide? It might've been an automatic gearbox but he was *driving* at last, checking the fuel gauge, king of the road. He hadn't envisaged a two-way trip. He hadn't known he'd be coming back. Oh man. Oh bad bad bad. And there were the dogs barking and howling as he pulled up. This is where all his spaniels came from too. The kennels. Howling for his blood, throwing themselves against the wire. Drip drip drip, but this was as far as I could go with him. It had all gone so badly across our fence. Then him dying in that ambulance.

PART TWO

The Getaway Car

XV

*T*he grit outside the Starlite Motel, Streetsboro. Cramp, exhaustion, we couldn't drive another yard. F said her face'd come off in her hands. Asleep on our feet we stood in front of the car and greeted the manager who leaned in his office doorway in a filthy undershirt. The day's heat hung round him, beer stains on his front, food halos, waistband thumb grubby.

– How far ya come? he said nodding at the licence plate.

– Connecticut.

– Pretty good, load like that. Come inside, ah'll see what ah've got fa ya.

We paid him in traveller's cheques for the room and he went over to the house for change. We looked round his office. Three half eaten TV dinners, a microwave on a chair, the keyboard with two screws missing leaned away from the wall, boxing photos hung, propped and tacked everywhere, most of them framed and signed. A stack of *Combat* magazine spilled off the table. But mostly there were suitcases everywhere. Every shape size and colour. On shelves, in corners, under the table, blocking the door, even three of them stacked on the microwave. I asked F if she'd ever been in a motel. Neither of us had.

The manager came back smirking. We looked across at the house and saw his mother watching from the window.

– Here's the key. It's a triple, okay? You doan want

them beds so doan touchem an I doan charge extra. Keep the key in the door, *outside*. Bolt's on the inside.

He saw us looking at the suitcases, all the names and addresses. J Chang denveR. John Lee, La Foirie. Mr Richard Pagano, Meeker.

– Oh those? he said. Well, ya find em sideways or just plain rubbed out when ya bust the door down. Some do the ole soft-shoe shuffle in the night. Others go for a beer an never come back. If they want their gear they know where it is.

Three double beds in our room. F chose the middle one and flaked. No more motels. I promised we'd pick green fields, we only needed one good sleep. I took a bath and slept nine hours without moving. F was still asleep when I fetched coffee and it was her turn to drive today. She stood half an hour in the shower then filled the tank, checked the pressures and headed out to the highway. I could tell the difference in the car, the smoother flow of F's driving. I'd only been driving two months by then. The car fitted her. She'd named it too and talked to it. Undaunted by highways, unflustered on inside lanes, passing trucks or just keeping on it with her spurs dug in till something faster came up. We were mirror-blind too. To cut back in I'd lean my head out the window and give her a cue. We were so top heavy it took a hundred yards to cross lanes. Those side winds off Lake Erie, the way they rocked us into swerves.

We looked out for breakfast turn-offs, somewhere quiet. Next exit had a globe with orange neon dots revolving round the equator. GAS POTATOES LOVE YOUR TRUCK BAIT & TACKLE 79 DEGREES HAVE A GREAT DAY MINI-MARKET RIDIN HIGH TOLEDO 130 MILES GAS. We found a track which cut through rye grass fields and parked in a clearing two miles off the highway. We brewed coffee and soup on the camp stove, sitting on the ground under a wide grey sky in the warm air, flat soft land, its few gentle undulations tapering into ridges on the green horizon. This was the elsewhere at last. Homeless and married, us out there. Just the drive ahead. We had no other life but this. The simple purpose we'd never known. It didn't matter if the bread had baked hard in the sun and tasted of polythene. Who cared about runny butter on the sleeping bags, sweat blisters on the Monterey Jack.

Then the DANGER signal. I knew myself better than this. About a mile away to the north was a clump of trees, a line of bushrow leading to another clump. The bank of a creek? There's a pond, I thought, amid the trees, must be a tiny pond about half an acre. What did it make me think I had to say? That at times like these I wanted to settle. Every evening I'd have to walk over those poxy fields, sun setting, fishing rod and a rusty old baked bean tin of night-crawlers, cheese roll in newspaper and a fag behind the ear. But this was just Ohio, and we were passing through. So what I really saw was somewhere you catch nothing, like you're born there by chance, a place with no choice, just the one pond. One day out of Gethsemane with F and I thought I'd escaped. This was Oakwood Hospital Ohio too and I was trudging out with doctor's permission to fish the Medway back of the council houses. No, keep driving till we're dead.

– Let's go, F said. This reminds me of Verity's ideal site for a mall.

Back on the highway we hit a passing downpour and the windshield gunked up from passing trucks full of root beer sucking us downstream. They cut in front twenty-feet off the fender, bumper stickers jeering: LIKE MY DRIVING? DIAL 1–800 EAT SHIT.

6 pm we were running out of Chicago Heights, Illinois straight at a lowering sun lodged in a forty-denier sky, burning a hole like a flashlight through a workrag. F said when her father was a boy they went to this pond for snapping turtles. He told the other boys you couldn't make

soup off them but they killed them anyway so he figured he'd better go along with it. He took the meat home and stuck it in the freezer. Next day he took a knife to it. The meat grabbed hold of the knife and wouldn't let go.

Smog, dust, fume-cloud hanging over Chicago so we sealed the windows and shut off the air vents. A red glow over the city through gaps in high concrete shoulders. Cars shot down feeder lanes in sprays, beaten up heaps of junk driven by nuts who sliced across four lanes blind. Ever read *Studs Lonigan*? F said. Because every car had a Studs in front, a Studs in back and six black dealers glaring at us out side windows. F missed the interchange. We followed this pit-holed double lane out along a mile of wire fence twenty feet high into acres of factory lots all deserted for the weekend. She pulled into an empty bus terminus outside a factory gate. We blanked on the map for ten minutes, aiming west at the sun, back down the pitholed road watching for directions and coming up behind this old Dodge piled with furniture, this black dude fifteen feet up in the air on a yellow sofa waving down at the fellow travellers. As we pulled by, granpaw shot a one-tooth grin from behind the wheel and we saw the smoking engine, the hood lashed down with twine. At dusk we crossed the central time zone and the Mississippi, a red sun setting on Iowa. My turn to drive.

I settled down for a night drive, F napped a hundred miles. After Quad Cities the traffic thinned to trucks and other night drivers. I radio zapped across flat dusty plains which smelled dry and deserted. Twenty-four-hour Country stations. Non-stop Evangelists said the sins of the wicked are marks upon the flesh, boils, scars, pox, rashes. In the all-nite shopping mall near Montezuma there was a dispute at the Sav-A-Lot checkout. A man had chrysanthemums and wanted change off his credit card. It was 3 am. The man said he came in every night so's his wife could have fresh flowers on the breakfast table. Sindee wouldn't do it, she didn't know him, it was the regulations. She snatched the chrysanthemums off him.

Two hours out of Des Moines 6.30 am we pulled off to sleep, 800 miles on the clock since leaving Streetsboro Saturday morning. There must've been a downpour in the night. We took a lane pointing south. Coon Springs 5, bumping down half a mile of hard road onto murrey, sliding back heavy in the slick, almost coming off the track.

– What do I do? I said.

F said put it in first and turn the way of the skid. We churned forward cutting furrows in the sticky red top. Ours were the only treads on it so we decided to pull up and sleep. Soft roll farmland growing corn on four sides. We found an intersection where a ditch ran under the road, shored to form a bridge, a grass verge wide enough to park and make camp. Hardcore in the gateway, a clump of saplings screening us on two sides. So quiet in the slight breeze, warm grey sky, spit-flecked air. We couldn't sleep properly, just dog-napped on the ground by the driver's door, ringing ears, making out trucks a mile off, scratching overheated limbs, grass rustling us awake again. At noon we rose and sponged down each other's naked skin in cold water, drying off in the breeze, brushing teeth with baking soda, slipping into clean shirts.

F took over. A few miles down the highway we followed the FOOD GAS sign into Soap Creek. Corrugated tin shacks and silo wraps, dirt parking outside the Shamrock Cafe. Oil drums keeled over in the dust. The dust went back forty years. Widowed sisters drove down from their farms in buckled Buicks and Oldsmobiles they'd traded in for the last one twenty years back. The cafe was a cattle house or gas station in the fifties. Some old paint said DANCING. Inside was like an old folks' home, maw, paw and their sixty-year-old daughter cutting up the gristle. The sheriff and his sidekick had the best seats, both feet on

145

the table with their guns. After breakfast F headed the Wagon at Nebraska.

The Missouri, into Nebraska and another weather change. Across the plains with the windows down. Covering the long blue sky was a white haze like hot milk skin. The highway glared white. Tyres monotonized over joins in the concrete. Wind pushed the mileage down. 170 a tank instead of 350. We stopped five times a day instead of three. The price of gas still rising. A dollar fourteen in Nebraska. Against the wind it took a mile from standstill to reach fourth gear, a top speed of 45 in overdrive. We crawled in third for fifty miles, dust-caked faces, half-way across America, the stink of pigs, silos rising like planetaria, billboards twice the size of Panovision, PIONEER VILLAGE FIVE MILLION SATISFIED VISITORS. Exits led to Hazard, Pleasanton, Eddyville and Broken Bow. BUFFALO BILL'S RANCH.

Sunday afternoon, even there. At North Platte the light failed and F handed over, sleeping till midnight, waking in time to see the strip of boards nailed across the sky like a ranch gate, WELCOME TO WYOMING. We slept well that night in a grit turnaround. The road ran on to Grover, Colorado. The Lodgepole County sheriff woke us in our sacks next morning.

– Ever-theen awlride? A steer kicked up dust half a mile away.

The wind hit us three quarters on, roping us down to the highway and we stalled against gusts unless we changed down to third as soon as it hit. Then the dead land joined in, unleashing showers of hot red grit-dust. 98 degrees mid-morning. Road construction, dust clouds a mile thick, progress down to a crawl, zero visibility, audible fogs rattling against the car. Through Medicine Bow the wind tore the polythene off the trunks on our roof rack. Tumbleweed bounced off the windshield in flurries of grit. On past salt lakes which smelt like sea gales, and lean-to's

146

set for take off, shacks called Milk Shake Bars with their single pumps every fifty miles. Between Wamsutter and Thayer the wind slammed grit against the car which took off the paint like buckshot. An aqueduct of cloud drove rain over the cattle range. Great slatted windbreaks shook each side of the highway. Like driving up an airport runway. The land made us silent, flinched at the wheel, waiting for the car to die, or the wind to lift us into the air.

F read all the way to Rock Springs, looking out now and then to wince at the rasping grey scrub, Spanish bayonets, red rock, parched haze. At Rock Springs mining derricks stubbed the skyline. Slag heaps, a smell - soda ash, gas or bitumen. We'd come to a mining hole at 3 pm, curving into town on a dusty wind. A Coca-Cola sign swings above a door. One old man blown bent in half up Main Street.

We drank coffee at a filling station and F asked for the rest room key. A woman on the checkout rang a friend to tell her about some news just in.

– Bobby says they got the li'l boy out. They was cuttn-away fur three hours. Ohhh Bobby says he still hayd that lil ole camera roun his neck an he was takin pitchers an awl of the men cudnim out. Cain you ber-lieve thayat? With his own daddy . . . well, like that in that cab? Delsey? Dun that make you heart come?

We approached the wreck site a mile out of Rock Springs, the red flares still lit. Down to one lane, a 300-yard snake going 10 mph. They were all standing there looking at the mess, the County Police, Highway Patrol, Fire Department. The concrete bridge was at the bottom of a long banked curve. For a quarter mile there were hundreds of twenty-foot rough-cut planks marking the slide like a pack of cards strewn across a table. The truck was on its side where it came to rest against the bridge, its few remaining planks having shot under it and piled up against the cutting.

It wasn't long before we came off US80 for keeps.

Highway 30 was paved, two-laned. Idaho, and we were suddenly alone on the road. Hills darkening in the distance, a long straight road across the plain and nothing on it. F pulled in and we ate an apple and took a photograph at the brow of a gentle rise where the valley cut away and the hill dropped to another plateau. We tried to forget the Wagon and fooled about for five minutes, cooling in a breeze which came off the hills, not the arid plains behind us. A truck passed and everything was silent again besides the blusting and the gravel underfoot. F said: show on the road, and started her up. She was in fourth doing 50 on the long slope, beginning to level off and give it gas.

– No power, she said. There's nothing there.

We rolled to a stop and switched off. It wouldn't start so I got out and lifted the hood. F knew about the plugs and the air filter. It wasn't them. We could see three miles down the empty road. We'd seen twenty from up top. Where we were on the map exactly was hard to tell. We'd passed Little Muddy someway back at Granger, but neither of us remembered Opal. Diamondville was ten miles on near Kemmerer.

We kept the hood up and the flashers on for an hour. First vehicle along was this beat-up old Chevy Wagon bumping to a stop in front of us. Big blond Norwegian in a mesh cap comes over, serious grin like the sun was in his eyes. The mesh cap said *Chevy Drivers go to Heaven coz drivin one is Hell*. There was an I luv New Mexico sticker on the rear fender. The woman on the front seat wouldn't look round the whole time. We got the tow rope hitched and the Norwegian said Kemmerer was only fifteen miles.

– I know no-thing for fixing off carsse.

The woman called out still looking in the mirror.

– Ronny . . . Ronny . . . Ronny.

We could see her fat arms winged along the back of the seat, her thick black hair, narrowed eyes in the wide mirror. She began to shake her head.

– Ronny. Ronny.

Ronny shrugged:

– Ah hiv chew hurry. My woman, ah be-cozj ah work on the ni-sheeft an it make trooble.

Ronny towed us to Kemmerer in time to catch Don's Motors. Kemmerer was a two-hill boomtown on the coal veins where J. C. Penney opened up his first store in 1902, The Golden Rule. Same year that Wm. Rootes Snr opened Rootes Motors in Hawkhurst, oh yes, *the* Rootes. The sun was lost in the back of the hills and gave Kemmerer a five o'clock shadow. Ronny had to cut us loose by the pumps because he couldn't untie us fast enough and he was agitated, his woman going Ronny Ronny you hurry okay? He called Don out.

– Theesh gice heff brooken down so hi breeng them heeya Don.

We all shook hands. Ronny drove downhill. Don slipped back into his auto shop leaving the boy in charge. He just stood there still and self-conscious, knowing we knew he couldn't do anything. Several times he whipped out a rag as if to start something. We let him fill the tank and scrape the windows clean. Don came back, same silent face as his son. Black mechanic's hair, specs taped up. He flipped them up on his forehead because of the grease on the lenses and poked about under our hood, pulling out the rotor arm.

– Yep, look at that. Burned out, see? Fraid you'll have to wait till morning when the auto parts store opens.

We didn't want to spend the night in Kemmerer so we didn't acknowledge that, just stood not knowing what the end of the matter ought to be, waiting for Don to make the next move.

– Pretty sure, he said after a while, I don't have one in stock right now. Best thing's to shove the car round the side here, way from the pumps, okay?

Don's was on a slope, the only level ground along the

side by the oil drums. Even with four of us we couldn't push the Honda up the slope so Don had to fiddle under the hood of his old pick-up to get that going to shunt the Honda up there with his fender. He chocked the back wheels then reversed into his shop. Again, we stood there with the boy. We didn't know what to do next, all of us looking down the slope into an empty town, the sun gone, hills purple.

F said:

– Must get cold up here nights? Seven thousand feet up aren't we?

The boy shrugged. He was transfixed by the Connecticut licence plate, unsnapping his eyes up at F when he thought she wasn't looking. He held the rag now like it wasn't his red rag any more, blowing his nose on it for something to do just as this cat snicked out from behind the oil drums. It flinched from the hiss of dry nostrils but kept coming forward when it saw who it was. F knelt.

– Hello kitty.

The boy mimed the words with his mouth, the same words, hello kitty, trying to see what it felt like to be this girl from Connecticut.

XVI

*D*ead Indian Road left Route 66 below Excelsior City, Southern Oregon, climbing into mountains, twisting on by Pompadour Bluff, Grizzly Peak, Breast Mountain, disappearing off the survey map at Grizzly Creek. Driving up in a full high sun, so hot we kept our elbows off the window trim, coming on construction work and ten-mile delays. We pulled up by a student with a STOP sign and a walkie-talkie. Stationary, it was furnace hot inside that car. F said she was of the opinion it didn't matter being late, that people who live up a mountainside forfeit the right to choose exact moments for visitors to arrive. I said:

– Yeah, well, no one else's applied for the job.

It was late July and we were broke. We'd got as far as Excelsior City a month back. It was no city, just the last town on the Oregon Trail big enough to stop and look for jobs in. We'd taken an apartment by the month. There were plenty of dishwashing jobs but none for me. I didn't have a Green Card and too many spot-checks on the kitchens made it risky. No one wanted hand-made fishing poles either. Then I saw the Youngbloods' advert on a bulletin board.

At the County Gravel Pile we took a track over pit-holed waste ground till we reached the new yellow iron gate. Kayty Youngblood had given us the combination over the phone but it took ten minutes to figure out, handkerchiefs over the hot metal, fingers slipping on sweat. The next half mile was flat. Grey dust clouding up behind as we drove at a crawl, touching bottom as we began to rise. The track was rocky now. Kayty Youngblood said we'd make it fine. She'd done it to the top in a hired hatchback.

– If she doan grip, run at it twice – it's oany loose dirt.

At the rate we were moving F calculated it would take an hour to drive the five miles to the Youngbloods' trailer.

– It's a quarter of three, F said. I have to be at work in one hour three-quarters.

Some dirt road. More like a dried-up mountain creek. I ran at the first big slope in second but she wouldn't grip. The back swayed and the engine cut. One more try at half the speed got us half as far. A longer run on the third ascent cracked the muffler on a rock. It was three o'clock. I slammed the door and looked up the track. F shifted seats and parked the car in the long grass by a digger. We started walking, feet slipping on the dirt pellets. Rocks jutted high overhead. Thin dry trees, roots gripped down between fissures, trunks leaning over at shadeless subsiding angles. The clearings hadn't grown back and the track began to twist and turn back on itself now the mountain took shape. After a mile of bickering heat and dust sticking on the sweat I started cursing the fucking Youngbloods. F said:

– Shuttup, there's a man up ahead.

He was sat like a rock fifty yards away through some scrub. F whispered:

– It's Sisyphus.

Sisyphus clutched the shaft of a thirty-pound sledge-hammer. I said:

– Hello, how far's the Youngbloods' trailer?

The man had dug a hole two feet square and a yard deep. Beside it lay a shovel, a belt of tools, a stiff hide pouch of 14" bolts. A brand new yellow iron gate leaned on the incline nearby.

– Ah righty, the man said. The Englishman.

He stood up, closed his eyes a second. When he opened them they were like brown ink burst on a blotter, hard as knuckle. We shook his huge encrusted hand.

– Dale Youngblood, he said. Ah see ya car didn make it up.

He pointed out yesterday's work. Blind, he'd sunk a twelve by twelve beam into a concrete bed, bolted on two gate hangers. No spirit level, just a tactile yardstick.

– Yep. He ran the whole length of an arm under his wet beard and dipped his hand in a coolbox packed with ice-flow and beer cans with dead bugs floating on top. Wanna beer either ya?

Perhaps no one'd told him the ring pulls weren't supposed to come off the cans these days. This one he flicked off the ledge. Fifteen feet down we could see about a dozen crushed beer cans scattered in the bushes. He sat, so we sat behind him and stared down the way we came.

– So Mister Englishman, where'dya leave your car? I reckon down by the digger, that right? Busted ya muffler on that ski jump, hey? Okay then, here's what I'll do. I've learned to be pretty fuckin mechanical. So when Kayty comes along with the truck we'll run on down an take a look, then we can go on up, see the trailer.

– Where is the trailer? I asked.

– Enda the goddam road. Last thing ya come to, straight upwards two miles and a half. Matter of fact ah'm buildin the road now maself. Gotta gravel it fore it rains and snows. Reckon a month clear, maybe.

He was talking about five miles of winding dirt track, nowhere for a truck to turn. Daunting tons of gravel.

– Yep, gotta do that in one week. Aimin to shoot down to LA next week. Kayty maya toldya. Just had ma first novel published. Now, we ain got no power up here yet an ah need power to write with. Bin five years in that trailer,

153

me an Kayty. Now we gotta son, needa house. Yep, got real pissed off a long ways back with human fume. Never wrote when ah could see em. Lost m'sight in a bear huntin accident.

He held one hand up in front of F's face.

– Kayty, he said.

A whole sixty seconds passed before we saw the truck, dogs running in front and either side.

– Kayty'll giveya copy if ya still wanna go up there. Called it Blind Drunk. You know they had me shave ma beard off an wear some fucking shoe salesman outfit with spectacles for the jacket shot; believe it. Fuck, they had me put on a shirt and hold some goddam kid by the hand I'd never met with. He's there, on the backa ma book. Some goddam kid I never knew, juss so's the human fume can feel easy, like the man can see. Oh wow he's one of us. Got a kid in school whose daddy wears a nice clean fuckin shirt.

Two black dogs bounded the last fifty yards in front of the maroon Chevy high-wheel like they were pulling it along. Three other dogs flailed alongside the driver's door. Dale Youngblood started howling and all the dogs spurted forward and fell on him in one wriggling howling black mass.

– BEARS, ma lovely Bear-asses, here-here-here-Bears, yeah-Bears, grizzly-Bears, money-Bears, jelly-Bears, care-Bears . . .

They frothed at the mouth and knocked the cool-box down the incline, water and cans and coolpacks tumbling out. Dale punched his mongrels, pulled their ears and rolled over stones on his bare back. Kayty Youngblood stood on the running board, an eighteen-month-old boy gripping her like a squirrel.

We left Dale sitting by his hole picking up beer cans, his wide flat hand moving about the dirt like a metal detector. As the truck moved off, the dogs abandoned him. Kayty said:

– They just have to run even in this heat. It's a hundred ten you know, and them rattlesnakes are moody. I'm just worried about Darwin here.

A mile on we passed a crater with a bucketful of green slime in the bottom.

– That's our pond, she said. Had a diviner up here a coupla months back when we moved up. He told us to dig right there. We hit a spring all right, but it dried. Right now we fetch our water up from Excelsior in two-hundred-gallon tanks.

The trailer sat on a mound in a clearing, slashed-down grass, one tree clump left to keep the trailer in perpetual shade. A view of the Siskiyous across into California, a distant view nobody could really get at because if you walked towards it the entire view disappeared behind the rising trees.

– We chose the blind side, Kayty Youngblood said, for the shelter, you know?

The trailer was fifty feet long and squeezed in among the trees, a septic tank sunk just off the clump. And those vehicles, scattered haphazard round the clearing: a red Porsche all sap rind and birdshit, two earth movers, another twenty-foot trailer, a spare Chevy with bits picked off. The rest was junk. Doors, axles, flat bed. Dragged and stacked into this corral sixty feet off.

– Oh well, she said, this is home now.

A failed smile from a life-long trailer lady. The tight jeans, red T-shirt, camel elk ropers and white ball cap free with the gas. Her face chubs reddened easily. Her expressions always broke into looks of incomprehensibility.

– Oh, Dale calls it his cracker box, she said, closing the screen door. Welcome anyway. Them rattlers come right up to the door now an that's rilly scarey, baby crawlin on the ground an that. They live down there under the diggers an in the Porsche, juss comin up when they feel like it I guess. The Bears worry em a lot too, you know? I'm kinda . . . oh, it doan madder, sit down if ya want.

The inside was brown and drab, neat and functional. They weren't hooked to a generator. There were no kerosene lamps or candles. F asked how she saw in the dark but she just kept tidying the seat cushions.

– I mean, F said, you mentioned you were studying again . . .

– Oh that? Well, ya know axshly I don't read in the dark. I mean I do everythin in the daylight. I gotta few candle stubs an that if I wanna look anything up. We got a flashlight too but, ya know after dark we listen to the radio, sleep . . .

F looked at her watch:

– We have to go. I work in a restaurant.

Kayty Youngblood opened a box under the table.

– Here, take this. It's Dale's book.

Blind Drunk, the title smeared across a snot-green sky. Two eye sockets, one with a fractured rent and charging bear, a hunting rifle and whisky bottle sunk in the other. Both had sight marks like a spy thriller.

– We doan want no drink or drugs up here, she said. There ain no board games nor TV neither.

– Am I hired then? I said.

– Let me tellya. We got a rilly good feelin off your letter, real positive.

F said: The Honda won't get up here easily.

Kayty Youngblood made F take the book.

– Dale's puttin in a road, honey . . .

Dale was still sitting by his hole and didn't look inclined to move till we pulled up right beside him. He let the tailgate down, hoisted himself up, legs dangling, beer in fist, dogs flipping on and off. He thumped the metal and the Chevy moved forward, the dogs racing ahead to the bend.

– Oh Money Bear! She beeped the horn. Money Bear

had settled in a rut ten yards in front of the Chevy and wouldn't budge.

– What are you doin there? Bear, just get out the way willya. Bear? Money Bear?

She edged nearer, staying on the brake, her voice rising.

– Bear? . . . Money Bear? . . . MONEY BEAR . . . She pulled up sharp, the dog just visible over the hood.

Dale shouting over the back:

– HEY HONEY FUCKING JESUS.

– It's Money Bear, Dale. He's juss lain there. He ain moved, oh god . . .

Dale let himself down and felt his way alongside. F held onto Darwin so Kayty could bite her fist and open the door when Dale was clear of the fender.

– Where is he KY? Bear? Money Bear? Come tya ole papa, Bear.

Kayty guided him along the rut and put her own hand on the dog's head and snatched it back, crying.

– I doan understand. He was okay juss now – he came down with us didn he? Oh god Dale, I doan remember. Wasn he with us at the trailer? How longs he bin lain here Dale? Anyone?

Kayty took Darwin who stayed asleep while she squeezed him and massaged his scalp. Dale knelt over Money Bear but couldn't get at him. The other dogs jumped on his back and rolled over Money Bear, biting and snotching his belly and leg flanks. F said we'd better help and we both collared a Bear each. The two loose Bears were growling low and plaintively, their mood changed. Flies piling in from nowhere to climb up Money Bear's nostrils. When Dale pumped the dog's chest a whole ball of flies popped out and its legs flopped and puppeted. Lock-jawed, one tooth stuck out from a silly grin. Froth leaked along the dry rubbered lining.

– C'mon Bear, Oh Bear c'mon Bear. Come orrrnnn Bear. Come . . . orrrnnn. Goddammit c'mon back to us

Bear boy.

On he went till it got like a chain gang out in the heat, Kayty chanting her round to fit his:

– Is it coz he wouldn drink? Did he drink? I tried to get him to drink. I mean they stopped at the pond, I swear I saw em drinking at the pond . . .

Dale put his hand under Money Bear's jaw and started the kiss of life. His belly went up and down, getting bigger with each blow. The two loose dogs had their pricks out and grabbed Money Bear by a back leg each, pulling in two directions. Kayty yelled:

– Stop that Bears stop that, and putting Darwin on the dirt rushed forward and started wrestling with the Bears. The other two dragged forward, yelping and snapping and wrenching free. Dale left off the kiss of life and growled at Kayty:

– You keep ahold o'the kid, dya hear? KEEP AHOLD – coulda bin a rattler, okay?

He stayed on top of Money Bear for fifteen minutes.

– His li'l ole heart's given up fa good.

He stood up and kicked the other Bears away. Money Bear flopped out over both arms, he stumbled his way off the ruts into scrub, feeling about for a bush, rolling the dead dog under it in paper-thin shade. More flies bunched up its anus and smothered its prick and eyes. They drank off its slobber, off Dale's slobber and the slobber on its belly from the other dogs.

– Coulda bin a snake bite maybe, Dale said. Oh Money Bear you ole dawg, whydya let a snake do that?

He spat a few times, closed Money Bear's eyelids. The flies landed on his hand then started working their way back in under the lids.

– G'bye ol Money Bear, friend. I juss know you're already chasin them fuckin rabbits . . .

At the digger, F backed the car out the long grass before Dale Youngblood felt like hopping down off the pickup.

– WHATYA GO AN START'ER UP FA? Be all fuckin hot under there now.

F said she was simply being wary of them rattlesnakes which just killed his dog. She said it was on his behalf, what with long grass, what with diggers and her being due back at work this minute.

– Okay okay, sounds like the connecter's busted anyhow. You get the part, I'll put'er in . . .

It was five o'clock. Three feet of shadow off the car. Back on Dead Indian Road we sat another twenty minutes on the STOP sign. F said Dale was like some War Memorial. I said more like Ozymandias.

– They won't phone, F said. They hated us. That's two jobs we don't have now.

– I fuckin know that, I said.

XVII

*T*hen Ena Tolstoy shutting shop on us like that. Ena told F that coming in late from the Youngbloods' mountain had nothing to do with cutting her four days a week down to two hours on a Sunday. It was just that someone had turned up. Someone from the Holy Land they'd promised a job to in the past.

The Tolstoys were Polish Jews from Leningrad who'd left their real name in the used name pound. They opened the restaurant in Excelsior because the birch trees reminded them of Russia. F understood this so she got along with Ena after a bad start just knocking on the door about the vacancy. Ena snapped without looking up. It was a stupid time to come, she'd said. And anyway, someone took the job a week ago so please go away and let her get on with the preparation. F left her number anyhow.

1.30 am a week later this fight broke out in the upstairs apartment. Blair & Skookie Yunk. You just have to sit up and listen to a fight like that, get the frozen yoghurt out the icebox, be ready to fetch Jack our apartments manager or the Peace Force.

We settled down, tobacco tin nearer the mattress, the lid an ashtray. This was a rancid sticky night with just the window screens up and half the block listening to Blair slap Skookie across the room, rasps of drunk slagging till she sobbed down on this long slope of wet words we couldn't catch, words that streamed down the back wall and put us off the frozen yoghurt which'd melted anyway. The ceiling breathed in and out with their clumsy accusations, like you couldn't fit all the beads on the string:

– You doan love me you doan love me coz you beat up on me yalways beat up on me.

– That ain't fuckin right, he said. I do yeah so fuck I do fuckin love ya s'fuck.

– How can you say that how can you say that when you beat up on me bruise an beat up on me agin . . .

– Bull-shit, he said.

Two stomps and he landed her against the door and all the dead bluebottles, dust and the loose glass from a crack and the dried-up sticky tape off the lampshade cascaded onto our bed.

– You doan love me see, Skookie said.

– I fuckin do.

– You doan love me Blair.

– No. I don't. I hate ya guts. I hate your fuckin guts. You've ruined my fuckin life.

– I ain ruined nothin but mown life. You've ruined mine, ah could've had anythin I wannid, money, a car, anythin.

– Ahhh wass wrong, Skookie-cookie doan like the way I do shit anymore huh?

Howling under her breath she let go in a widow's grief, only the way it sounded she was beating herself into it and leaning against the door the way it shook our wall and ceiling.

– Kill me kill me kill me you'd bedder kill me now do it now kill me now coz if you doan it's the last chance you're gonna get coz I'm gonna kill you Blair an ma brother'll killya an I'll come back an killya an ma cousin Floyd'll killya an uncle Preston an Orville . . .

She was tumbling down the wooden steps and we saw her run into the road down Lincoln Drive in just a T-shirt,

Blair leaving it a bit then bawling SKOOKIE in bare feet, trying to run:

– Aw shit fuck ah, so he had to go up again and put his sneakers on.

About ten that morning the phone rang and it was Ena Tolstoy. She wanted F in there right then to do prep because Skookie was her dishwasher and had skipped to California, that is quit yes, owing to family crisis at 4 am.

F and Ena talked the whole time through food prep and after closing when they all sat round the candles, Ena and Stan Tolstoy, the waitresses, eating Ena's Russian specials which the Californians wouldn't touch. When Stan wasn't there Ena said she'd always wanted to work with animals, not cook for Goldnecks who came in for dinner at 6 pm and were gone by 6.15 pm. She'd once worked in a Russian zoo feeding elephants and giraffes. She came from a family who didn't like touching. She didn't even let Stan touch her in the restaurant. The temple which sponsored her family's emigration from Russia had gathered to meet them on arrival. The woman delegate had walked forward and kissed her grandfather. *Welcome to America*. He hadn't even waited to get her name or his luggage, just pushed her off and in Yiddish had said:

– Never do that again lady, herding his family into the waiting taxis.

Ena met Stan in Virginia. They were 'defected' scientists working in a nuclear plant where they were never actually given any work to do for six years so the CIA could monitor their adjustment without risk. They weren't allowed to read but they had to sit at their desks and look busy. They designed dream houses on their computers and Stan said it drove him nuts. His colleague killed six years with absurd calculations, like how many baseball bat blows it'd take to kill a quarter-ton Virginia Pig. When he paid for the experiment to take place on a nearby farm Stan said that was enough, time to get out and start a restaurant.

Stan had been a Red Army conscript during the Hungarian uprising. He was told they were going to fight America because America began the uprising. They'd set out to fight the West on foot. Stan's Division only had four Studebakers left over from World War II and they were going to sail over the Bering Straits in Liberty Ships built at New Orleans in 1941, ships only welded to last three years. Stan had never seen a Russian weapon. He'd carried a wooden rifle his whole military career.

One Sunday night I drove down to pick up F and sat across from Tolstoys' in the Elk Brotherhood parking lot. Since Stan made Ena cut F's days to Sunday they hadn't spoken to me or invited me in for the leftovers. Stan snapped at Ena. Ena stopped talking to F and Stan ignored her if he could. We were all of us out of place, out of our depth. There was no honour among immigrants, because we were not exiles. We had no fondness for the old country and we'd begun to hate the new one. This Sunday I could see something was really wrong when F stepped out the front door instead of out the kitchen alley. Stan had just said something weird.

– Ask your husband what the hell he thinks he's doink. Does he wanna get arrested or what does he want?

F had asked what he meant but he said:

– You ask him, he knows what I mean.

As usual I stank and had a two-day grit on my face and knew if I went in there now he'd treat me like a bum. But we'd already been skunked by the Youngbloods and now these Tolstoys were driving the wedge under my nail. I was in the alley and slamming open the kitchen door telling myself I was doing it for F too. Stan was counting up his credit slips by the till. He looked up like I'd caught him with his fingers in it. I went all breeches and brogues.

– Would you have the goodness to explain your message, Mr Tolstoy.

163

Stan backed into mumbling, the only audible nonsense was that it didden matter, eet was nothink.

I paced forward leading my arrogant infantry.

– I'm sorry Mr Tolstoy. That's not good enough.

Stan put the pen down and took his specs off.

– So, you don't know what you are doink on Marndy night, eh? No? I remind you. I was out the back when I hear sarm-one wrenchink off my door handle so I run inside to catch this thief and switch floods on. I light up whole sidewalk. There is no mistake, I see you runnink away to Post Office.

Ena was standing in the kitchen doorway holding her wineglass in two fingers, the red wine drained into her face. Stan hadn't told her this.

– My door handle, it cost fifteen dollars and more to have fixed. I take it off F's wages. Why you do it? Are you crazy or what?

– I'm what, I said. *You're* crazy Mr Tolstoy, you and that crazy Leon. Ask Leon where *he* was Monday night.

Leon was his nephew. No one else wanted him so he'd dumped himself on the Tolstoys. He ate and smoked all day, dropping food and ash all over the house. He practised knife-throwing in the yard, sticking birds and butterflies and the neighbour's cat which they'd had to pay the vet's bill for. The only English he knew was some military words he'd picked up in the Israeli Army. He'd learned one army trade – how to kill a homo sapiens with a knife at distances up to twenty yards. And one civilian trade – the enamelling of false teeth. He'd spent all his money in Excelsior on a Lincoln gas-guzzler but he couldn't drive. Stan offered him an air ticket home to Tel Aviv but he'd refused to go and wouldn't give a reason.

I could've enlightened Stan. I knew what being Leon felt like. Double or quits, nothing to lose. No one asked you to be there. Every night, Leon went down the restaurant and sat doodling at the staff table, doodling these androgenes

164

floating in tiny rooms, electric flex plugged into their backs. I'd seen these androgenes in Farm Villa, the only difference from Leon's was that in Farm Villa they had British Standard plugs on. Stan didn't like it, patients' art. He used to throw his hands up and shout at Leon, Do your English. Do your American history. How you gonna pass citizenship test?

Leon was ugly. Face crushed in, flat tree stump head, belly like a sack of dirt, always on the scan for loose change, out the till or off the tips plate.

– Well Mr Tolstoy? I said. How dya know it weren't Leon?

– You tryink to frame Leon, Mr Josh?

– No.

I already knew Leon had an alibi. I just needed to sink lower. Leon wasn't going to recover from Monday's humiliations any more than I was. He was finished. Not like me, someone would come pluck me out with a rubber glove, Mr Tolstoy. Poor Stan. For him Monday was when someone tried to wrench his door handle off, not the day Leon hit the bottom of his own cesspit. The restaurant was shut on Mondays. On the Sunday night, Leon had packed his bags and Stan had taken him down to Sacramento and dumped him on the freeway at 6 am. Leon had wanted to go to New York by hitching up US80. By Monday evening, Stan was back in the restaurant when his door handle was fingered. Ten minutes later the Police from Pollack Pines phoned to say they'd found Leon by the roadside, only a mile from where he'd started, thrown from a moving car for a reason they didn't care to unravel. Stan drove the seven hours down again to fetch him back.

– Please, I think we leave my nephew, Mr Josh.

– Well if I had to live with you, I'd tip a packet of corn-flakes in the bath every morning just like Leon does.

Stan said:

– Get out of my business. You're like a flea on an iron dog.

XVIII

*A*tlanta had been dead fifteen months when I'd phoned Mr Fairweather whatsisfuckin name all those Christmases ago.

– What do you want? he'd said.

– I thought I might pop over . . .

– Why? he said. Why exactly?

– It's Christmas, I said. For a chat and a mince pie.

– A chat about what?

– Just a chat.

– You mean a chat about life? Is that it? Why can't you tell me now?

I'd said I didn't know, really . . . it was Christmas after all, I was a bit down, you know, that's all . . .

– Well, he'd said, I'm sorry but that's impossible. We're going away for Christmas, to New England actually. We're going tomorrow in fact, to spend Christmas with Atlanta's family. I doubt we're coming back. I feel we belong there now. I don't want Ashley upset, you know. Thank you for remembering us. Goodbye.

– Cunt.

Even my parents had a purpose and a kind of contentment they'd never had before and I saw how wrong it was to stay at home, especially with Pearl just getting over Bill's suicide. They'd all spent their anger and got nothing for it.

You'll have to learn to drive, the old man said. Oh yeah, I thought, drive old Chittenden's car up Bedgebury. No, move, face life and get a job. Driving. Nagging, he was now. Rights and wrongs. The whole root of my problem was No Drive. I couldn't see it. I'd never drive. Why should I?

I'd lay on the bed and fall asleep shivering under the coverlet all afternoon. My one human contact was the weekly visit from a psychiatric social worker in her nice P reg. Austin Allegro. I'd walk her to it, watch her start it up, put it in gear and stuff, then stand there while she turned round at the bottom of the road and came back past me in third, a nervous bony smile as she went to her next patient. I wrote and said I was in love with her and she was taken off the case. The bloke they gave me said I should read *The Savage God*. He drove the same Allegro and wasn't allowed to tell me what Miss X was driving now. In case I . . . in case I what?

Had I confused escape with cars even then? Or cars with love? Cars were illusions. I'd hung on to that belief until I went to America. Cars had been illusions because they'd died before they got you there. You'd have to fix it. The money you kept by to spend at your destination went on the car. When the car worked you couldn't afford to run it. Then you couldn't afford to fix it. You sold it for scrap and it was a downward spiral into soiled dungarees and filthy nails, Germolene smeared on chassis gashes, elbow too weak for the monkey wrench, lying in the bottom of the world with your hands lit by the runny eye of torchlight. There *was* no other was. And as for mechanics, you couldn't trust mechanics. Sandy'd proved that. He'd worked with them in their garages. Garages were daylight robbery. He'd made out the invoices himself. What had mattered was the old man's torchlight robbery for the auto-didact. I didn't have it so there was no point was there? I hadn't needed a car to kill myself.

I'd taken the bus to Oakwood Hospital the week before Christmas, aged nineteen and a half. On my own, mid-morning, sitting over the wheel hub watching the verges blur past. I felt slightly sick in this modern, automatic double-decker. The once-infallible country bus service of my childhood in ruins. Half the routes abandoned, Hawkhurst Bus Station closed down, the single-deckers scrapped. Old green coaches rotted in the long grass behind blackened sheds at village garages all over West Kent and East Sussex. My one small suitcase had a change of clothes and a toothbrush. No evidence of life so far. As empty as a mind can be. Making it up as I went along, losing.

Months later, after I'd ceased to exist, I joined the hospital library. There were hundreds of brittle yellow Polish books published in Warszawa and Krakow in the thirties. There was *Wireless World*. AA books. Enoch Powell's *Collected Poems*. *The A-Z of Tropical Fishes*. And the book I took out. *Reminiscences* by The Marchioness Curzon of Keddleston G.B.E., my parents' employer in Bodiam. She'd been an American, born in Streetsboro, Ohio. And if I palmed the compulsory Mogadon the night nurse dispensed like clockwork, I could remember my dreams.

XIX

*W*hen we'd descended the slope at Milkweed Lane for our drive across America the rain was chucking down and the car felt like a lop-heavy stranger. It was 2 am.

– Well, I'd said, here we go.

– Yep, show's on the road. Oregon or Bust, F said.

3,500 miles ahead of us, over the Great Plains and mountains. Ours had been a marriage made by the willingness to risk everything. In a pact like that you trust each other and the car equally. You exchange existences. The mechanic we'd had service the Wagon said that in Oregon cars rust from the inside outwards. We only cared about getting there.

F was sorry to leave in the dark, no one to see us off or wish us well. They'd all said she was throwing herself off a bridge. She said she was throwing herself onto one.

As we rolled, the downpour began to ease off. We'd loaded the Honda in the rain after a fortnight's packing, our list running to several sheets. We'd filled ten U-Haul boxes, one chest, two steamer trunks, three stuffbags, rubbish sacks, pillowcases, rucksacks, travelbags. Everything else had gone in loose, wedging gaps. Bach's entire output on record. Ten iron skillets, eight kerosene lamps, 300 books, twenty x 500-size tubs of vitamins, twelve pillows, three comforters, 75 lb of clothes, three boxes assorted junk which had to be unpacked and wedged loose, and a lead owl which weighed 12 lb.

For us Oregon was what we'd read in Ken Kesey and what F's old English teacher said because he had a cabin there. It meant downpours and rainforests. It was as far west as you could drive. There were shacks in the hills you could rent for dirt. I'd build rods how they wanted them and call them poles if I must. Great trout and steelhead state, Oregon.

So, with the back seats flat and a roof rack, we took everything. Trunks and stuffbags lashed to the roof under polythene, the rest so wadded and rammed there wasn't one inch left inside. The back sagged, the tyres bulged, stuff fell out when you opened a door. Getting in the front seats was like squeezing into a cockpit. It required assistance and the temporary removal of all the up-front essentials like maps, tapes, pullovers, food, thermos, flashlight, first aid kit. But the moment we settled in we were used to it.

The house was instantly behind us, locked, dark, past. We sat awhile with the windows down listening to the rain kittling through the blue spruce, on wild roses and honeysuckle with its deep fresh clean scent, and we could hear individual rains on the choke cherry and grape arbour, the roof shingles and bird feeder. The peepers yimmered on the pond and the bullfrogs belched. The click of seatbelts. The rustle of cigarette papers as we rolled a few for the road. Sitting there at night was already a journey because the smells and the rain clupping on the polythene was new and felt like something we'd aimed for in our life together. Soon the windshield wrinkled over, the windows steamed up and I stepped outside with the shammy and wiped the passenger side first to see F waving the arms of the little bear travelling on the dashboard with us. I was scared then because life had gained too much I didn't want to lose. I didn't yet know how you went about protecting it. I'd

170

never been responsible for happiness before. Because everything was so beautiful, all I could think of was how appalling losing her would be.

The engine started first turn and we held hands for half a cigarette. Then headlights on, inching slowly down the drive and into Milkweed Lane. It felt like driving in glue with lead tyres. It took twice the usual distance to get up into third, and bounced an extra hundred yards after hitting a bump. To swerve round a dead skunk or shredded tyre I needed a hundred yards to re-align.

F said:

– It's gonna eat up gas, specially cross them plains.

And another wave of fear, as if back in London we'd made some kind of suicide pact under philosophical duress, the way we saw our destructions in our knowledge of each other and ourselves, because of the bad opinions of friends and relatives. Without F, I'd no defence. Beulah Stafford had been right. Verity had been right.

I didn't even have a driver's licence so I'd no right sitting at the wheel. My visa had run out at midnight, so I'd no right even being in America.

F was at work in Excelsior the day of the San Francisco earthquake. News came in as the sun dipped in the hills. They were all talking about it on the coffee shop terrace, even the quiet bums took the stitches out their lips and came over to split the day's dog-butts at my table. One of them said the whole Bay had a power outage. Hundreds of dead bodies. And there was this guy he knew who was going to tip his mechanic ten grand for wrecking the guy's truck. This mechanic was supposed to have fixed it ready for a trip down to Santa Cruz that day. Only the night before the mechanic took off with the truck on a date with his girl and wrapped it round a utility pole. It was back in the shop again, having a new shell put on, so the guy didn't go to Santa Cruz. The way the guy looked at it, he

171

would've been on that bridge about the time of the earth-quake. His truck would've been 4" thick like a gymnastics mat the way that bridge collapsed, and he'd've had a face like that:

I looked up. The bum held up the edge of his flat hand. I stared at it.

– Hey, he said, you look like you recognize that face, man.

I knew F wasn't in San Francisco. That week she had a subbing job at Bi-Mart, stacking shelves three hundred yards away. I was driving to pick her up in an hour. From Excelsior it was a nine-hour drive to San Francisco. I'd dropped her outside Bi-Mart at 8 am and heard her man-ageress say:

– Hey you guys'll be going down with this truck of stuff.

That meant she'd be getting into Bi-Mart Santa Cruz about the time of the earthquake, 5.03 pm Tuesday October 17th. The next thing I knew I was running round Bi-Mart with a wet face, bumping into people and tripping over boxes. I found F putting new price strip holders along the hardware shelves.

F drove into Excelsior one morning when everything was still yellow with cold sun and I stood at the door smoking. When she drove back with that magazine she'd bought I was sitting on the stoop. She pushed past me, ditched the magazine and threw up in the sink because she'd seen me dead in the front seat of someone else's car. It was a brown car, just sitting there in the middle of Main Street outside the pharmacy, a short trail of broken glass and oil, hazard flashers on, holding up the traffic. The front wheels angled outwards and the right fender was crushed in. All four doors were wide open and a bunch of onlookers were star-ing at this person on the front seat. F pushed through, just to get by. A woman with a baby spun on her. She'd said:

– Hey lookout willya.

Then everyone noticed F and she was funnelled down to the open door. They knew she was married to the dead driver. They kept saying so. Then who was this chubby blonde with a dislocated jaw and a Walkman round her neck? But F knew I was dead, somewhere else if not there. From the sidewalk a voice said:

– Dya know that lady honey?

The lady went, uuuuuuhhhhhh, but she'd broken her jaw. F cracked her head on the door jamb getting away.

XX

*W*e did plan a suicide pact. In case, against the worst, instead of keeping a cyanide capsule round your neck, like F said Beulah did. We'd go up Little Hyatt Lake. Just pick a day with a cold skin on the sky, white as your fingernails. When the sharp end of a killer's wind cuts across a winter pond. When the air's left shivering over clean polished water.

The future isn't a place to arrive at in the dark. We'd never never never dreamed of that. Blowing up against a fence in Excelsior City. F dishwashing, while I honed my pessimism to a point sharp enough to stab us both.

F had found Little Hyatt one hot late afternoon in high summer, driving down a stumbling unmapped track, a 5 mph dust, the car white from parched earth. Lazily, from four days' camping, one mountain lake to the next, four hopeless days. Poisoned crapfish bulldozed into heaps. Dried out creeks. Hanged owls on poles along the highways.

Little Hyatt was a damned two-acre pond down among pines and evergreens, a tumbledown mill, rushes and lily pads, green pasture and this old dam where the brown silt water fell to a stickle over beds of cress. We wanted to dream and tell stories. We forgot Excelsior and Oregon there. We were in New England or Sussex or Normandy. And we were simply lost.

It was like I'd frozen F on the verge of happiness. She'd

married me that June, a long evening in the soft warm drizzle beside the old cemetery in Sharon. The Judge in a white raincoat recited Dover Beach then summed up with: Life is not a bowl of cherries, but there are plenty of cherries in the bowl. An hour later when we were shucking corn in the garden and fanning the coals, the Judge drove up in his Brougham hot under the collar and breathless. He'd forgot one bit of the ceremony.

– I pronounce you man and wife, he said.

So come November the mist descended off the hills as far as Luna Vista. Mid-morning came a fish-eye sun, pale soak, loose cloud fluke drifting like steam, dew on cafe tables. It was time to leave Excelsior, that fake city, before we lost sight of each other. F said it was like running back into a burning house to pull me out. She said leave that rubbish in there because she was pregnant. We had to decide what to do.

At the duckpond in Lithia Park we watched a young couple video themselves sitting on a bench. The woman held a spray of maple leaves, the man threw crusts for the ducks and stroked the woman's hair with one finger, kissing her on the cheek as she stiffened, intimidated by the camera. His clapperboard fell off the bench. He abandoned her, running forward shouting Cut, clapping his board like a pair of snapping jaws. He kicked the ducks away and snatched the breadcrusts off the ground. He chalked a new scene on the board and shouted Action. The woman turned her profile to the lens to show off the bulge in her belly.

By the restrooms, husband, wife and son watched their little girl play in a sandpit. The man had no arms. When he walked into the urinals his eight-year-old boy followed him without hesitation or summons. We laughed, grateful that we could always laugh. Point it at that bee, son. But he probably just flipped it out dutifully then stood aside, waiting to shake the drips.

We even named the kid we didn't intend to have, the

way Americans named their towns after hardships along the trail: Bitter Creek, Gunsight, Stark, Recluse, Rocky Bar, Sodom. The way now, with the false hope, they named their children Loving, Paragonah, Helper, Sweet. We called ours Psychiatrica, Prolixia, Oakwood, Atlanta. I chucked F's beret in the stream and we called that Moses. She was still laughing as she arranged the abortion over the phone and we walked back through the park with stale crusts to capture our last moments as an intimate family. Now we had this passenger to nowhere, this backseat driver.

F said:

– Let's pretend to kill ourselves.

She said it might free us. We could make mental effigies of ourselves. These would commit the suicides, bury the effluent. We had to do something. Our first summer had just dried up.

F took the scenic route to Little Hyatt, up Dead Indian Road as far as the logging track at Hooper Spring. Just past the Youngbloods' turning we picked up an Eldorado with a bumper sticker: MY SON IS A JEWISH CARPENTER. Up in the mountains it was winter. We rose 1,000 feet into scattered snow and there was cat ice on the streams and icicles like swords on the falls. We could hear the ice forming and feel our tongues stick to the air.

At Little Hyatt we made our effigies by standing near the water and slopping out the painful thoughts, like sticking two fingers down your throat. We were both so polluted we could step out of ourselves and leave a visible outline. F said the idea then was to step into one thought only, about each other, a distilled thing, which would sound like a wind chime if a thought could hang in the breeze. I thought of when I'd wake from dreams, the moment when I'd open my eyes and turn to her. Her eyes would snap open too, still asleep. She would see me and squeeze my hand. In the morning I'd tell her this but she never remembered, so I never knew what she saw or dreamed in those few seconds. It was like second sight and I felt so safe.

We bucked down the dirt at the foot of Green Springs Mountain, hitting flocks of mist which curled across the Wagon, an icing mist chiming on the metal. We rubbed warmth back into our hands, hands we'd immersed in Little Hyatt when drowning our effigies, letting the water spate and quiver and fin through our fingers. Making sluices and loopholes. Making a free wish.

We came off Buck Point whining in third, a Hundred Hour Dark Roast slapping in the thermos cup and steaming up the windshield. There was a policeman sitting in his skunk at the foot of Maple Hill under the leaves, grazing on the dark sky near The Hungry Woodsman. Our hi-beams burned his face so I dipped them but the offside beam blacked out on low. He hesitated, then heard us singing our tops off, singing along with The Vagabond from *Songs of Travel*. Perhaps he didn't like seeing our windows down on a cold night. He gave us the full siren like we'd already got the edge on him. He had to cross the highway. We were already half-way up Maple.

I pulled over and the skunk parked behind, lights flashing. F said:

– Don't get out.

The Peace Officer stood at the window, torch and gun drawn.

– Hi, he said. I'm Peace Officer Cahoon. You have a defective low-beam. I'm going to ask you to step out of the car slowly so I can see your hands at all times.

He stood back as I did that.

– Now, what are you doing out here?

– Joyriding, I said. F laughed.

– Driver's licence.

– I don't have one, I said.

– I have to ask you for your immigration papers.

– I don't have any, I said.

XXI

*P*eace Officer Cahoon pulled off Peachy Avenue through the drizzle into the lot behind Lois Lanes Bowling Alley. Through the busted fence the trailer park looked like a used dog pound. The frail brush, those runs alongside the trailers. Repairs postponed. Birdshit stucco. Tarps rucking off in the wind. He said he'd kill me if I tried anything. I said I was only in the deportation tank. He reminded me I was still under house arrest and that he was just being nice, driving me to the cafe while F was in the clinic shitting on America, oh excuse me, he said, having an abortion.

He shoved the car into park beside the busted fence and chucked his toothpick out the window.

– I'll watch from here, okay? You go on over, take ya time. Have two coffees, three, I don't care today. Big muffin? Enchilado? Could be ya last meal. You ain goin nowhere.

He'd kept saying that. You ain goin nowhere.

– This is nowhere, I said.

So I sat on The Beanery terrace at the corner of Peachy and Route 66. The Beanery was a hang-out, the place you gathered if you weren't suburban. I was just relieved I didn't have to listen to Cahoon for ten minutes. He'd talked in the car non-stop all morning, back and forth from court-house to apartment, to the clinic . . . His voice had become the landscape.

178

Once he'd pulled into a parking space at Lithia Park and left me to doze as he fed the ducks Alka Seltzer. It made him laugh to see ducks fart their way across the pond like burst balloons. He spat and slammed himself back in the car.

– Dork hungry yet? Ah'm fra corn dog.

Cahoon was from Medford, another town, another America thirty minutes' drive south, the industrial belt. Excelsior City was the dead end on the Oregon Trail before it crossed the mountains and stopped at the ocean we'd all set out to reach.

– Kind of ashamed today aincha? Cahoon'd said.

– Yeah, I'd said, as I matter of fact I am. Aren't you?

We'd been sitting on a stoplight at the intersection, Siskiyou Boulevard and Route 66. Cahoon drummed the steering wheel of his patrol car, clicking a Tic-Tac lid in time with the blinker. The flat summer sky had finally gone to seed. The November sky had been darkening all morning. Since June the blue had clouded only twice.

– Might rain, I said.

Cahoon had said:

– No point it rainin where it ain't supposed to, right?

It'd only rained on one day in Excelsior that summer, and me and F had stood on the steps under the porch, marvelling at the annual rainfall in twelve hours. A canopy of thunder on the hillsides for a whole day before the first clod of rain smacked down, whole bucket stains on the dry concrete road. In five minutes there were mini rapids shooting between the apartments and out into Lincoln Drive sweeping away take-outs, Burger King rafts and Fried Chicken windjammers. Everyone came to their porches to cheer their boats on.

– Like Moby Dick filmed in a bathtub, F had said.

But I was already dumping my fallacies on her about life flowing away that fast, and that if for any reason we found ourselves alone again, would our notions of being alone still coincide?

She'd begun to miss herself already, having to resist my flooded history. Let it seep away. All you can do with it is construct more weird sculpture. She didn't want any more sculpture.

So we'd watched the sky flickering like a loose connection. There were 3,500 lightning strikes that day. Some hit the 600-year-old pines at Boise.

Cahoon tossed the Tic-Tacs onto the dash and stuck a toothpick in his teeth.

– Nope. Look at it this way. We get nine inches of rain per year. Up in Bandit Springs it's a goddam duckpond two hundred inches deep. See ma point? Oregon's wet as water but not up here. It's why some they like to call Jackson County, California.

He speared some gristle, held it up to the windshield. I told him all I meant was the light had changed. The Cadillac slurped forward.

– YEAH'M WATCHIN. Ain't no light in Jackson County changes without me comin ta hear about it.

Peace Officers in Excelsior City all looked like Cahoon. Thin moustache, thin face. Short, thin-brained, bullet-proof Beef Jerky skin, yellow clip-ons over spectacles. They drove alone or pedalled mountain bikes along sidewalks.

– I meant the bloody sky not the stoplight. The clouds. They're rain clouds.

Cahoon's vocal cords tightened into piano wire.

– Rain? Like ah just toldya, we ain't never hearda that commodity.

He swung to the inside lane behind a Dodge Ram with some black Gothic script on its tail gate:

𝔐𝔈𝔗ℌ𝔍ℜ𝔎𝔖 𝔗ℌ𝔒𝔘 𝔄ℜ𝔗 𝔄 𝔖ℌ𝔍𝔗ℌ𝔈𝔄𝔇.

– Why dya think them Goldnecks been comin up here? They wanna own somma this dry land, them oldy worldy hansome wooden houses where yaint gonna gitya bar-bee-

Q quenched in no Oregon monsoon. Californians oany got golf umbrellas, ain't that cute?

Then he'd pulled into the lot behind the bowling lanes and I sat out on The Beanery terrace watching the clouds catch hillsides like smoke under ceilings. Cahoon kept his door open awhile, sat out alone in the empty lot. Feet on his dash, puzzle book, sucking on a Bic he'd got from Jittery Joe's Haircut House in Phoenix. I was beginning to feel angry, but it was too late, or useless to fight back. I was watching the sky, feeling the air, and thinking *carp*.

XXII

*I*n June, after we'd found the apartment in Excelsior, I made a couple of carp rods and we went up Emigrant Lake asking about carp. Old boys trolling jiggers would spit and say nope, scratching under their ball caps like I was a snoop. Carp, faggot, nigger. Same word to them.

– No carp in Southern Oregon. Made damn sure o' that, son.

I found some twenty miles south at Gold Ray Dam, a backwater of the River Rogue. Found them in the dead bit where the cow pokes couldn't poison the water because it would leak into the river and kill the steelhead. Somehow the carp had established themselves in the rancid, popping water. Carp that swirled in angry sulks and shrugged off water like it stuck to them. My kind of carp, so I stuck it out the first afternoon. If this was where they were, then sod the hot dirt and sheets of cardboard and the three bags of litter you have to pick up before you sit down. It was fishing. But I soon learned that every revelation there began with a car coming along the track.

Heard the first one a mile off too, a rammed–up black Datsun clobbering along the dirt and coming to a standstill behind me. Two of them stamped down the bank.

– Hi there. How zit goin, friend?

The other one saw the water.

– Aw shit. It's all shit-up there, Leo. Een gonna pud a line through that crap no way.

– Hi, Leo repeats. What's doon, friend? Any action?

They looked puzzled when they saw the whole picture and bent over to look at my rods. That little tremor on the alarm. Leo wore his Slam Dunk T-shirt and red ball cap. In one hand a six-foot jigging pole with a little spinning reel and a red cantilever box. He chucked all that into the ferns so's he could deal with the jumbo milkshake from Burger King. His sidekick stayed back at the barbed wire fence twanging on his short pole. Had his jeans tucked in his socks, tough commando. Little runt black hair kept flippin in his eyes like he'd slept on it badly. Kept tossing his head back too, keeping his nose high, kicking divots as far into the pool as he could. Then Leo spots a fish.

– HEY, heyheyheyheyhey Gary-Gary, quit foolin. Gitya pole set up. Right there, see em? Bluegill, swimmin under this fella's pole.

Leo opened up the cantilever. He'd written his name inside with marker pen mixing upper and lower case so he didn't have to join the letters. LeO BuKTeniCA. He took out his deli tub of nightcrawlers and chucked a 6" wriggler at Gary.

– Brit incha? Leo said. Use nightcrawlers much?

He dug out some rubber frogs and a rusted ball of hooks till he found a pack of rubber nightcrawlers. Gary said save a dollar and stick em on ya dick. Leo said they're good-lookin and he aimed to try them when he ran out of live ones. Kept looking at the stranger's gear though. Couldn't quite get what was going on here.

– Yeah . . . hey Gary-Gary, in that long hole there, ah c'n see them snappin. Juss jig it slow now . . .

All the carp had pissed off. I anticipated a bad end so I pulled both baits in. Leo was transfixed.

– Say friend, cain't say ah know what make of poles ya got there. They sea poles or what?

183

I couldn't tell how innocently he asked, but I did know it was the kind of ignorance which turns bad. Gary hits a strike from a bluegill.

– Damn skunked it, Leo.

Hits another straight off but the nightcrawler whips out the water and slaps him in the face. UGHH CRAP PURRR PURRR. Leo said he'd get the hang of it. They hook themselves. Gary-Gary was like a jumping jack.

– Sheeee-eeee.

Leo said: Gary-Gary's hot for it. Baby cousin. Can't go wrong up here any. Bluegill, crappies, bass. Hey, took a bass seven pound a coupla months back. Skinned it for Red Eye. Likes em in the pan, Red Eye.

I was packing away right under their noses, trying to hide my gear as best as I could knowing none of it corresponded to what Leo thought fishing stuff ought to look like. You couldn't get actual carp gear in America, so I'd made the rods and the big landing net from tackle shop scraps. They were well made though and looked authentic, so Leo was on the double take about it all. He kept asking me this and that: ever caught bluegills? You got bass in Britain? You say them's sea poles now?

– No, I didn't say.

– So what are they then friend, c'z I ain never sin the lark o' them poles you unnerstan.

The trouble was Leo didn't like the poles, fine, but this wasn't one fisherman talking to another.

– They're carp rods, I said.

– Come agin friend? They're what? Where?

– I said carp poles. Carp. I'm fishin for carp.

Every time they thought of me from then on they were going to spit puke. I'd made a dirdy-dirdy word. Poor Gary-Gary on his first clean fishing trip holding his jaw out, his nightcrawler stuck on his shoe watching Leo for a sign to stab me in the eye with his bluegill pole. Leo drew his lips back all right.

– Corps? Jeezuss. You like *corps*? Zat what them aiggs is on ya rig foh, corps?

I said they weren't eggs they were chickpeas, garbanzos. I held one up in my fingers like a sticky bogey.

– Hell, Leo said, shaking his head, ah sure as . . . you hear that Gary-Gary? Corps. Ah've seen em swimmin under ma boat man! But sheet ah wouldn let no corps in ma fuckin boat, no way, oh woh woh woh woh ah cain stan em. Ah mean nobody friend, you unnerstand ah mean you doan seem to unnerstand, NOBODY won't touch no corps t'even git their hook back. Ah stuck one with a crossbow too an the water wen red fa days an all the bluegill was floatin upside down. You wanna ruin ya maw n paw? Juss tell em ya goan fishin fa corps. They're junk. They drive out the trout an turn water muddy. Ya cain ketchum anyway they're so sly. Ah doan like sly fishes in ma creek. They was put here by Germans too. Didn't you know that friend?

Well I hung about with shame running down my leg as Leo rigged up and jigged his crawler through my pitch, yanking up bluegill and crappies, both of them counting loud as they threw them back.

– Number nine hey, bigger one too, they're pullin good Leo.

They massed a shedful. In half an hour we had rubber fakes and a Big Charlie Brown Mugger hanging in the tree and gut-hooked crappies floating upside down in the scum. Yeah, Leo'd got me into jigging with a slice of crawler to get them corps out my head. So in the dusk we were standing on the railroad track squashing bugs, good fishing buddies long as I see how wrong corps is.

– So long, friend.

And I think fuckin cesspit as I walk back to the car, but what could I do?

XXIII

I stared over the railings at the unstubbed butts flicked out car windows. Bel-Air 100s. Some Luckys on the stoop. Cahoon slammed his door on the drizzle and dozed off. His head leaned on that shotgun poking barrel-up between the front seats. His windshield clouded over. Drizzle swept across the car in short flurries.

A few tables away on The Beanery terrace one of Excelsior's drifters sewed purses made of old jeans from the Free Box. The finished purses sat in a basket strapped to his handlebars. He'd written on this strip of Kellogg's box: $5 each piece. An onion sack bulged with empties off the back. Diet-rite, 7-Up and Root Beer cans worth a dollar per twenty. We'd seen him most days that summer, but even he was ready to go now. He'd dumped his sandals for a pair of 800-gram all-weather boots, two sweaters, wool pants. I could see he didn't belong in Excelsior for the winter. Just a week back some woman had loaded him and his bike into her pickup and they'd driven off. Next day he was pedalling back in down the bike lane like he'd done this false migration or some freak emotion had blown him off course. He made me feel bad too, like my love for F was the freak emotion, like any migration I could make was false. I wondered how he could just sit there, knowing he had to go, why he hadn't fucking gone.

Through The Beanery window I could just make out my

and F's For Sale card on the bulletin board. After we'd sold the Fuzz Buster nobody phoned, and I could see myself dumping our belongings in the Free Box. The dry yellow foothills were reflected in the glass. The jaundice yellow of summer and Fall had gone. November turned patches of light into strips of early snow. The coldest points frosted blue in the afternoons. Blizzards were down to 4,000 feet in the Cascades and Siskiyous. Weather reports said to keep off the mountain passes. All the 4x4s had their ski clamps fixed. That summer's boats were roped down and under tarps in the driveways. Little Hyatt Lake was cut off now.

Leaves turned instant copper in Lithia Park. Along the boulevards they turned the quick yellow of old wallpaper in the morning, fell off the trees by day and got sucked up overnight by dedicated crews driving vacuum cleaners with searchlights. Dawns were chill and dry. Sprinklers stayed on along the sidewalks into winter. Any breeze was like a gasp of discontent and set the uncollected leaves rittling aimlessly into the road. Between 1st and 2nd Street the banner strung across the store fronts announced DOMESTIC VIOLENCE AWARENESS WEEK.

People once drifted into Excelsior City without purpose, caught on its edges and wanted to stay. When Cahoon drove me to The Beanery, this coffee jerk who'd never spoken to me and F before – and we'd been in there all summer – pointed at the patrol car with a list of questions.

– Trouble? What trouble? Whadya mean immigration trouble? Whadya mean ya wife's in hospital trouble? Dya wanna coffee drink man, on the house?

And this coffee jerk couldn't think of anything shittier than being turned out of Excelsior City for all time.

The lights came on inside The Beanery. All the faces were chewing motel ballpoints under hot air blowers. Ambient music leaked out the walls. Excelsior was a base camp for mystics and pilgrims to Mount Shasta. I met one out at Big-Buy, one of those warehouses with fifty-foot-high shelves and everything boxed. The assistant drives a fork lift and serves you in a yellow helmet. The pilgrim tapped me on the shoulder.

– Ever been up Shasta, man?

– No, why?

– It's got powers. You come down different. I can see your aura now. You got a purple aura man. You're out of tune.

Then the Goldnecks moved up too when California real estate prices hit the roof. Limousines appeared on Main Street. The little banks fattened up. The little stores were closed down by the real estate agents. Logging companies saw the way things were going and began to rip the hearts out of redwood forests 500 years old, last home of the white-eared owl. We signed the petition and the white-eared owls appeared overnight on bus shelters, swinging from a noose. The real estate agents sponsored new bumper stickers: IF ITS HOOTIN I'M SHOOTIN. KEEP OREGON CLEAN – GET A HAIRCUT. This was the place we were being thrown from.

A car pulled up against the fence. A man in a checked sports coat turned his collar up against the drizzle and tied a nervous dog to a chairleg out on the terrace. It kept shifting and moved the chair with such a jerk it took off. The chair was chasing it so the dog licked down the steps and up the bike lane towards Cahoon. The man chased the chair shouting Mothera Christ. The sky had lowered two-thirds down the hillsides. It felt like the end of the ride too.

Drizzle turned to rain and Cahoon called me over, beckoned me for chrissake with the blue flashing light and one pipsqueak on the siren. Sports coat led his dog back down the bike lane, one hand dragging the nasty nasty chair. The dog's tail thick as tow rope struck out at the enemy air. Cahoon was moody.

– See that asshole with the dog? Can't keep a job or a woman an even his mutt runs off with a goddam chair when his back's turned.

XXIV

*I*n summer, carp are night feeders. Me and F opened our campaign on Gold Ray Creek one July evening, setting up for a night. At sunset the air thickened with mosquitoes as far back as the car. We had to wade through them with our hands. Mosquitoes up our nose, in our ears, biting down our throats if we breathed. It was too hot to dress against them and they were immune to every repellent we tried. The bites swelled into hard lumps, red raw buboes after scratching all night. The only relief was a cold bath.

So we tried the dawns instead. Too short. The sun was up and hot before we'd settled in, and the feeding spells were too erratic. As July advanced the carp moved up the island to a jungle pool impossible to reach. Then F needed the car for work. The days were just too hot, sun squealing on shadeless banks, rubble like embers underfoot. The track iron ganched and clunked. Crickets skiffled on our nerves and the dirt singed into dust. At dusk the temperature sat heavy in the 80s. It never rained.

Some rare evening a dry stillness might descend to relieve the scorch. The sun dipped behind the hills, a cupboardful of cool air dropped off a mountain breeze. Nature turned inward, shy and delicate. The barometer swung and trees tensed and trembled. One evening I was crouched behind the rods, flexing fingers, holding onto each breath

189

as it came. The wait was over. One slack line was about to spring tight and the water erupt. My skin was like a web across a doorway. A carp rolled in the creek. Single file the others quit the jungle pool and made their way down. And that was as far as I ever got. Mosquitoes rose out the bare earth and drove me away.

The chance to catch a carp was always a race against time. If I thought I'd beat the dusk, someone would show up to spook the fish. Floaters were assassins. Not the lazy nuisance of messing about on a creek, no sedate drifters barefoot in a sunhat. These pirates scuppered whole shoals with scend and pitch, heave-to landward right through both my lines, backcasting without ever wondering why I was sitting there with two poles looking concerned. They thought they were being friendly when they asked me to move so they could haul their boat up the bank and dump their beer cans in the undergrowth I'd been using as cover.

All summer they launched anything that floated into the scum. And this was out in Void Corner by fuckin Vacuumsville. Where did they come from? All the slipways were marked with beer cans on twigs or fried chicken boxes weighted by stones, plastic wrappers round bushes, bright red styrofoam milkshake buckets jabbed onto sticks rammed in the gravel. Back ashore they tossed their land-marks into the creek. Some days I'd find ten pick-ups sit-ting along the track, boat clamps empty. If F was with me, we'd just head back to Excelsior City or drive up a moun-tain pass and sit there with a bird spotter's handbook.

Creek water was always dead calm, choked stagnant, low oxygen with the dam sluices shut. By mid-August the creek dried up and I don't know where the carp holed up and didn't care. I made a few steelhead poles for a shop in Medford. They said don't bother going back up Gold Ray Creek as I'd never catch a carp out there.

I did go back in Fall and found the place stripped down

for winter, new brown water full of leaves, dead weed, broken reeds drained of greenness. A sky devoid of swallows. Beavers finishing off their grey dams. You could see no one came there any more. That hollow, whittled loneliness of the last place on earth you want to be.

How could that have been the place where I'd stood that July? When a stiff wind had blown up from the dam, the tail end of stowed winds off mountains, the whole channel became one swept ripple like static sand ribbed at low tide. The carp started rolling everywhere, crashing heads and backs, tail flips, bursting out along the margins. At last. I'd take them on one at a time. Then this rust-cluttered yellow Hondamatic nobbled its way along the ruts towards me, front offside fender smashed, a side-window blocked in and taped up with grey trashcan liner. It parked right beside me and an old man and his son got out, the old man gripping the top edge of the passenger door, surveying the trees and rock behind him. The son opened up the trunk and took out two bright red six-foot spinning poles and two fold-up garden chairs. Father and son wore red and blue plaid shirts and pale blue denims, only the old man's had the bib. They both took black tubs of Skoal Bandits Smokeless Tobacco out their breast pockets. Spat the old stuff out soon as their feet hit the ground, picking out new dips, the son keeping his cigar stub going the same time. The old man chewed that New Wintergreen flavour. Juice stains down his denim, pulling on a red ball cap which said *My worst day's fishin's better than my best day workin*.

He took up his pole, leaned it on the door, line uncoiling at his feet, plastic bobber knucking in the wind, a size 4 baitholder catching in his turnup.

– Aww git the damn hook out Bo.

Bo knelt over and disgorged the hook while the old man saw across at who the hell I was standing on the railroad track like a man trying to remember up an enemy or two

191

and not deciding right. He drew his .38 from the Uncle Mike hip holster he got last Christmas, looking anxious when he couldn't see the sun shining on the leather. He unclipped the gun and squinted on the contents. Bo went round the back of the car for a slash.

– Shoot, the old man said looking at the hole in his turn-up, then back up the track at the stranger.

– Howdy. Ain sin you b'fore, hev we?

The gun stayed aimless at the stranger who said no, wishing the carp'd keep down now or they'd get shot at.

– Aim never ta go fishin these days without ma revolver.

Bo came round yanking on his zipper:

– That's a fuckin pistol, dad.

– You keep out, Bo! Juss lemme tawk ta this fella. What ah'm sain's this, son. Bout three murders every week in these parts, see that? Thet's why. Hell they doan give Jack . . . Shit. They come off the highway. Hell, they ain gonna care. They're back in Californya like they was never anywhere else.

Bo and the old man fished for half an hour in the wind's teeth. Their chairs kept blowing over when they stood up to untangle a backfired cast so they packed it in.

By evening the wind had turned and dropped. I was settled in the rampicks, a handful of bait across the margin weed where nudging fish sent up clouds of silt. I tackled up slowly, confident I'd catch, Bo and the old man just a figment. My first cast had just hit the water when I heard a Ramrod snap the atmosphere in two. The driver put it through the floor and came off Gold Ray Road in a rubber smoke, hacking down the embankment zero to 50, one wheel on the sleepers, a skid and two-spin finish.

I wound in quick and broke the rod down reasoning they didn't know I was there and didn't need to if I stayed tucked under the bank. The Wagon was parked way up on the road at Snake Bend. The Ramrod ate into the place. The water heaved and flattened as carp keethed off into snags. Waterbirds kicked and beat their way to cover. The air reeked of dust and burnt fuel. I was scared then and started shoving everything back in the rucksack and looking for a way to escape. The V8 died down.

– Yee-hawwww, and two doors burst open, Dolly Parton on the boombox fifteen yards away.

There was still a chance they wouldn't find me even if they walked to the edge and looked over. I lay flat under what I was beginning to think wasn't an overhang at all. Maybe Bo and the old man would come back to get something they'd lost and there'd be a shoot out. Bo and son hadn't impressed me as gunslingers. Ramrod and sidekick were killers.

One of them started pitching rocks in over the back of the truck. On and on like he'd gone berserk, hitting the far margins.

The other one said:

– Donny you asshole, just punch that bolt thing willya.

The tailgate clapped down. Two thirsty pokes kissed open two each from a six-pack. Someone'd upset em. They'd burned up Gold Ray to get away, but Lester had had enough of Donny too.

– You doan stand a hog's dick in sawmill's chance, Don boy, s'doan spit shit with me, okay?

– Aw, that's fuckin great comin from you Lester. Your life's bin Snafu all along, know that? Shit, you de-serve Barbie an you de-serve ta puke teeth over snuff dippers like that . . .

– Fuck you rubber lips if I ain had enougha your rachitt jawin for one night, okay? You cain even make it with an oil can who chainsmokes, whose gallbladder's took out, who's done three liver biopsies an shits blood three years outa every four . . .

This went on till after dark. The mosquitoes forced me out. Mosquitoes and the possibility of a rattlesnake sliding along to drink. I had to pull myself up onto the railroad

193

track right under the Ramrod. One of them lay in the back humming, sparking a lighter over and over. The boombox drowned the sound of my footsteps and I managed to stand up without going to jelly and walk quickly up the track, staying visible in case they thought I was sneaking away with their jack or something. The other poke was out in the dark somewhere. When the music stopped I heard what sounded like a hole getting dug so I flew up the track to the Wagon and the next song on the boombox wailed out in the night air. A railroad song. No, that was the train a mile off whistling where it always did. It was running late. Donny and Lester must've thought it went through on time. They'd parked smack on the track. I wanted to let it come, the big rusty Cotton County goods train out of Medford. I wanted it to round the bend and smash into the Ramrod. It would tip over and fill the creek in, kill the carp, kill everything so I wouldn't have to go back there again.

XXV

*T*he clinic was on the other side of Excelsior on a steep hill up Luna Vista. A 3 pm wind sprang up scratching on the birch leaves. Luna Vista looked down on Interstate 5 a mile away between the City Exits. An empty road all the way to Tombstone Mountain. The wind felt warmer and veered south-west. Light cloud shifted off the hilltops along the valley. A rumble of thunder. A grey patch of sun. The first welt of rain whacked into the hood. Cahoon made a pained face.

– Bedder git yaself in there quickedy spit.

F was asleep in a double room, the other bed still empty, all her clutter strewn across it. I sat on her bed and shook her awake.

– Listen, I said. I'll die if I have to go back to England. You said you'd think of somewhere.

I was used to her being one jump ahead of me, the way she dealt with our invisible business, leaving me the maps.

– I'm coming out tomorrow, she said. Don't worry about it.

– Why're they keeping you in anyway?

– They just didn't like the blood tests.

– I'm not going to England, I said again.

– You have to, she said. We'll think of something after that.

I stood at the window pulling a dry ball of hair from her brush, twisting it into a miniature hank and pushing it into

195

my back pocket. The rain cracked down. We only had a few hundred dollars left and what we'd get for the Honda when we sold it. It was still sitting in the lot outside Safeway with a For Sale notice on it. The Judge at the courthouse said he'd give my $60 bail money back if I didn't go near the car again. Then I'd be escorted to San Francisco International Airport and put on the first available flight to London. F was free, of course, to accompany me if she so wished, and paid her way, but they advised her to obtain a visa. The British Embassy had refused her one because I was a deportee. I was scared. I knew no one in England who'd put us up anyway.

– Trust me, F said. Just trust me.

Outside, the air felt electrified. A soothing rain as I toured the hospital lot, already sleepless.

Cahoon was shouting at me to get in the car. He said he was driving to my and F's apartment so I could get on with packing up. By East Main courthouse the first heavy thunder roll shook the valley like furniture shifting in the room next door. Excelsior City dimmed to a pit-town under dust-caked lamps. Cahoon dropped me off and said:

– You stay in now. I might call in like I'm supposed ta. Wanna go down Safeway later?

The dismantled apartment. We'd never had any furniture. In the chill it was naked and temporary, nowhere to sit but propped against a wall. Two rooms with half-packed cartons. A Free Box pile and the rest for sale. Taps dripped. Filthy bathroom. I sat outside on the stoop with a tin mug of stale coffee. When the rain picked up I came in and threw stuff on the piles. Jack the apartments manager came by on his rounds, scratching a week-long cornfield on his face. Rolled cuffs, blue anchors from the wrists up. He shouted from the road.

– How's it goin? You people still in jail?

Chin scratching and rivulets like a broom on a workshop floor.

196

– Ah'm gettin a wash standin here. Say, guess life's gone kinda dull eh? No? She's newer than new huh? Leavin us Friday? Well say hello to Ringo for me. Boy, you ain ever hearda Ringo Starr?

It was dark when the storm passed on and heavy rain set in. Cahoon turned up at five to seven, wipers on fast like his car had a temper, blue light bursting on flash. Down Lincoln Drive he cursed the heater.

– Got hands like a turkey. There must be a dead rat crawled in there. They do that, crawl inta car engines.

In Safeway I bought bread and tinned soup. Cahoon ate a bowl of chili and took a 100-mile coffee out to the car. Our Honda Wagon was parked fifty yards off with the For Sale sign on it.

– Mind if I check the Wagon over?

– Cool by me, he said.

Just the sight of that car made me want to drive. Take a parting shot, leave a paint scratch on this fucking country. It took me two seconds to figure it out. I checked the tyres, went over the route from here to the creek at Gold Ray Dam like I'd never done it before.

In the police car, Cahoon said: Sorry bout the new hot air system. You don't smoke, I don't fart.

He took the corner laughing. No indicators, no looking. We hit the East Main flack, undipped beams coming out the stadium. Outside the apartment he said:

– Ah'm takin my kid out now. Ever seen the noo Batman movie? Okay now, stay out them nightclubs bloke. This'll be your last night in America from what I've bin hearin . . .

At midnight more rain spilled down the guttering. I dozed on the floor wrapped in a comforter with the radio on as the Mexicans hoovered on the floor above. The Japanese couple woke me up for good as crockery splintered against their kitchen wall, screams like a tape on fast forward. In the next silence urgent knuckles rapped on my door. The freak-head drummer from next door getting wet on the stoop.

– Eh, yeah, uh, saw your light, man. Domestic violence week, yeah? We're in Hell City again. Like, not on is it. Think we should eh get the landlord over?

He splashed off in his mocassins to fetch Jack as a Japanese boy in his early twenties slammed the front door opposite and walked off into the dark, hunched in a leather jacket, rain drumming on the shoulder pads. Jack came round and banged on the door. The girl was four foot six, bare feet, yellow T-shirt, black undies. There was food, broken crockery and crumpled paper strewn along the passage behind her.

– Eh, you okay Eyumi?

– I am very well thank you, Jack.

– Oh, well eh bust-ups have to be paid for . . .

She slammed the door on him. He shouted across at us.

– I tried didn't I? I always try. Nuthin ya c'n do, juss the kinda place this is. Ya gettem, ya throw em out after a month.

At one in the morning the Mexicans started hoovering again. I tied some carp rigs, oiled the reels, wiped the grit off two carbon rods, thawed some bait and packed a rucksack. A note for Cahoon pinned on the bedroom door. GONE FISHING.

Lights still burned in half a dozen apartments. Rain hammered on my jacket every gust. I walked fast, pools of porch-lit water on the concrete ribbed by wind. I stayed off Siskiyou Boulevard and kept to East Main, past the courthouse and the electric gates of the Police Station, threading across the cemetery and out through a hole in the fence behind Safeway. I went straight for the car with the key already palmed. The engine started first turn. I peeled the For Sale sign off the window but left the other, Oregon or Bust.

Four Hawaiians ran across the lot to their V8 Slugbug.

Shaped like cornsacks, puffing and groaning. They scrummed in and four Snickers wrappers blew back the way they'd come. Safeway was open twenty-four hours. The other customer parked his Bronco at the doors and left the engine running with the doors locked, a hunting rifle strapped to a rack on the back of the cab. I waited to follow the Bronco out. Safety in numbers. I made a three-point turn and indicated right into Sherman Street just as this Highway Patrol came off East Main. It slowed but kept going right up to the supermarket doors. I rolled the window flat and took deep breaths. In ten minutes I pulled off the ramp onto a deserted Interstate 5 North, shoving the Wagon into fifth.

XXVI

*I*nterstate 5 was dark and empty, the tyres hissed and clubbed on the concrete sections. The rain head on, worn blades rubbed at the glass, the swivels on the line ticked against the fishing rods. Distant yellow squints in the rearview, then a convoy of trucks loomed close and flashed to pull out, rocking me sideways, hurling filthy blinding spray. I had to slow up till the road cleared and I could build up speed again to a steady 50. Bear Creek Radio signed off. Another line of trucks sent me scuttling off at the Talent Exit, down Valley View Road staying north on Route 99 at a steady 45. The road to Phoenix was a sheet of water. I dropped speed because the car began to aquaplane.

After Phoenix the lights were green all the way to the Medford intersections. I skirted lumber yards, floodlit sodden metal, walls of peeling boxcars, switch engines, a dilapidated caboose. Southern Pacific. Cotton Country in rust-blown yellow lettering. The stoplight at the Jacksonville intersection burned cold red and my dead radio hissed like the drizzle as I tuned along the AM. I was tired and slipped the heat on recycle by mistake, leaning out the window to gulp the cold wet air, fighting sleep.

Through Medford the lights stayed green. An OPEN sign flashed over DONUTS IN HEAVEN so I turned in under the angels on donut clouds with donut halos. At the drive-up window I ordered an apple donut and sat in the lot, coffee in a tin mug from the thermos. I was waking up. Part of this was sharing it with F, the way I still gathered things to tell her. Before we met we'd considered ourselves so inviolate within our solitudes, self-sufficient, curled round our grievances undisturbed, those unspent pieces from a hoard of stolen coins. Then we'd met like two burglars breaking into the same house. We'd added our hoards together, swapped methods and so on. And she'd provided the get-away car. I felt it round me like a collaborator, still a new sensation to wonder at, a born-again driver.

Men in pick-ups on their way to work an early shift pulled into the lot for a $1 donut coffee. Thinned-out rain. Sky still dark but less dense, the long middle of night almost over. I took a stretch outside. Dawn wind stirred elsewhere along the valley.

Back on the road in thicker traffic, everyone had coffee on the dash at intersections, red faces, coughing on the first smoke. Route 99 through Medford, all the stoplights red. In ten minutes I hit the speed limit out of town and picked up the railroad again, running a string of motels with green and red neon VACANCIES. Trucks turned out the lumber yards. Dogs slunk from bin to motel bin. The smell of dead skunk stuck in the drizzle through Central Point till I pulled in at the Mobil for gas.

It was open country after the bend. I crossed Interstate 5 on the overpass onto Tolo Road with its smooth wide bends and new yellow lines. I could just make out Lower Table Rock against the cloud before a long climb, grit-stone over the railroad bridge, sharp at the Gold Hill inter-section till finally you hit Gold Ray Dam Road. From here the way undulates, an unmarked track, past the Pine Tree Saloon, two deer watching on the next bend disinclined to bolt, just stumbling out the glare of hi-beams onto the grass verge. Dead skunk in the air again.

Under a mile now, the road fell through mist off the river, forcing me to slow and dip the beams. Deer cropped

201

ferns beside the railroad track and the road began to cut along a rising ledge still following the river. Land rose to the left, coarse pasture, dry red earth. Rubble tracks to ranch houses set well back, their blue bug zappers glowing in the cold bugless air. Objects caught by the headlights. Mailboxes, newspaper shots, name plates. Wayne & Paulette *SIPPLE*. **ABBOT.** Lloyd **Geppert**. A dog's eye reddened in a swift turn, barking thinly, tacking backwards up a driveway. The last house. From there the blacktop continued a quarter mile, rising to a bend where the rocks just sheared then dropped to the dam.

A hint of dawn abreption, bleached cloud as the daylight was unearthed. A slight breeze picked up. The sky behind Table Rock lit up a second, stretching at the dark. White oak and ponderosa pine truncated where the cloud refused to lift. This was where white settlers met Takelma Indians in 1850. There was an airstrip up there now.

Dropping down to second for the Snake Bend. Pull-ins overlooked the backwater and railroad track. One hot summer afternoon I'd pulled up here sharp behind an old Dodge flatbed, plywood sides hinged down. An old timer nearby stooped under the rock-shade scooping up two pieces of a rattlesnake decapitated by his shovel. Flung the bits on the flatbed with five other dead'ns.

I parked down the embankment twenty feet above the water at a dead-end against the rockface where the yellow dusty earth was coated in litter. Beer cans, take-outs, monofil. The ferns were pale and the brambles had turned. The ceanothus was dead. I switched off, opened the doors, listened. The car creaked, cooled in the ticking drizzle, wind blowing off the dam end in weak gusts. Dry scratching foliage. Leaves fell, withered crispate. I could hear the faded pearl of water running off the sluice. It was this vicinity of the dam which interested me now. The carp wouldn't be in the stagnant pools any more. Come winter, they'd be in the deep water by the dam.

This was Gold Ray Dam, built across Rogue River in 1903. Now the vegetation had died back I could see how it formed the lake and narrow backwater along one bank of a leg of mutton island. Trees and thicket still made the island impenetrable. In summer the water was yellow, brown or green, always sluggish, stagnant in pockets. Now it was black in the dawn light. The home of beavers, turtles, mallards, tufted ducks, crested grebes, cormorants, owls, sparrowhawks, herons. A steelhead might stray up, a few rainbows, brook trout. But the creek species were bluegill, crappies, bass and a small head of Common Carp. One fish I'd seen several times. Forty lb plus.

The train sounded some way off, maybe under Tolo Bridge clearing deer off the track. Leaning on the car I heard the birds tune up, felt the land stretch. Four muted blasts on the train whistle. A sord of mallards beat off in panic. The first kunk along the rails, a stampede of dull iron through the embankment. I crossed the track in no hurry. A beaver fluked over a log. A sudden gust rippled the treetops. One long dolorous note from the train and a blue heron started beating its wings. An unseen animal flacked deeper in to the island thicket and a lone grebe tore up the creek and dived under. Coots lowered white shields.

Marginal water was screened by bramble, willow, alder. Only half a dozen gaps along the whole creek, the nearest in a culvert, exposed but simple to fish from. A concrete pipe for the run-off. Loose gravel rip-rap, a favourite launching shute for floaters. The adjacent pitch was better, cut into the end of the bramble thicket, scooped under rock and a canopy of red birch sapling. The water level was still down, the marginal shelf exposed. At its widest the creek was thirty yards. From the embankment I could scan the main pockets or tuck down with good back cover to fish the margins.

A burst of short pulls on the whistle as I stood and

waited for the train to pass. A sharpness in the wind cut through my eyes to the back of their shells and a carp rose in the clamour. It heaved against the air, stealing power from the charge and rampage of tons of metal boxcars and flatbeds toppling ker-thung ker-thung ker-thung. I could even hear it in the creen and strain and kunk of flanged iron, uncoiled steel and rattling chain. Another carp side-jacked under the brambles. Then a third rolled against the wind. Bronze-flanked, fully scaled, a belly in the halflight delicate orange and flaxen. It went down like a scuppered ship tail first, eyes like marbles. The big forty, packing it on for the winter. Looked fifty plus now.

I had some bait ready in the catapult. In one swing I slacked the elastic down to range and fired. The chickpeas hit dead-centre in the flat spot and in the same movement I hopped back from the rails as the train cut off my view of the creek. On and on went the empty wagons. It darkened while they blocked me out. But the moment they passed the silence was passed on as light, and the day began. The drizzle eased to a spatter and I could feel the sudden rise in temperature, the lipper of warm wind pushing fallen leaves against sunken branches. The red lamp on the caboose curved from sight on the bend and I was over the track and dropping on hands and knees along the bramble thicket. The carp was still there bubbling and clouding, moving towards a gravel plateau six feet off the tumbled willow. Here the water was high brown, flanked in pondweed where the shoal had rooted and gone, a dead branch jutting from below the thicket. The stink of decomposing fish rose in the wind. I was ahead of the fifty now and chucked another handful of peas a rod length out into five feet of water. I sat and waited. When next it rolled we were eye to eye. I could see the dull grey wem across its shoulder where Ramrod pilot or Bo's old man had taken a scale out with a bullet or speargun. Rolling again it shoved head down into soft waddings of duckweed, gill covers like welded lanx. I daren't go fetch the rods down yet. I couldn't move and risk spooking this fish. My immobility turned to cramp, the tension of a sleepless night, the impulse to stand and get it over with, just lose the fish, fail, accept defeat and get out of America.

A push in the wind, a spit every few seconds. I lit the stove and put a soup tin in a pot of water. Took a piss, washed my face and hands, rubbed the glaze out my eyes and ate my way back to life. I took just the one rod, tackle tin, landing net, rod rest and bait. My foothold on the rubble held, knees clicked as I crept squatward along the embankment, back to where I'd last seen the carp. The stink caught me in the face. Wet grit scratched my coat in need of waxing. I faced upstream on one knee and pinpointed the gravelpatch, latitude bankside stump, longitude willow rampick. Scum rolled up the margins, rising and falling in the windsway and wash of dead leaves. I baited with a single chickpea, clipped a $1/4$ oz peardrop sinker to the running swivel. The first cast had to be spot on or I'd snag on the re-wind and dredge a ton of crap through the swim. Bail arm open, line tight to the spool, index finger triggered taut, I swung through a motion to test the balance, left eye taking aim, waiting for that hollow in the wind, a lull in which to centre my next move. When it came I cast in sorrow. I mean it didn't really matter. I couldn't afford to need perfection and some things had to stay irretrievable. When you change, the past changes too. When you cast out, *everything* goes unless you really cut the link.

It kicked on a twig on the outswing but the bait stayed firm. I snapped the bail arm over before the lead hit the water. Dangerous but I didn't need to feather the cast and jack-knife on the bow in the line. Still, you shouldn't cast like that and I was lucky being accurate. I sank the rod tip just below the surface, three quick turns took up the slack. Rod on the rest, clipping on a red squeezy bottle top I'd kept from England, a bite indicator on a 12" drop between the butt rings. Slacken the clutch, anti-reverse on. The bottle top swung in the wind. Then the wait. The hoot of wind playing over an empty mind, fiddling dead leaves as a truck rumbled up a dirt track a mile off over the river, a white sky wind with a slight shift to the north, angling down the margins, cold-hearted too when it came off the brambles, flacking like polythene taped over a broken window. A homeless sound, it made me wonder what a waste of time this was, the old loneliness driven home like a nail. One split second and my perception changed. From carp fisherman to con, degraded and ridiculous. From Farm Villa to Gold Ray Creek, it was always the place, not me. Degrading places without choice. Another dead end backwater.

XXVII

*W*hen the wind pushed hard off the valley it brought rain and the water flattened in a sudden downpour. Scum shifted and the line slackened off. My coat stiff as card as the rain thudded on the hood and I couldn't hear much else. The bait had been out an hour and a half. I must've spooked the carp. The drift was towing my line and dragged the bottle top up against the rod. I lifted it to correct the drag but the line was caught and worked its way under the scum into a snag of litter and weed. Flicking the tip I felt the line rasp. A steady pull and it tightened hold, the line solid after a few turns on the handle, the reel cucked from grit backsplashed into the gears. I wound tight and clamped to the breaking strain walking backwards, the snag groaning up the line as the rain plucked it. Bubbles popped round the snag and I slackened off; the thing heaved down so I try again and the line parted above the swivel knot. A dead carp turned over as I wound in the slack and nearly gagged on the bloated stink, a bleached corpse, adipocere, crawling, about 18 lb. Shot in the swim bladder with a hunting rifle.

Back in the car I sat with the window down and rain slanting into my coffee, fighting the urge to light up. It was 8.45 am. Pack up. Get back to Excelsior, Cahoon would never know. Just leave the gear in the car and sleep it off. I stretched, walking the embankment, not interested in concealment now. Down to the rampicks through a cut in the brambles, curious for a last look, sliding sideways down the rubble to a standstill on the ledge three feet above the scum. Muddied, churned water, silt clouds hanging over the gravel plateau. Rain in heavy drops like under a tree. Cloud, heavy grey scud. And there were vehicles passing on the road now. A Ranger stared down at me from his Blazer, even nodding at my raised hand. A trail bike shot by like a hornet. I was back at my usual place in the world again. Asking the familiar question: why had I failed?

The answer was simple. A carp that big could be as old as me. A thirty-three-year-old carp with a bullet hole. I was fishing for it on the gravel patch. It just wouldn't have made a target of itself again by swimming over a gravel patch. Even the bluegills and crappies avoid the cardboard lying on the bottom. In English waters I'd seen fifty-yard-long shoals of roach move in blue twists just to avoid swimming over fridge doors. I once hooked a carp on a car roof though. A yellow Ford Capri sitting in ten feet of water in a Hertfordshire gravel pit. I baited up the roof and fished at night, hooking the carp at dawn. I lost it when it swam in through the driver's window and snapped me up on the steering column.

On the eve of expulsion, without F's gifts of logic, there was an accident. My mind must have hit the past head-on. I wasn't looking where I was going. All I remember of the accident is the sheer relief of thinking: I can't go any further. I was staring into the creek. The biggest carp I'd ever seen turned slow, just under the surface. Everything I'd done before now counted for nothing. You don't fool a fish like that with a chickpea on a hook. The fish wouldn't fool me either, packing on its winter fat, butting and sucking at these clumps of weed-like mane, fibrous wigs still teeming that late in the year with shrimp and pea-molluscs. It stripped each clump, blowing wads in founts to the surface. I tossed a single chickpea into the weed. The carp turned to scruti-

208

nize but the pea was swept away, lost in the gurge of giant caudal fin, a fin big as two hands. Only the carp made a gas mask mouth and sucked the pea in from two feet away without a fraction of suspicion. Because . . . it was lodged in a ball of weed, like an egg in a nest. Looking for more, the carp dived back into a clump up to its gills.

I crept backwards to the car, hands shaking as I stripped down the old rig on the other rod, keeping the snag leader but whipping a hook to the shank on a 24" 10 lb trace, biting on a split shot 2" from the hook. Down in the birch swim I couldn't find any of this weed, nor in the run-off under the rip-rap. The margins were too clear from all the boat launching. I flung my coat in the back of the Wagon and took the rod, net and bait back into the brambles till I saw the fish again. I picked the smallest pea from a handful, one with a tight seam and a dark blemish. It held well on the hook bend, the point well clear, but I couldn't see anything to use as weed. The fish rolled six feet from the bank. I could've pulled a thread of wool from my jumper. The best idea was to cut a lock of hair and bind it on . . . But I had one, in my back pocket, flattened like a hackle for dressing salmon flies. The hank of hair I'd taken from F's brush at the hospital. Fine, dry, off the underside where it often matted. Just needed a drub and one end pinched into a twist, tied above the hook with a strand of wool plucked off my pullover.

I was on automatic now and in one sweep the bait sailed out and I twitched it back till it sank and the line uncoiled off the water-film, slipping forward. It came to rest six inches under the surface in the weed and I couldn't tell the difference. There was no wait. The carp tilted up and backed off, pumped its operculum, mouth opening like a yawn.

I didn't need to strike. The carp kicked into the weedbed and the hook pulled home as the slack whipped taut. I leaned into side strain and fell back into brambles, the water lashed to foam before the carp took control and slammed the rod into a half circle, the cork handle creaking. One shrug of its shoulder and ten yards of line screeched off the reel before it thumped to a sudden halt in eight feet of snaggy water below the willow. I pushed the net down the rip-rap and slid after it on my heels, winding line to stay tight on the fish. Twenty feet between us, the line starts to grate. Head shaking, tail kicking. I was going to lose it. The usual procedures were habit. Hand plucking, sinking the tip, waggling the rod side to side. Still deadlock. I put the rod down and opened the bail arm, picking up a rock and lobbing it just downstream, trying to spook it into moving. But the carp stayed lodged and buried in . . . unless it'd come off, so there was panic as I picked up the rod and wound down again till I felt a kick. I could wait.

When line began to peel off the open spool I lifted the rod. I watched where the line entered the water to check it wasn't snagged and the fish had actually freed itself so it wouldn't kite on a tether when I engaged the pick-up on the reel. As it tightened, the line trawled leaves. The carp was thirty yards upstream now. Dead willow leaves clung to the rising line like men in old newsreels who should have let go of the airship ropes. Up they go till they plunge wriggling like elvers hundreds of feet to certain death. We said we'd never do that. F said we'd let go the second that rope tightened. But I didn't.

The rod curved and flattened. I clamped down, refused to give the fish an inch. The line held and the carp boiled inches off a rusty mooring pole. It hesitated. It wanted to wrap me round the pole. Only it set off on a run, up the length of the creek, towards the dam.

I went through passport control at Gatwick and waited for F. They asked her why she was visiting England without a visa. As soon as they stopped her I knew we wouldn't get through. It wasn't my fear they picked on, it was F's happiness they detested. Her faith in our existence. Her refusal to lie.

– To live with my husband, she said, pointing at me.

Her grin was private. Those words should've been our dignity. Our exchange of anxiety contained our knowledge of the last nine months. The grin which changed my life. To the Immigration Police it was unnatural, under the circumstances. It focused their attention on me too. They ushered her aside. An immigration officer took my arm and said he'd accompany us to our luggage.

– Her mother lives in London, I said. We're just visiting her, then we're, you know, moving on . . .

– That's not what your wife said. If she is your wife.

He was a young Tory in a blue suit and striped blue shirt, white fingernails, public school blond. MI5 trainee. When he saw our pile of luggage he was jubilant.

– Open it, he said. And we had to open it in front of everyone. We'd even brought the lead owl and the pewter cranebills, our skillets, F's heirlooms, and my home-made fishing gear.

– You've come to set up home, he said to F. Look at it from my point of view. You haven't got a visa so I have to ask questions.

We followed him with our trollies to the detention pound. It was mid-afternoon. There were four others from our flight detained. One of them was on the phone in the windowless lounge, bare brick painted yellow. He was a fresher in grey slacks, dark stubble and bloodshot eyes.

– Look Mrs Spillers, you've gotta help me, you don't understand. They're sending me back on the first flight. It goes to Denver Colorado. I only came through England to give your daughter back her drum kit. I'm from Boston. Fer chrissake, they're sending me back to fucking Denver Colorado with your daughter's drum kit . . . I just wanna go to Paris, and get a job . . .

211

There was no privacy. We were questioned standing up. Three feet away, the high school graduate sat back to front on a plastic orange stacker chair. Greasy stubble and a pointed sneer under a woollen army cap.

– Don't tell that motherfucker, he kept saying.

F's face was burning. Her acne looked like acid thrown in her face. I kept telling myself it won't happen. We refused to smoke too because we'd promised to give up together. Only the way things were going we were five cigarettes from the end.

– Hey motherfucker, the kid said. Where can I buy an SF Weekly?

– Denver, Colorado, Tory said.

– Excuse me motherfucker, I'm just goin for the turtle soup and green salad . . .

The door had been left ajar and he took off through it.

– Idiot, Tory said. He won't get far.

An alarm sounded. There was shouting, a scuffle. Half a minute later he was back, out of breath.

– I didn't even get to see Buckingham Palace.

– Here, Tory said, giving him a quid. Get a Coke.

To us he said: How much money do you have?

We had a $3,000 bank draft for the Honda and a few dollars' cash. There was a Coca-Cola vending machine on the wall which took pound coins. Everything was designed to make us angry and intimidated. It made the decision to deport the detainees simpler. F was on her way to Denver. The Fresher was on the phone again. He wanted his mother to drive to Denver and pick him up. She wanted him to take the Greyhound.

– With a fuckin drum kit? Get real mom, he kept saying.

Me and F gripped each other, skunks on the roadside. The questioning became superfluous. Did I have a job? Did I have an income? Did I have an address? How could I assure them my wife wouldn't be a burden on the state? Or that we wouldn't go on the council list.

– What's wrong with that? I said. I was raised in a council house.

There was a lot wrong, he said. The burden of proof: could I support my wife without recourse to state benefit? He didn't think so. In fact, he had my records.

He came and went, always referring to an unseen boss. For F's sake, he said he wanted to act with discretion. He could be flexible, but we had to be straight. We were the only couple in the room and his hesitation implied compassion, but it was clearly institutional. How long did we intend to stay? We were so tired now. We didn't even want to be in this fucking country, I said.

He took F to see his boss. When they came back F was shaking her head. She was being deported. They wanted to put her on the next flight to America. Denver, Colorado.

– Hey welcome to the gang, the kid said.

– What about me? I said to Tory.

– You can do what you like.

– I can't go back to America can I? They only deported me today.

– Yeah, I know, he said. Tough. Do things by the book in future and you might not complicate your life.

F said:

– What about France? Can we go to France, together?

He went to see his boss.

– That's okay, he said, if your husband pays for his own ticket and finds an airline to pay for yours.

I was given half an hour. If I wasn't back by 5.30 pm, F was going to Denver. I had to push all three trollies of luggage from arrivals to departures. None of the banks would negotiate the bank draft. I didn't have a bank account. I changed our dollars into fifty quid, put the luggage in storage and went from one airline to another begging a deportee ticket to Paris. Swissair gave me F's ticket and did me a standby discount for fifty quid on the 6.20 pm. On my way through departures I heard the final boarding call for

Denver. F was being escorted towards the boarding gate by immigration security. I began to run, shouting:
– Let her go, let her go, I've got the tickets.

XXVIII

Sometimes I dread how my feelings will turn before I've even hooked a fish, and the search is on for other satisfactions which are there already, but which give way under stress they're not designed to endure.

At L'Etang de Crève-Coeur in Normandy, a shoal of six Common Carp idle in the afternoon sun in a clear shallow bay. They sense my presence but inch away with no particular hurry. Three brace, between 5 lb and 7 lb apiece, bronze green and Prussian blue. They are so certain of their place that as they leave the bay, they tilt on their keel, suck down a waterboatman, spit out alder cones.

I throw a handful of cat biscuits onto the surface. Lightly, no fuss. This upsets them and they break ranks into single file. Their impulse to get away from me is urgent now, only the last one out hesitates and sucks in a cat biscuit. I take advantage and flick a freelined Felix inches off the carp's dorsal. It turns tail as if to snap. Slows. Sips. The astonishment in that fish as I hook it. I feel its panic on a short line like it's pulling on my guts. Four of the shoal vanish in a flash but one stays beside its troubled mate. The hooked fish makes short runs, darting turns up and down the shallows, throwing itself onto the surface, and all the time its mate follows and even copies it with the same look of astonishment and agitation. I can't watch this and I slack off the line so both fish stop and lie near the bottom side by side, heads touching, all their palpitating gradually slowing and the water calms, becomes clear again. Tremors, the fish are shaking. After five minutes working its mouth it's still hooked, so what choice do I have but to tighten up and start again? Only now it's recovered its strength and everything takes longer than it should. Its mate swims the whole way with it, right to the landing net rim, but when they're separated it bolts into open water even though I unhook my captive in the water and slip it back over the net rim in seconds. It makes fruitless runs in search of its mate along the route of its struggle before sinking out of sight into open water. Just fuckin weep.

HABITUS   James Flint

A hilarious satire on the state of humanity that
entwines the troubled lives of Joel, a mathematical
genius, Judd, the disaffected son of a Hollywood
star, and Jennifer, a precocious schoolgirl, as they
search for meaning in the millennial world.

£6.99   1 85702 832 5

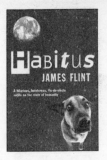

SHOPPING   Gavin Kramer

Alistair Meadowlark is an English lawyer in Tokyo
struggling to understand the strange new world
around him. Then he falls in love with Sachiko,
would-be starlet, aspirant businesswoman,
consummate shopper and pocket-sized *femme fatale*,
and his culture shock is complete.

£6.99   1 85702 958 5

**All Fourth Estate books are available from your local bookshop,
or can be ordered direct from:**

**Fourth Estate, Book Service By Post, PO Box 29,
Douglas, I-O-M, IM99 1BQ**

Credit cards accepted.

Tel: 01624 836000   Fax: 01624 670923

**Or visit the Fourth Estate website at:
www.4thestate.co.uk**

*Please state when ordering if you do **not** wish to receive further
information about Fourth Estate titles.*